Dangerous Dancing

Best wishes,

Dick Standring

4520-STAN

DANGEROUS

DANCING

RICHARD STANDRING

To order additional copies of this book, contact:
Xlibris Corporation
1-888-7-XLIBRIS
www.Xlibris.com
Orders@Xlibris.com

About the Author

Richard Standring is a retired publishing executive who spent 30 years in all areas of advertising, from an agency account executive, to space salesman, to publisher. He is also an experienced pilot, with over 3,000 hours of flying logged in a wide variety of aircraft, many of which he owned. He retired from advertising in 1993, and flying in 1995.

His first novel, **HUSTLE** was published in 1989 as a salute to the many enterprising space salesmen of the '60s and '70s. He is currently working on a sequel to **DANGEROUS DANCING**. Having lived in several large cities (Boston, Cleveland, Detroit, Philadelphia, Providence & Pittsburgh) the author and his wife now live a quieter pace in Cookeville, TN, where he plays golf most of the year. He also writes poetry & short stories. A collection of selected short stories, essays and poems will be finished soon under the title: **SOMEWHERE ALONG THE WAY.**

Readers who wish to comment, can reach the author on the internet at: *www.standring@cookeville.com*. To read some of his poetry: *www.poetry.com*.

CONTENTS

Accidents can happen... anyplace, anytime. Sometimes, it's the wrong place, the wrong time.

What if it wasn't an accident? Yet the police seem fairly certain it was. Why bother digging further?

It depends on who arrives at the scene first. And, if they ask enough questions. And, if they don't make hasty conclusions. And, if they have enough time. And, if somebody really cares. If not, it gets written off, move on.

How many times, and in how many places, Does this scene play out to an expedient end? Without anyone ever discovering the truth? Because...the search for the truth, takes time. And the journey, is not a straight line.

Many people have something to hide. When asked, they may try to evade the question. Dance around it, so to speak. If that person has a motive for murder, Then that suspect could be a... **dangerous dancer*.**

* A "dancer" is police jargon for a person who tries to evade direct questioning.

Author's Comment

This is a fictional attempt to answer the question, how could a murder be written off as an accident? Keep reading and you might find out. None of the characters in this novel are real, anyone having a name similar to one mentioned, has my apologies, it is just a coincidence. All names of people and places of business are figments of my imagination. The same is true for the names of the boats; they are just imaginary. While there are numerous marinas on Jefferson Ave. in St. Clair Shores Michigan, I deliberately did not mention the marina by name because the one I visualized, does not actually exist. Nautical Mile does exist, however.

There was a time, about twelve years ago, when I considered publishing a local magazine and naming it DETROIT VISITOR. It never materialized, remaining as an idea only. As for the pizza franchise mentioned, the name couldn't be located, at the time I wrote this novel. It is possible that someone has since used the name. If so, it is only a coincidence, nothing else. The restaurant mentioned at the former Herndon airport (in Orlando) does exists. I recommend it to anyone looking for a good meal and great atmosphere.

My special thanks to Captain Gary J. Franey of the Clinton Township Police Dept. for his help, and useful suggestions on investigative procedure. He is Commander of the Criminal Investigations Div. So, it's with a modicum of pride that I say, "gotcha!" for he, too was surprised with the ending.

Richard Standring

Chapter 1

"Listen to me, Vince, this isn't going to work. No matter what you think you know. This time, you're dealing with some dangerous people, who won't fool around with you. They can make you disappear. Don't you understand that?" The person sitting on the sofa opposite Vince was trying to reason with him, while waiting for another person to join them. It was getting late; too late for the advice to sink in.

"Yeah, well I guess you don't know me as well as you thought you did. I know a lot of important people in this town," he took a final swallow of his drink and started to stand up. His first attempt was unsuccessful. Looking at his Rolex, he saw that it was 1:10 in the morning. Was it really that late? Had he been drinking for 2 hours? He had to get outside quickly, so he could vomit. This time, he managed to rock forward and use the momentum to keep moving in a crouched position. Stumbling toward the door, his knee struck a low coffee table. The pain was dulled by the acute awareness of the coming surge of sour bile. He managed to make it through the doorway, and down the three steps.

He was surprised that he felt so bad. Normally he could hold four or five Scotches and still maneuver. Perhaps it was the gentle rocking motion of the boat. His legs felt wobbly as he leaned over the side. There was no wind. The water was calm. Only the slight slap of water could be heard against the gleaming white hull. It was a good thing the boat was in its berth, and not in open water, where there would be more motion. His rubber legs would not support him. Vince had to grip the side with trembling hands, as he leaned out as far as he could. A second upsurge was coming. He could feel his stomach contract. He didn't want to make a mess on the side of this beautiful yacht, so he leaned out further, his belt buckle scratching against the white fiberglass rail section.

"Ughhhhhh...." It was the last sound Vince heard before his head hit the nearby piling. Unconscious, he was unable to wrap his arms around the protruding poles covered with green slime. He never heard the splash of his body entering the cool, dark water, now mixed with his floating discharge. The only sounds were the squeak of a plastic fender protecting a nearby yacht, and the quiet footsteps of someone hurrying down the wooden dock, somewhere in the darkness.

THE DETROIT NEWS–July 19, 1999

Vincent D. Blessing, Age 60, a longtime resident of Birmingham, MI died on Sunday. t is presumed that he accidentally fell overboard from a yacht and drowned. The accident occurred at a local St. Clair Shores marina. Police are calling it an accident, pending further investigation. The name of the yacht's owner was not released. Mr. Blessing was a successful advertising executive. He is survived by his wife, Emily and his daughter, Mrs. Susan Deckel. Funeral arrangements have not been announced. Additional details about his death are not available.

CHAPTER 2

To help maintain the peace and tranquility of another quiet Sunday morning, Sergeant Gary Mitchell elected not to use the siren, just the flashing strobes. Traffic was light, since it was still early. A drowning accident had been reported at a marina, interrupting his breakfast plans.

"People should never die on Sunday mornings," Gary grumbled to his partner. "It disturbs the natural order of things."

"Is there ever a good time to die?" his partner asked, trying not to spill the coffee.

"Best time is on a Monday night. That's not my shift." He chuckled at his own joke.

The flashing strobe lights from two St. Clair Shores police cruisers pulsed an eerie and diffused glow into the still lifting fog, as they raced quietly along Jefferson Ave. They were headed toward one of the nearby marinas. The Detroit area along Lake St. Clair was about to experience another hot, Sunday in July.

Detective Lieutenant Nick Alexander was just reaching his halfway point on his daily 3-mile morning run along a strip known as the Nautical Mile when the police cars raced past him. He was glad they hadn't used their sirens. A few seconds later, his pager went off. He was on call for any important incidents. He had to fill in as Duty Officer, because of the vacation schedule. As a detective, Nick's primary responsibilities were to investigate homicides and robberies. Right now, it was too peaceful along the lake, and too early, for any criminal activity. However, he wouldn't be needed for something like a traffic accident, so he increased his pace, heading back to his apartment a block away. It was the closest phone.

15

Two patrolmen were searching the wet corpse lying on the wooden dock. Both were soaked, having struggled for several minutes to get the heavy body out of the water. The third officer, Sergeant Gary Mitchell, remained dry. He was taking pictures with limited success, using a Polaroid camera, while trying to finish his coffee. The security guard stood behind him watching with amused interest. This was the most exciting thing to happen, since LaMarr Jennings took the security job three months ago. He was the one who discovered the body floating in the water, and had called the police. Then he called the marina manager, Howard Swane, who wasn't pleased to be awakened at that early hour. The police cars arrived just a few minutes after his call, since the St. Clair Shores Police Department was just nine blocks away, also on Jefferson Avenue.

"Uh, pardon me there Sergeant, if I was you, I think I'd wait a few more minutes 'till all this here fog clears out 'fore takin' any more of them pictures." LaMarr could see that the prints weren't coming out very well. The flash created an instant glare against all the hanging moisture. Whatever LaMarr lacked in formal education, he more than made up for with common sense.

"Tell you what you can do, stand back over there by the gate, and make sure nobody comes over here." Gary knew the man was right. He'd wasted almost an entire pack of film so far in his haste to get everything recorded before the Duty Officer arrived. He just didn't need any suggestions from a civilian wannabe cop this early in the morning... or any other time.

Reluctantly, LaMarr retreated back to the gate, which he'd left standing open. A 6-foot high chain link fence separated the gravel parking lot from the dock area. The office was on the other side of the parking lot, near the marina entrance. LaMarr stood by the gate and lit a cigarette and thought how stupid cops could be at times like this. He sensed

the Sergeant's annoyance. The Sergeant had taken his statement, slowly writing everything in his little notebook. Because he was nervous, LaMarr spoke fast, and the Sergeant
had a hard time keeping up.

LaMarr hadn't been too surprised at finding the gate unlocked when he checked it. Boat owners went back and forth
to their vehicles and left it open all the time. For it to remain
locked, he'd have to stand there all night long like a sentry.
He wasn't about to do that when he could see the gate from
the office. Discovering the dead man floating in the water
had unnerved him. For a few moments, he was uncertain what
to do. Now, he was wishing he had checked the body before
calling the police, because the man was sporting a big gold
Rolex. The watch had to be worth some serious money.
LaMarr wondered if the watch would ever make it into the
personal property bag with the other items they found on the
body. Now that Detroit had a new gambling casino, LaMarr
was always suffering a case of the shorts. That Rolex could
have helped him recover some of his recent losses.

"Hey Sarge, did anyone call for the meat wagon?" One
of the patrolmen yelled.

"Yeah, someone from the ME's office will get here eventually. You guys better check out the boat when you're finished there." Gary hoped they could wrap this up quickly.
He was looking forward to a big Sunday breakfast at Zero's,
his favorite restaurant. He knew Lieutenant Alexander was
Duty Officer this week, and hoped he wouldn't bother checking on this simple accidental drowning. It was fairly obvious
to him what had happened

Gary didn't like working with Nick. He didn't like anyone who didn't have a sense of humor. Nick was far too serious. He also asked too many questions. He asked questions
nobody would ever think about asking. Gary's job had been
mainly patrol work before being promoted recently to Sergeant. He'd worked with Nick on several robbery investiga-

17

tions and listened to his never-ending questions. It just about drove him nuts.

In public, Nick always referred to Gary as, "Sergeant". In private, he called him, "Mitchell" never, "Gary". In retaliation, Gary always referred to Nick as, "Lieutenant" in public, and called him, "Nick" in private. He also referred to Nick as, "that pain-in-the-ass" in the locker room, whenever Nick wasn't around to hear him.

At 52, Nick Alexander still presented a rugged, healthy profile. His lean six-foot frame was in sharp contrast to Gary's stocky appearance featuring a growing beer gut. Nick was just starting to show some gray hair at his temples, while the rest of his crop was still predominantly light brown. Gary was sensitive about losing his hair. At 38, he felt he was too young to have skin showing on top. Once, Nick had overheard some of the patrolmen tease Gary about having worn his football helmet too long in high school. It was one of the few jokes Gary refused to laugh at.

Gary knew the Lieutenant would want lots of photos for the case file, even for an accident. People got drunk and sometimes fell over the side of boats. Michigan had its fair share of boating accidents, ranking high among the states with the greatest number of registered boats. Gary knew the report routine and what needed to be filed with the Coast Guard, the Sheriff's office and the State Police. He was thinking about that as he loaded a new pack of film into the camera. He thought about asking the nosey security guard if he wanted his picture taken with the wet corpse. That would be worth a few laughs back at the station.

"Sarge, we're done with the stiff. You gonna take some shots of the boat?"

"Yeah, might as well. It'll impress the Lieutenant." Gary had to walk back by the fence and still couldn't get the entire yacht into the picture. It's gleaming white fiberglass hull now reflected the morning sun. It was a sixty-foot Bertram that dwarfed most of the other yachts in this section of the marina. The long sleek bow protruded out into the central waterway of the marina. The stern section faced the parking lot fence and gate about 100 feet away. There was an open slip on the side where the dried vomit disgraced the otherwise beautiful boat. The enclosed bridge was on the upper deck. The salon door opened to the rear section where the fighting seat had been removed. Gary walked back and stood in the aft section taking more pictures.

Meanwhile the still dripping body of Vincent Blessing laid on the dock, a dead witness to the scene being photographed from every angle. One shoe was missing. A patrolman covered the body with a blanket, leaving the wet stocking foot exposed. So far, all the motions duplicated what would have been done for a traffic accident. The only exception was they didn't have to take any measurements. As Gary took his last photograph, he saw the Lieutenant's unmarked Ford stop near the gate. Gary wasn't looking forward to the next half hour. It would be a hundred questions about some of the most unrelated things ever imagined. His headache arrived, and breakfast would no doubt be delayed. Gary had been thinking about Shirley, his favorite waitress at Zero's. They flirted with each other regularly. It was another of his more enjoyable routines.

Gary had become reasonably thorough in his preliminary investigations, but he never seemed to measure up to Nick's high standards. That was the main reason why Gary had taken so many pictures. No matter how Gary would anticipate Nick's questions, there would be something he overlooked, or hadn't considered. Nick had many more years' experience, so there was a lot to learn yet, and a high price to pay for the tuition. Nick had been on the force for 28 years and had a reputation for being a loner with the other officers. He didn't hang out with them after work, like Gary did. On the other hand, Nick did enjoy a close relationship with the Chief. The recent rumor going around at the station was that Nick's latest girlfriend had left him. So, it was a good bet that the Lieutenant was probably sleeping alone this morning, unless he got lucky last night. In which case, he wouldn't be here now. Gary thought the guy went through a lot of short-term relationships. If he was as big a pain in the butt off duty, as he was on, then Gary wasn't surprised that Nick had trouble maintaining a steady love life. But that was his problem.

Gary had a hard time admitting that Nick looked much younger than 52, and was no doubt in better shape. Gary needed to lose 30 lbs. while Nick remained trim from all the running he did every morning. Since Nick's divorce, he had become a workaholic. It served to convince Gary that too much dedication to the job could definitely impair one's social life. Nick was a prime example of that theory.

"So what have we got here?" Nick walked directly over to the body, lifting the blanket. Gary was unable to read any expression on Nick's face. The man looked serious all the time. Nick arrived dressed in tan slacks, a white golfer's tee shirt and boat shoes. He could have passed for one of the boat owners. His hair was still wet from his quick shower.

"Looks like the man had too much to drink and fell overboard while pitching his cookies." Gary pointed to the dried vomit on the side of the yacht's hull. It was a definite violation to its elegance. "We had to fish him out of the water." This would make the forth accidental drowning so far this year.

On his way to the marina, Nick had stopped at a nearby deli for a coffee to go. He took short sips while admiring the big Bertram. He'd seen a brochure on the Bertram line of luxury motor yachts, but this was the first time he'd actually seen one this close. Nick's experience with boats was restricted to the 16-foot run-about he used for fishing with his son, Nickie Jr.

"So who is he?" Nick asked, taking another sip of coffee.

"Victim's name is Vincent Blessing. He's sixty years old, according to his driver's license. Lives in Birmingham." Gary was referring to his notebook, hoping Nick would notice. "Had a couple of hundred on him and some change. Also, he's wearing one of those expensive Rolex watches. Watch must have stopped, 'cause it reads one-eighteen." Gary figured that additional bit of information might impress Nick.

"Must be one of those cheap knock-off watches then. A real Rolex is supposed to be waterproof." Nick bent over and covered the exposed stocking foot, adjusting the blanket.

"Oh yeah? Well, he's not going to complain about the warrantee now." Gary's voice carried, and the security guard by the gate laughed at the joke. Nick ignored the humorous attempt. Most of Gary's jokes were in poor taste, or just corny. However, it was that casual, joking attitude that made Gary popular with the other men on the force.

"It might help us establish the time of death," Nick continued. Looking around, he saw an ambulance with more flashing lights backing up to the gate. The security guard was directing them, glad for something to do. A crowd of curious gawkers would be arriving soon. They always reminded Nick of vultures. "You figure this for an accident?" Nick asked.

"Looks that way to me, Lieutenant. The way I figure it, the guy drank too much Scotch. There's a bottle about half empty on the counter inside. One of the low tables seems to be moved, so maybe he hit it going for the door. It's a wonder he didn't stumble on those steps. Anyway, he seems to have made it to the side over there. Probably lost his balance, or slipped and fell over." Gary pointed to the area where the vomit could be seen. "My guess is, he hit his head on one of those pilings. You can see some splinters and the abrasion on the victim's forehead." Gary hoped that Nick had plans for his day off and would leave soon. That would allow enough time to finish up here and still enjoy breakfast.

"I guess it could have happened that way. Any wit-

21

nesses?" Nick took another sip of coffee. Except for the corpse, it was the start of another great day, particularly here on the water... on a luxury yacht, with the only sound coming from a few screeching seagulls. Early morning was Nick's favorite time of day. Too bad the victim couldn't share it, he thought, as he watched the body being removed by the Medical Examiner's team. A patrol officer would follow the ambulance to the morgue. It was standard procedure, even though an autopsy wouldn't be performed until Monday.

"Nope. It was pretty quiet around here, according to the security guard over there. He's the one who found the body. According to my notes, he says he heard some music and voices coming from here around eleven, nothing loud. He was making his rounds and the gate was locked. When he checked again at six this morning, he found the gate ajar. He also noticed the salon door was open, but the lights were off. He figured someone forgot to lock the gate. That's when he found the body floating in the water over there. He called it in soon after that." Gary closed his notebook, having given what he considered a pretty complete account. No doubt it wouldn't be enough for Nick.

"They keep that gate locked all the time?"

"Sure. Just look at all these pleasure palaces. There's a lot of money floating around here. They have to be careful. Visitors have to check in at the office, and the security guard brings them down, unless the owners let them in. Either way, you have to be expected... just like in those expensive high-rise apartments. Only difference is they don't have an elevator here." Gary looked around to see if anyone else enjoyed his observation.

"Yeah, right. And, this, ah... Mr. Blessing, is he the owner of this yacht?" Nick suspected he wasn't, based on the way the victim was dressed.

"Don't know that. The security guard didn't recognize him, and he doesn't look like a boater. I haven't had time to check the registration yet." Gary had planned on doing that next, before the Duty Officer arrived. He knew the routine. He hoped Nick wasn't going to make a big deal out of a simple accident like this one. If it had happened sometime during the week, when Nick was busy, he wouldn't even be here. It wasn't a homicide, or a robbery, so there was nothing to interest Nick. Unfortunately it was a Sunday, and Nick didn't seem to be busy, so here he was, asking questions, killing time and causing Gary to be late for breakfast.

"Anyone know if this boat was out last night?"

"Not while the security guard was on duty. He comes on at ten, and leaves at eight." Gary anticipated Nick's next question.

Nick stepped inside the salon. Out of habit, he pulled on a pair of white latex gloves. The salon had a blue, long curved sofa that was color coordinated with the drapes and the two chairs. There was a teak entertainment center, containing a large TV, a VCR and a stereo. The countertop dividing the salon from the galley was white with teak trim. Nick sniffed the empty glass and noted the almost empty bottle of expensive Scotch. A plaid sports coat was thrown over the end of the sofa. Nick picked it up and examined the label. It was a size 48, which seemed to match the victim. A gold Cross pen was hooked on the inside pocket. Nick turned to Gary, who was watching from the doorway.

"Did you find any keys on the victim?"

"No sir, haven't found any keys yet. They're probably in the water somewhere."

"Uh huh, yet he didn't lose his change, did he?"

"Keys are different, Nick. Mine get lost all the time."

"Hmmm, so how did he get in, if the security guard didn't bring him? The gate was locked, right?"

"Well maybe he had a key, or someone met him."

"But nobody reported the accident. So if there was someone else here, why wouldn't they try to help him?" Nick

23

walked into the galley and noticed two glasses in the sink. One of the glasses had a very slight hint of lipstick, as nick held it up to the light. Both had been washed, no drink residue. Nick opened the dishwasher; it was clean and empty. The galley had more cabinets than Nick's apartment. Opening them, he found most were empty except for a few plastic dishes, bowls and more glasses that matched those in the sink, and on the counter. Each displayed a small gold anchor.

"I can't answer that. Maybe they left before he decided to go swimming. Maybe he was in the doghouse with his old lady, and came out here to be by himself." Gary could think of better things to do in a place like this. "Having a pad like this could sure improve your social life, eh Nick?" Gary said it without thinking and momentarily held his breath.

"Sure could. I couldn't afford the berth rent, so it would be out of the question for me." Nick continued forward, down three steps and found the master stateroom on his left. The door was open, he was greeted by a king-size bed. There wasn't a wrinkle anywhere on the top cover. He walked into the adjoining head. The shower was big enough for two people. That appealed to him. The sink and vanity were spotless. Inside the medicine cabinet he found a bottle of aspirin, a bottle of Dramamine, for motion sickness, and some Band-Aids. There was also a partial bottle of Maalox. The wastebasket under the sink was empty. Nick was taken by how sterile the yacht appeared. He didn't see any personal items. No pictures or trophies on the walls. The other two staterooms were equally neat. None of them appeared to have been used recently.

Nick returned to the salon, then went topside to the cockpit area. The instrument panel held an immense display of dials and switches. The radar screen was on the right side of the chrome wheel. Just below, was a recessed area with three handsets; two were telephones. Nick picked up one of the handsets and heard a confirming dial tone. He knew the yacht had twin diesel engines. This was confirmed by the dual throttle quadrants, each color-coded with two levers on each side of the wheel. The fax machine was on the left side, a perfect location for reading weather reports as they arrived. The tachometers showed 810 hours each, so the boat, while relatively new, wasn't a dock queen. It had some use, but was well maintained. Nick couldn't find a ship's log, or registration documents. They were obviously locked away somewhere.

Nautical charts were stored in a lower cabinet. He recognized the hand-held global positioning unit on the shelf. Nick lifted one of the seat cushions on the bench seat opposite the captain's seat and found a pair of German high-powered binoculars, a portable hand-held two-way radio and a flare pistol. It appeared the boat was well equipped for emergencies. Under another seat, he found life vests and a first-aid kit. He climbed down, wondering what this magnificent boat was worth.

"So what do you think, Nick?" Gary asked meeting him.

"I think... we'd better have a talk with the marina manager and find out who the owner is, and what the victim was doing here? Find any keys yet?" Nick wanted to spend more time inspecting the yacht without any distractions. He'd stop back later when Gary was gone.

"No, still looking. Doesn't appear that anyone has been playing house here."

Nick had to agree with that observation. If he could afford something like this, his love life would be considerably different. For the past six weeks, it had been a big zero. And that had been his fault. He was getting tired of short flings and one-night stands. He'd had too many of those since the divorce. Each one had left him feeling more depressed and frustrated. His dedication to his job was the real reason. He had to cancel dates at the last minute, when there was a robbery to investigate.

The other reason was, he refused to discuss any investigation outside the department. His last girlfriend, Gloria, was excited about dating a cop and tried to get Nick to talk about his work. When he wouldn't, they became limited in what they discussed. Mainly it was about her work at the clinic, or sex. She thought he was great in the sack and in the kitchen, but boring elsewhere. Nick knew she was right, and didn't blame her when she gave him notice. His ex-wife had done the very same thing. Nick was proud of the fact that he hadn't fooled around while he was married, even though he'd had opportunities. Since the divorce, he'd fooled around a lot, and still he wasn't satisfied. Perhaps the right lady would change all that... some day.

Nick was still holding the empty coffee cup and started to deposit it, then decided to carry it outside with him. He had seen a large trash barrel, with a lid, near the gate. Gary followed him out onto the dock. He was hopeful to wrap all this up quickly, and still make it to Zeke's for a couple of eggs over easy, with bacon and a side of hash browns. His stomach was sending him a signal he needed food, and his bladder was telling him he'd had too much coffee. Now he was just waiting for Nick to leave.

"It hits me as a little strange that he was left here alone. Someone must have seen, or heard something." Nick wasn't talking directly to Gary, more to himself. He removed the gloves and scratched his ear, thinking about the way the victim was dressed. He wasn't a boater, so he must have been a guest. If so, who was he with, and why was he here? The circumstances were just a little strange, even if it was an accident. Someone should have called for help.

Nick walked to the gate, lifted the lid of the trashcan and deposited his empty cup and latex gloves. He spotted a tan towel with a blue stripe. It was identical to the towels he'd seen in the galley, and in both heads.

"Hey Sergeant, check this out." Nick threw the towel to

Gary. He instantly recognized it as being from the yacht. The towel didn't appear to be soiled, just wrinkled.

"I wonder what that's doing out there?" Gary asked. The towel looked new. There was no reason to discard it that he could think of.

"Maybe we should dust for prints inside the salon area," Nick suggested..

"Hey Lieutenant, this is an accident, not a homicide. What do you want with prints?" Gary knew he'd touched a few things. Only Nick had bothered to put on gloves. And dusting for prints would take time. Breakfast was out of the question now.

"Maybe the victim is wanted for something, somewhere. Who knows? Just humor me on this one, okay?" Nick proceeded to the marina office, taking note of all the cars that were in the parking lot. One of them probably belonged to the victim.

4520-STAN

CHAPTER 3

Howard Swane didn't appreciate having his sleep interrupted. He hated having to dress quickly and hurry to the marina office. He wasn't due into the office until noon. His assistant, DeWayne left early... again. That meant the office had been left unattended, except for LaMarr, who no doubt took a nap on the couch. The day was not starting well for Howard.

"Great! Just freaking great. Look at all those strangers out there in the parking lot," he barked at LaMarr, who was the only other person in the office. "Pretty soon they'll wander in here, looking for the bathroom. LaMarr, tell all those people out there that the restroom is out of order. Go on now, do it." Howard motioned for him to get out, then proceeded to make a hand lettered sign for the bathroom door.

Nick passed LaMarr on his way out. He smelled the fresh coffee on the sideboard in the office and didn't bother to ask, he just poured himself a cup.

"The restroom is out of order, and this isn't a restaurant," Howard snapped.

"Well, I must be in the wrong place then. You the manager?" Nick flashed his badge.

"Yes, and I'm sorry. I thought you were one of those out there," he pointed with his chin.

Nick figured Howard to be in his early forties. It was easy to see he was overweight. Nick noticed the brass nametag attached to a double-breasted blue blazer with the nautical crest. It seemed a bit of a mismatch with the jeans and striped sports shirt. Howard was perspiring even though the office was cool. Nick didn't have any doubts that the man was wearing a hairpiece. It had been put on in haste, and wasn't quite

28

straight. Taking all this in, Nick smiled. Swane wasn't far from swine, and Porky would be an apt nickname for Howard.

"How can I help you, Lieutenant?" Howard cleared his throat.

"I understand your night man discovered a body floating in the water near that big Bertram over there. Nick was about to mention the name painted on the stern of the yacht, then decided to wait.

"Yes, what a horrible thing to happen. Do you think it was a suicide?"

"Too soon to speculate on that, but I doubt it. The man didn't leave a note. Who is the owner of that yacht?"

"Let's see, our records show the owner is Freeman Enterprises. It hasn't been here very long. It arrived last month from Port Clinton I believe. Port Clinton is near Cedar Point."

"Thank you, I know where Port Clinton is, as well as Cedar Point." Nick could remember going to Cedar Point when he was a kid. It was a popular amusement park just outside Sandusky, Ohio. "The dead man appears to be a Vincent Blessing. Did he happen to register here when he arrived last night?"

The manager checked his register, turning his back on Nick. It was an annoying move. "No, he didn't. Someone must have met him. I wasn't working last night, or I might have noticed."

"Uh huh, do you have an address and phone number for this Freeman Enterprises? We need to get in touch with them soon."

"Sure do. I have it right here. Mr. Phillip Freeman is listed as the principle. Normally we don't give out that information. It's confidential, but we want to cooperate with the police in every way...."

"Yes, of course you do. We could use your help in asking the other boat owners if they saw, or heard anything last night. If any of them did, have them contact me, okay?"

"Sure thing. Glad to do it. Of course some of the boats left for the weekend, however I'll check with them whenever they return. Tell me, Lieutenant, did the man fall from the yacht, or the dock?"

"It appears he fell from the yacht. The name sure is hard to forget." Nick decided that Swane was more concerned about his insurance liability than the man's death, and doubted that he'd be much help. The name on the yacht was, **The Other Woman**. It would be difficult to maintain a yacht like that and still have a mistress, Nick thought. So maybe the yacht was a suitable replacement for another woman.

"Oh you mean, **The Other Woman**? Yes, I suppose it is a little unusual, but we see a lot of crazy names around here."

So far, this entire investigation seemed a bit crazy. Nick walked over to the sideboard and helped himself to some more coffee. He really didn't want any more, he just liked holding the cup in his hand while interviewing people. He'd found that having a prop was better than using an open notebook. It made people feel more relaxed. Nick had a good memory for details, so he took good mental notes, later he always transferred these onto paper. He had learned a long time ago that whenever he took out a notebook, to write down everything a person said, they said very little. Casual conversation worked best for Nick. Mitchell on the other hand, still needed the notebook method. And, he still needed to be a better observer of small details.

"I'd like to know if Mr. Blessing was ever a guest here at some other time. Mind if I check your guest register for the past few weeks?"

"Uh, I don't know about that, Lieutenant. The other boat owners could get very upset with me if they knew I gave out that information. We have to respect their privacy. You can understand that, can't you?" Swane moved the clipboard from the counter to the top of a nearby filing cabinet. It was almost childish.

"Of course. I can see that you're very concerned about privacy and security here with all those expensive yachts out there. Which leads me to wonder how it is that Mr. Blessing got in? Your gate was ajar, when the security guard checked it at six. It seems to me you should be a bit more concerned about that. If I owned one of those million dollar boats out there, and I knew you were lax on security, I'd be all over your ass."

"Well, you do make a good point there. And I'll see to it that the gate is checked more often. Perhaps I'll have a sign made, insisting that all owners and visitors should be sure to close the gate." Swane took a pen from his pocket and jotted a note as a reminder to have that done. He also planned to have a good talk with LaMarr about talking so freely.

"Please call Mr. Freeman and ask him to come down here. Also ask him for a list of visitors to his boat since it has been here. I'll wait." This needless run-around annoyed Nick.

"I'm sorry, Lieutenant but I really don't want to call Mr. Freeman at this early hour. I'd much rather you took a little peek at the guest register. You won't tell anyone will you?" Swane dabbed his forehead, then nervously patted his toupee. He instantly discovered his problem. He pushed the clipboard at Nick and disappeared into his office, closing the door. Nick smiled, and shook his head in wonder. He was sure Swane could be a snooty bastard, and doubted that he socialized with any women. If Swane owned that Bertram, he'd probably change the name to The Other Man. Nick chuckled at the thought. It was more in keeping with something Mitchell might have said.

Checking the guest register, Nick discovered that Vincent Blessing had in fact been a guest, along with several others on June 12th at 8:15 AM. That was a Saturday. Nick was jotting down the names when Swane reappeared. His wig was now in place and the man was composed. He saw that Nick still had a cup of coffee in his hand, then looked past Nick and saw LaMarr helping himself to a cup.

31

"LaMarr, I think you'd better see if there's something you can do outside. And leave that coffee cup in here. I don't want everyone to think this is a restaurant." Having scolded LaMarr, he turned to Nick. "I trust you'll forget about any of the celebrities you might have noticed on the list." The man sounded like a true gossip.

"Not a problem. Thanks for all your help." Nick left thinking, if they needed anything else, Mitchell could handle it. He didn't think he could stomach another session with Swane. He spotted the security guard talking with some people in the parking lot and signaled for him to come over.

"How about showing me how you found that gate," Nick said. Together they walked over to the entrance, where Nick saw the gate still ajar. The patrolman standing there quickly flicked his cigarette into the water as they approached.

"You got to pull that gate closed, else it stay open a little, like it be now. Thas just the way it be, when I came by doin' my rounds. And thas just what I tole the Sergeant. " LaMarr had the ability to shine people, particularly white people. He did it readily out of habit, gesturing with his hands in an overly animated fashion to attract attention.

"So when you noticed the door was open on the boat, were the lights still on?" Nick asked, ignoring the man's act.

"I don't rightly recall they was on. No, I'm pretty sure they was off."

"Okay, the door was open. You told the Sergeant that you heard music when you came by around eleven, checking the gate. The gate was locked then, wasn't it?"

"Yessiree, the gate was locked. Next time I checked, it wasn't locked, so I looked around like I'm suppose to do. I peeked inside over there, but I didn't see nothin', and I didn't take nothin'. That's when I saw the man in the water. I almost shit my pants when I saw the body. So I ran back over to the office and called the po-leece."

"You touch anything in there?"

32

"No sir, nothin', I didn't touch nothin' in there. I just peeked in the door, then when I turned around, there it was."

That answered one of Nick's lingering questions. He wondered how it was, that the security guard even saw the body floating in the water. It would have been hidden from anyone standing at the gate. However, from the raised salon door, it would have been easily seen.

"When you peeked inside, was any music playing?"

"No sir, no music. And them lights weren't on either, 'cause I remember it was a little dark inside."

Gary heard the interrogation and came over. "Sorry to interrupt you, Lieutenant. That towel you found matches those on the boat." Nick already knew that. "You figure this for a homicide, or what?" Gary looked over at LaMarr and indicated he could leave.

"I guess we won't know that until we see the autopsy and toxicology reports. I want you to place someone on watch here. Nobody goes on the boat, understand?" Gary nodded. "Any of those cars in the parking lot belong to the victim?" Nick was thinking about the rules they had just broken. Technically, they should have a search warrant for the yacht before proceeding, unless a crime had been committed. This one could still go either way. To protect himself, Nick decided to get a trained evidence technician to go back over everything, after he got a search warrant. Meanwhile, nothing could be taken, except the victim's body.

"Just about to tell you. While you were in the office, we found that black Lincoln Town Car over there unlocked. The car is registered to the dead man. Same address as on his license. We found his briefcase in the trunk along with some golf clubs. I opened the trunk by using the remote button inside the glove box."

Another patrol car arrived with two officers, to help keep the interested onlookers away from the gate area. Nick stepped onto the boat again. As he entered the salon, he saw a policeman wearing latex gloves, dusting for prints. He was busy lifting a piece of tape from the empty glass on the sidebar.

"You finished in the salon area?" Nick asked.

"Yes sir, but I didn't find much. There are prints on this glass, the arm of the chair and outside on the railing where the victim went over. That's it. You'd think there would be more than that. A lots of smudged prints on the door. Most of them are no doubt ours. And nothing on the bottle over there. It's been wiped clean. Same thing for the glasses in the sink."

Nick sat down on the sofa with a yellow lined pad he brought from his car. He started making notes of all he'd learned so far. As he began writing, he was interrupted by Mitchell.

"Lieutenant, I think we just might have a problem here. I guess you know about the prints already?"

"Yes, I know. Somebody doesn't want it known they were here with Mr. Blessing last night." Nick was still pondering that point. .

"Well, it might have been a woman. There's a little lipstick smear on one of the glasses in the sink. Of course we don't know how recent that is. I checked the beds carefully and there's no sign of a romp. And nothing in any of the waste baskets either." Nick already knew all this. "I was ready to chalk this one off as an accidental drowning, now I'm not so sure." It was the first time Gary had shown any real concern about the strange circumstances.

Nick turned back to his note pad and started listing a few items:

Who turned out the lights?
Music heard @ 11:00–Who turned off the radio/tape player?
Why no fingerprints?
Towel in trashcan–Was it used to wipe the fingerprints?
Who is Vincent Blessing? Why was he on the boat late Sat.?
Who else was with him? Why didn't they call the police?
Check out Phil Freeman. Relationship to the victim?
No keys! Lost, or stolen?

CHAPTER 4

Nick finished his notes and reviewed them. Having a few minutes alone, without Gary telling him things he already knew, allowed time to assess the circumstances. The second item on his list of notes held his concentration. He looked over at the stereo, stared at it for several long seconds. Then it dawned on him that a tape was still in the tape player. He walked over, took the eraser end of a pencil and hit the eject button. Using his handkerchief, he removed the tape. It was a country & western collection by Patsy Cline, one of Nick's favorite artists who died years ago. Her signature song was "Crazy". Nick thought that was particularly appropriate for the present situation.

Nick looked in the drawer below the stereo. It contained dozens of tapes and CDs, mostly classical and oldies from the '50s & '60s. He looked for the empty plastic case for this tape and didn't find it. On a hunch, he slipped the tape into his pocket. He'd have it checked for prints later. Perhaps whoever turned off the tape player, forget to take the tape... if they brought it. It would have been an easy item to overlook during a quick departure.

With a heavy caseload already, Nick sure didn't need another one. If they could find some keys, and if there was a logical explanation for why the victim was here, and why it wasn't reported sooner, Nick was willing to write this off as an accidental drowning. But, not before he had more answers. So far, this wasn't shaping up as an easy one to finish quickly.

Walking back to the parking lot, Nick saw a tow truck backing up to the black Lincoln. Gary was directing the driver, and saw Nick approaching.

4520-STAN

"Hold up for a few minutes while I take a quick look around," Nick said.

"Okay, but I don't think you'll find anything, Lieutenant. I already checked."

That alone, was sufficient challenge for Nick. He started with the ashtrays, then lifted the carpet pads, and looked under the seats. He was rewarded with finding a quarter and a toothpick. The glove box had a pair of sunglasses, the owner's manual, registration and insurance papers. He pushed the trunk release button and walked to the rear of the car. So far, Gary's report was accurate.

Inside the big trunk, he found an expensive, black leather Gucci briefcase. The lid was closed, but not snapped shut. There were several magazines, some literature, another gold Cross pen and some business cards that indicated Vincent Blessing was Midwest Regional Manager for a publication Nick didn't recognize, but it matched one of the magazines in the briefcase.

A pair of black and tan Foot Joy golf shoes, with a pair of socks rolled up and stuffed inside each one lay next to the golf bag. The bag held a set of expensive Callaway clubs. The victim obviously was a serious golfer. Nick was curious why the golf shoes weren't inside the pocket of the bag. That's where Nick kept his shoes. Out of curiosity, he unzipped the side pocket and withdrew a large manila envelope. Inside, he saw what looked like a business proposal for a pizza franchise. It was a strange place for the envelope. Why not in the briefcase, he wondered? Nick decided to hang on to the envelope and read the contents later. So far, that was 2 possible piece of evidence he'd taken, neither of which Gary had seen.

"Okay, I'm finished here. Remove the briefcase, golf clubs and shoes and tag them as personal property." Nick wanted to be sure they didn't become lost along the way. The clubs alone had to be worth a thousand bucks.

"His wheels were almost as clean as the boat," Gary

commented. He noticed Nick take the envelope and decided to wait until later to inquire about it. He hoped it wasn't something important that he'd overlooked.

——— ——— ———

Nick hated having to face grieving family members. It never got easier, and it wasn't something he could put off until Monday. He took Gary along and made him drive while Nick went over what they had so far.

Upon reaching the Blessing residence, Nick admired the late model silver Porsche in the circular drive. The house was a brick Tudor surrounded with tasteful landscaping and similar-looking homes, all in three hundred thousand plus category. Nick debated about calling first before arriving, since there was a good chance the family might be attending church services. Nick indulged Gary's growling stomach and they had stopped for a late breakfast before making this unannounced visit. It was agreed that Nick would handle the brief interview with the family. Gary was to watch the reactions. They would compare notes on the way back to the station.

"Hello, can I help you?" the young man opened the front door as they approached, and before Nick could ring the bell, or knock.

"Yes, I'm Detective Alexander, and this is Sergeant Mitchell. Is Mrs. Blessing available?" Nick estimated the young man to be in his mid-20s. He had long, blond hair parted in the middle. He was dressed in a plaid sports shirt and Jeans, not the usual attire for someone attending church.

"Can I ask what this is all about? I'm her son-in-law," he said nervously.

"What is your name?" Nick asked still standing in the doorway. He hadn't bothered to show his credentials. Sometimes he liked to wait until he was asked. It gave him a subtle

———

37

clue about how the rest of the interview would go, touchy or easy.

"Uh, my name is Paul Deckel, is there some sort of a problem?"

"Paul, is Mrs. Blessing home? We need to talk to her about her husband, Vincent."

"Is he in some kind of trouble?"

"No, he's dead. Any trouble he may have had is behind him. Now, may we please see Mrs. Blessing, so we may give her the bad news?"

"Oh wow, I can't believe it. Vince is dead? I don't know how Emily and Susan will take this. Please come in, I'm sorry to leave you standing there like that. I thought maybe you were here for something else."

"Before we go any further, Paul. Could you tell me who Emily and Susan are?"

"Right. Sorry, Emily is Mrs. Blessing, Vince's wife. And Susan is their daughter and my wife. We were just having some brunch on the terrace. Follow me." They walked down the hallway, through an ornately decorated living room, through French doors out onto a patio. The two women were seating at a round table drinking coffee. The remnants of brunch were still in evidence. Three settings, so obviously Vince wasn't expected.

"Emily, the police are here. They say Vince is dead." It was a rather blunt and strange pronouncement, for an introduction.

Nick introduced himself and Gary and offered his condolences. He hated having to do this to people, intrude on their privacy, and give them shocking news. Mrs. Blessing never left her seat, nor did she get up to shake his hand. She sat there just staring at him in total silence for a long few seconds. Then she covered her mouth and shook her head in disbelief..

"How did he die? Was it a car accident?" She finally asked.

"No, he fell overboard from a yacht at a St. Clair Shores marina, and drowned sometime late last night, or early this morning. Were any of you aware that he was there?"

"Oh dear, this is just terrible. Vince always plays golf on Sunday mornings. I thought he got up early and went to the club, as he usually does. I have no idea what he was doing out last night. I never heard him leave. Are you sure it's Vince?"

Nick explained that the picture on the driver's license matched the victim, and the car's registration was also in his name. While he was explaining all this, the daughter ran into the house crying. So far, she was the only one shedding tears. Paul stood behind Emily's chair shaking his head in silent disbelief.

"When was the last time you saw your husband, Mrs. Blessing?" Nick asked.

"Let me think, we had dinner here, all four of us. Susan and Paul left around eight, and I went upstairs to bed around ten. I said good night to Vincent, he kissed me on the cheek and said he wanted to do some work in his office. I guess that's the last time I saw him."

"So you didn't hear him leave?"

"No, but my bedroom is at the far end of the hall and I watched television for a while, so I never heard anything. What was Vincent doing on a boat?"

"I wish I knew the answer to that question, Mrs. Blessing. It appears that he'd been drinking. Did your husband usually drink?"

"Oh Vincent would fix himself a drink before dinner sometimes, and he might have a nightcap before retiring. He wasn't what you'd call a heavy drinker, if that's what you're asking." The lady reminded Nick of an Aunt he was very fond of. Both were very proper, always polite, and hid their emotions well.

"I see. You mentioned his office, is that here?" Nick had already seen Vincent Blessing's business cards with this address and a Post Office Box number, so he assumed the man worked from home.

"Yes, you passed by it on your way here. Paul can show you where it is, if you'd like to see it. Paul, why don't you show these gentlemen where Vincent's office." Turning to Nick, she asked, "Is there anything else I should know, officer?"

"Not at the moment, Mrs. Blessing. I would like to take a quick look at your husband's office. Perhaps I can find something that would explain why he was, where he was found. I'll keep you all posted on anything we learn." Nick gave her his card. This time, she stood and held out her hand. It was a formal departure.

Nick was pleased with Gary. He'd remained quiet throughout the exchange so far. They followed Paul back to the entrance area. The office was off to one side. Paul pushed open the door, then stood aside allowing them to enter. Nick turned on the overhead light, even though the room was well lit from the sun coming through the front bay window.

It was a comfortable room with a large executive desk dominating the middle portion of the area. Behind it was a matching walnut console with a computer terminal. One wall was covered with photos, mostly of Vince with other prominent people. There were a few plaques and certificates of appreciation. A large brown leather sofa sat in front of the bay window. A high winged-back chair was on each side, forming a conversational grouping. A low coffee table in the middle was covered with magazines. Nick took it all in carefully, and noticed that Paul remained standing in the doorway, watching him with interest.

"Just exactly what did Vince do, Paul?" Nick asked casually while examining the desk and the desk calendar. It was open to Friday, July 16th. There was one page for each day of the week. On Friday, Vince had printed several appointments. Nick noted the printing was precise. He flipped back a few weeks and saw similar notations. Flipping forward again to Saturday, he saw a hand written note, '*Pick up special info at club from Henry*'. On the reverse side of the page was Sunday, today. There were no appointments or notes.

"Well, uh, he was in advertising. What I mean is, he sold advertising space in those magazines you see on the table."

"Apparently he was pretty successful. Was he a good golfer?"

"Oh yeah, Vince was good at everything he did. Had an eight handicap and played several times a week at the country club. Is there anything special you're looking for here?"

"Well, I'm trying to learn as much as possible about Vince. Not only who was he, but also what kind of a person he was? Was he well liked?"

"Well sure, there were people who liked Vince. There were some who didn't like him, too. He could get kinda pushy at times. And he was pretty free with his opinions."

"Uh huh, did he give you much advice, Paul? You know, 'you ought to be doing this', that sort of thing." Nick was thinking of his son, Nickie, Jr. Paul reminded him a lot of Nickie, Jr. only the hair was too long. Paul was perhaps a few years older than his son.

"Are you kidding? All the time. I had to listen to his advice every damned time we came over for dinner."

"That Porsche out there belong to you?"

"Yeah, actually it's Susan's. When I saw you out there, I thought maybe she'd gotten another ticket, or something."

Nick raised his eyebrows slightly and looked over at Gary. They would need to remember to get the license number on the car. Apparently the daughter had a heavy foot, and a fast car to do it with. He guessed the car had to be worth close to fifty thousand, it had spoiled written all over it.

"Tell me something, Paul, is your wife an only child?"

"Yes she is." Paul couldn't understand the Lieutenant's line of questioning.

"And was the car a gift from Vince?"

"Yes. It was a graduation present when she got her degree in Liberal Arts. Vince was very proud of her. Particularly since he never finished college."

"Well, I'd say he did pretty well regardless. Just what is it you do for a living, Paul?"

"Me? I uh, sell printing. Why?"

"Just wondering. You and Vince must have talked a little shop, both of you being in the advertising business. Did you know any of his customers?"

"Not really. He talked about some of his clients. You know, like the ones he sold space to. His assistant, Ruth would know more about his clients than I would."

"I'll try to talk to her tomorrow. Does she also work in this office?" There was only one desk and Nick couldn't imagine two people working in this same room together.

"I think she's on vacation this week. But yeah, she works here in this office. She's usually here alone. Vince pretty much stays out of the office during the day. He's either calling on customers, or playing golf." It was as if Paul had read Nick's thoughts.

Nick saw a blinking red light on the telephone answering machine. Without asking permission, he reached over and played the messages. There were three. The first, "Hey Vince, this is Jack. We're teeing off in about five minutes. Where the hell are you? You can catch up with us on the second hole, if you're running late. And don't forget to bring some money, ha, ha, hah." The message was followed by a date and time. The call came in today, Sunday at 9:15. The next message, "Hi, it's Ruth. Just wanted to remind you that I won't be in on Monday, so you'll have to pick up the mail. I'll be back probably Thursday. Bye." That message came in at 9:33. The last message was a hang up. Obviously Ruth wouldn't be available to question tomorrow.

"I'd like to borrow this appointment calendar," Nick said.

He was admiring the black leather cover. The pages were removable. "I could use something like this. It's really nice."

"Yeah, it was a present from Ruth. I guess it's okay to borrow it, but I don't know why? Is this the way you handle accident investigations?"

"The Lieutenant likes to turn over every stone," Gary interjected. He'd remained silent as long as possible.

"What's Ruth's last name?" Nick asked. She had a pleasant phone voice.

"It's uh, Lambert. Ruth Lambert."

"Tell me something, Paul, how did Mrs. Blessing feel about Ruth working here?"

"What? I don't know what you're implying, but whatever it is, believe me, Emily doesn't get involved with Vince's business activities. Before Ruth came along, Vince went through several secretaries. She's the only one that lasted." Paul sounded defensive.

"Why is that? You think he tried to fool around? Or was he just difficult to work for?"

"He was difficult. I don't think he fooled around. He wasn't like that. He was only interested in making money and playing golf. He wasn't interested in anything else."

"This Ruth Lambert been here long?" Once again, it was Gary's question, and well-timed. Nick noticed that Gary had been taking a few notes as well.

"I think she's been working for Vince for about a year and a half. She's more than a secretary. She handles some of Vince's accounts. He relies on her a lot."

"Sounds like a good arrangement. Is Ruth Lambert married?" Nick asked.

"No, as a matter of fact, she's divorced. But... she has a boyfriend, and like I said, messing around wasn't something Vince would do. He and Emily got along real well."

"Uh huh, but they slept in separate bedrooms," Gary said with a smirk.

"That's because Vince snored. I don't know where you're going with this, but you're asking a lot of personal questions. I don't think I can help you any more."

"One last item before we leave, Paul. I think you may know the boat Vince was on."

"What! Why would I know anything like that?" The young man's face had turned red.

"Because you've been on that boat before. When I checked the visitor log at the marina I noticed Vince had been there before also. He was there with several other people that day and you were one of them. So what was that all about?"

"Hey, that was a business thing involving some sort of a presentation. Vince asked me if I wanted to go along and maybe do some fishing, so I said sure. Turns out that I was the only one who did any fishing. The rest all stayed inside. I don't think the owner was too pleased that Vince brought me along."

"Okay, and was Phil Freeman there?" Nick asked.

"Yeah, he and some other older man were making some sort of pitch. They had a flip chart and all that stuff. I didn't pay any attention."

"Did you know any of the other people there?"

"Nope. I didn't know anyone. And that's the only time I was ever on that boat. Was that the boat Vince was on last night?"

"Yes it is. Apparently he was meeting with someone. I'll probably know more after I talk with Phil Freeman. Meanwhile, thanks for all your help, Paul. Why don't you give me your phone number, in case I have any other questions."

Paul Deckel gave Nick his business card and walked them to the door. "Sir, is this by any chance a homicide investigation?" Paul asked as they were leaving. He was looking at Nick's card.

"No, for now it's just a set of strange circumstances that we have to sort out." Nick said as he stopped to admire the

Porsche and get the license number. He shot Paul a thumbs up. Paul continued to stand in the open doorway and watch them leave.

"Hey Nick, that last question was sort of strange don't you think?" Gary asked as they pulled away with Gary behind the wheel.

"Yep," Nick had to agree. He flipped the pages of the calendar sitting in his lap. If he had an appointment to meet someone on that yacht, it wasn't on the calendar, only the note to meet Henry at the club earlier to pick up something. The calendar was the third item Nick had taken in his growing collection of seemingly unrelated objects. Something bothered him about the calendar. When he first started to examine it, he noticed Paul looking apprehensive. Paul also seemed to know about Ruth's vacation plans. Maybe he'd played the phone messages earlier. If so, what was he doing in Vince's office? He also knew that she had a boyfriend. And he blushed a few times when her name was mentioned. Nick wondered if Ruth was attractive. Perhaps Paul had a crush on her. Nick thought about the time he introduced his girlfriend, Terry to his son, Nickie Jr. It had been an awkward moment with Nickie staring at Terry's beautifully sculpted breasts under a white tee-shirt, sans bra. Like Paul, he blushed when he realized he had been caught staring.

"Find anything interesting in that calendar, Nick?"

"I don't know yet. Vincent Blessing was very precise in printing all his appointments, even his golf tee times. That message on his answering machine indicated that he was expected earlier this morning, yet it isn't noted on today's page. I find that a little strange. And the note to meet Henry at the club was hand written, not printed. That's a definite departure from all the other pages on the calendar. From what I see so far, the victim was a creature of habit and probably very predictable. If he didn't play around, then last night was a departure for him."

"In more ways than one," Gary added with a chuckle.

And so are you, Gary thought to himself as he drove. Nick looked at small things and made a big deal out of them. Gary felt pretty sure that the victim probably had a date with some bimbo who took off on him. After all, his wife slept in another bedroom. That told Gary everything he needed to know. He'd wait and see how long it took Nick to come to the same conclusion.

CHAPTER 5

It was another typical hot July Monday. Nick reviewed his plans for the day while running his regular 3-mile routine. He hoped to see the Medical Examiner's report sometime later in the day. Since this wasn't a homicide, it wouldn't get a high priority. It was however the start of a new week. Weekly assignments would be passed out, and progress reports would be evaluated at the Monday morning meeting. It wasn't much different from any other office job in that regard.

Mr. Freeman, the owner of **The Other Woman'** was out of town on a business trip and wasn't expected back until late that day, according to his secretary. She indicated that she might be in touch with Mr. Freeman, and that if he called, she would relay the message, 'to get in touch with Lieutenant Alexander, about an accident that had happened on his boat Saturday evening'. Mr. Freeman's secretary seemed pretty sure that he was still in Orlando. He'd flown down on Friday on the company plane, so his actual return time wasn't known yet.

Nick had a lot of experience with secretaries who liked to protect their boss's privacy. Instinct told him when they were being specifically vague. They made it seem as though they were giving you facts, when in reality they were blowing smoke around. It wasn't the best way to start. Now Nick would have to wait to see how worried Mr. Freeman was about an accident happening on his boat . . . while he was in Florida. Was Vince making it with Freeman's wife while he was out of town? Was Freeman even married? Nick made a mental note to check.

Phil Freeman's call came in at 12:20 PM, a time when

47

most people would be out to lunch. Nick had opted for a yogurt at his desk, while reviewing another case file. Freeman was still out of town, and had just received the message. No caller ID appeared on Nick's phone, so he was apparently using a cell phone to make the call. The department didn't have the latest phone tracking equipment yet.

"Mr. Freeman, thanks for getting back to me so quickly. There's been a fatal accident on your boat and I have a few routine questions. Where are you calling from right now?"

"I'm in my hotel room in Orlando, why?"

"Good. Give me your number there, and I'll call you right back." This was always a good way to confirm a person's whereabouts, and Nick used it routinely, more out of habit.

"Why don't we just take a minute and do it now, I'm leaving soon for a meeting, no need for you to call me back."

"I have a call holding on the other line that's rather urgent so I'll get right back to you." This wasn't a complete lie in that Nick did have a call holding, but it wasn't an urgent call. The smoke he'd encountered earlier made him a little wary of Freeman and his associates. The man obviously had money, and that meant a needless run-around to prove that he was also very important. Nick had played the game hundreds of times in various forms. His hunch told him he was about to play yet another stupid game.

"Then I'll call you back in exactly ten minutes." Click. Nick asked the reception desk where that last call had originated? The Desk Sergeant confirmed that it must have been from a cell phone, since a number didn't appear. So Nick had no real way of knowing if Mr. Freeman was actually calling from Orlando, Florida, Birmingham, Michigan, or somewhere in between. When Nick had one of his famous hunches, he took every precaution. He told the desk Sergeant to put a trace on an incoming phone call from a Mr. Freeman when it came in. Nick wanted to know the number just in case they were disconnected again. If a game was being played, he wanted to know early, so he could adjust his interrogation accordingly.

The second call came in at 12:35. Phil Freeman explained that he could only speak for a brief period, he was scheduled for an important business meeting. He planned to fly back sometime tomorrow and they could of course talk at some length then, if it was absolutely necessary.

"Mr. Freeman, I appreciate you calling me back, and I realize how busy you must be. Do you know Vincent Blessing?" Of course Nick already knew the answer.

"Yes . . . I know Vince, why? Is he in some sort of trouble?"

"Not now. He drowned Saturday night. He fell over the side of your boat at the marina."

"My God, how terrible! What on earth was Vince doing on my boat?"

"That was my next question to you, sir. Did he have a key?"

"Of course not! I've been out of town the entire weekend on a business trip. I gave no one permission to use the boat while I was away. And I certainly wouldn't have given Vince a key. I didn't know him all that well. We're talking about a very expensive piece of equipment, Lieutenant. Was there any damage?"

"None that we could determine. You might want to contact your insurance agent about the accident. They can get a copy of our report later this week. One more question, Mr. Freeman, how long have you known Vincent Blessing?"

"Why? What has that to do with his death?" Nick hated when people responded with a question, rather than an answer. It was a form of dancing around the issue, which always meant more questioning. It was something Nick specialized in, much to Gary's chagrin.

"Just curious how you two happened to know each other."

"Yes, well we can discuss that at another time, right now, I'm late for a meeting . . . ." Click.

49

"Thank you, Mr. Freeman for . . . ." Nick was about to say "all your help" when he was cut off. Freeman seemed more concerned about damage to his boat than with Vincent's death. He was obviously a man preoccupied with money. He liked to dismiss people. And, he was devious.

Phil Freeman hadn't been very cooperative, and he wasn't in Orlando when he had called. The call had been placed from a cell phone again. The Desk Sergeant thought it might have been made locally. He had to check with the local carrier to confirm that. It would take a little time. Fifteen minutes later, he had the confirmation. The call originated from the Dearborn area. Why would Freeman pretend to be calling from Orlando when he was here? Nick had a feeling this case would continue to get more complicated as he searched into the life and death of Vincent Blessing, super advertising salesman, father to a spoiled daughter and a man who played a good game of golf. There had to be a bit more to know about him and his recent activity. Nick hoped to fill in those blanks. Paul Deckel, and perhaps the absent Ruth Blessing, would no doubt be able to help him. He doubted that the widow, or her daughter, Susan would be able to supply much information.

Nick still had three unrelated pieces to this developing puzzle. There was the Patsy Cline tape that still needed to be checked for prints. There was the envelope with a business proposal he'd taken from the victim's golf bag. And there was the desk calendar. Each item had an unanswered question attached.

Nick had a 2:00 appointment to meet Paul Deckel. This time they were meeting at a small coffee shop just outside Birmingham. An informal place provided just the right atmosphere for asking some difficult questions. Nick wanted to know a lot more about Vincent Blessing, and Paul seemed to be the best place to start.

"You can go ahead with the funeral arrangements. The

Medical Examiner has released the body," Nick said stirring his black coffee. He used to use cream and sugar, so the stirring habit remained.

"Then Vince's death was an accident?" Paul seemed relieved.

"I suppose so. I haven't had time to review the report. There's no evidence of a struggle, or violence that we could determine. And, we've ruled out suicide."

"If that's the case, then why do you want to talk to me? I've told you everything I know."

"I want to get a better profile of what Vincent Blessing was really like. Like I said yesterday, the more I know about the man, the sooner I'll discover why he was on that boat, and who else was with him. So far, no one has admitted being there, or witnessing the accident."

"So you're continuing with the investigation?" Paul's disappointment showed.

"Sure. Aren't you interested in learning the answers to those questions?"

"Of course. I didn't mean to appear not interested. It's just that you seem to be treating this more like a homicide, or at least with a great deal of interest. Do you investigate all accidents this thoroughly?"

"Yes, when there are as many unanswered questions as there are in this case. Have you spoken to his assistant yet?"

"Yes, Ruth called and Susan told her about Vince. She's returning from her vacation early so she can be with Emily. She was shocked of course."

"I'm sure she was. Tell me about Ruth ah . . . ."

"Ruth Lambert. Well, she's very... efficient. She knows most of Vince's customers, and I think she gets along with everyone very well. She got along with Vince, which was a miracle."

"How's that?" Nick watched closely as the young man attempted to answer.

"Until Ruth came along, Vince went through a lot of secretaries. Couldn't keep anyone more than a few months."

"Why? Did he try to play hanky-panky?"

"Nah, Vince wasn't like that. He was 60 years old. His main interest was golf, making money and, trying to impress people. He was just difficult to work for, that's all. He yelled all the time. His bossy manner didn't go over too well I guess."

"Then Ruth came along, and things changed?"

"Yeah, they did. Vince didn't scare her the way he did the others. She ignored his outspoken manner and rude behavior. So, they got along fine. I think she knew as much about the business as he did, but I doubt that Vince would ever admit that."

"So he came to rely on her?"

"He sure did. She took over a lot of his little details, and that freed him up to play more golf."

Just then their waitress came over to refill Paul's iced tea and Nick's coffee. When she left, Nick noticed the way she walked, her buns shifted from side to side in a manner that appealed to him. It was a sexy walk. He continued to watch her and noted that Paul hadn't missed her somewhat exotic departure either. It helped Nick with his next question.

"You think maybe Vince and this Ruth Lambert may have had a thing going?"

"What!" The question had unnerved Paul, he appeared to be upset and caught off-guard. "No way. Ruth is a very... attractive woman, who could have her pick of any man she wanted. She'd sure want someone a lot younger than Vince."

"Really? So she's attractive too? How old is she?" Nick was more interested in Paul's description and opinions, since this gave Nick a handle on Paul. Nick really wanted to zero in on what their relationship had been like, and this was one way to get there, by talking about women.

"I don't know, forty I guess. I never really thought about it much. Why?"

"Well, I saw the way you looked at our waitress. You were admiring her ass when she walked away . . . ."

"So what? You were, too."

"I know. I think she's kind of cute. And since I'm single, I may ask her for a date. You on the other hand, are married, so you only get to look." It was something he might have said to Nickie, Jr. He had to be careful not to assume a fatherly role here with Paul.

"So what's your point, Lieutenant?" Paul hadn't touched his drink, and he was acting more annoyed than nervous today. He kept flicking his head so his hair would stay back. It was a mannerism more suited to a woman. But then, he'd been an art student.

"My point is, all guys get horny at some time or another. And I don't think you, me, or Vince is any different in that respect. You tell me Vince didn't fool around . . . ."

"I said, I didn't think he fooled around. He was my father-in-law for God's sake. We weren't buddies. We didn't talk about pussy. We talked about advertising and printing . . . and golf, of course. Those were his favorite subjects."

"How did Vince act around Ruth? Was he considerate, or pushy like he was with the other secretaries?"

"I already told you, they got along just fine. Vince had respect for her ability. She's a very intelligent person." Nick noted that Paul was being careful in how he described the woman. Was it possible that he was smitten with her, even if she was older than he was?

"And she's attractive. Was she flirty around the office?"

"I seriously doubt it. Vince wasn't there that much, and Ruth has a boyfriend." Paul flushed when he talked about Ruth, this didn't escape Nick's notice.

"She got big hooters?" Nick was deliberately pushing him.

"Pardon me? Oh, you mean tits. Yeah, they're beauties." Now Paul's face was completely flushed, and he knew it. He looked down at his drink to avoid Nick's eyes. Yes, the poor lad was smitten, Nick was sure of it. He also seemed to know she had a boyfriend.

"Uh huh, you talk to her much?"

"Not really. Sometimes when I had a quote I wanted Vince to look at, I'd stop by. That's about all."

"Tell me more about your job. Who is it you work for?"

"I, ah, I'm in business for myself. That is, I have a small printing business."

"Uh huh, and did Vince help you in any way?"

"I don't understand your question."

"Yes you do. You're a bright fellow who knows more than you are telling. And I'm the guy you're gonna tell it all to, bit by bit, however long it takes." Nick decided it was time to get tough with this rich kid, who seemed to have a crush on his father-in-law's pretty secretary. It wouldn't be the first time that a young man fell for an older woman, married, or not.

"Okay, what is it you want to know exactly?" Paul seemed tense, yet resigned and a little exasperated. It was like anticipating a dentist appointment, not fun.

"Did Vince set you up in business, or help you out in any way?"

The question hit Paul like a punch in the face. He was surprised. It took him a few seconds to collect himself before he could answer. "How . . . ah, how did you know about that?"

"Paul, just answer the question. A simple yes, or no, will keep us moving along here. I'm trying to learn how well the two of you got along. Were you partners?"

"No, nothing like that. Vince loaned me some money, to help me get started. I was selling printing for another company when Susan and I got engaged. We met in college. Vince thought I should start my own business, so his daughter wouldn't have to starve when he retired. It was his constant dumb joke." Paul looked out the window, just like a kid in school waiting for the school bell to ring, so he could go home. Then he looked down at his hands, avoiding Nick's direct gaze.

"Okay, so you started your own printing business. How is that working out?"

"It's okay. Actually, I do pretty well. Vince introduced me to some of his friends."

"They give you any business?" Nick found Paul fairly easy to read. Paul would stammer a little when hit with a surprise-type question. And, his face would blush when he was caught in a lie, or embarrassed to have to reveal something personal. For this reason alone, face-to-face questions could never replace phone interviews. Sometimes the body language was enough to tell Nick what it was he wanted to know, regardless of the answers.

"A little. Of course they didn't know I was Vince's son-in-law. We kept that a secret."

"Oh, why is that?"

"Well, like I told you, not everyone liked Vince. Some of his customers hated having to do business with him. If they knew we were related, I wouldn't stand a chance."

"Uh huh, so he pushed some business your way to help you out. Sounds like a pretty thoughtful thing for him to do."

"Yes and no. I had to sign a note for the fifty thousand he loaned me. And I had to listen to all his bullshit over dinner every Saturday night, when we were there. He liked to brag about himself and criticize others, including me. He was a very self-centered man."

"I guess that's the price you pay for marrying a rich man's daughter. You have to measure up in some way."

"Yeah, you got that right."

"Tell me, Paul, how come you didn't mention being on that boat until I brought it up?"

"I guess I didn't think it was all that important, is it?"

"I don't know yet. How's Mrs. Blessing holding up?"

"You won't believe this. She's in her garden making a special flowered wreath for the funeral. I told you, she's a very unique woman. Doesn't openly display much emotion, but she's hurting inside, and trying hard not to show it, for Susan's sake."

"And how is your wife doing?"

"She's taken this very hard. She isn't like Emily. She can't keep things hidden inside. She's been crying a lot. I don't seem to be doing a very good job of consoling her. I don't know what else to do." Paul was twisting his wedding ring, not looking at Nick. Another few years, and this could be Nickie, Jr.

"What does your wife think about Ruth Lambert? Did they get along?"

"Uh, I guess so. I think she resents the fact that Ruth and Emily hit it off so well."

"I see. Tell me, Paul, what kind of music did Vince like?"

"He was a jazz buff. He had a lot of old thirty-three records. Why are you asking me about music?"

"Well, my picture keeps getting clearer all the time, thanks to your help. I believe you mentioned that you met your wife while you were both attending college."

"Yeah, art school. I didn't get any degree, okay? And Vince threw that up to me every chance he got. Wanted his daughter to marry a banker's son, not some art school-drop out."

"Well, all things considered, you don't seem to be doing so bad. Vince must have wanted to help you, or he wouldn't have loaned you that fifty grand to get started in business."

"Susan is the one who got him to do that."

"So it took awhile to gain his acceptance. I can picture that happening. Best thing to do in your case would be to learn to play golf, and get good, so you could give the old man some competition, where it counts the most to him."

"I never became that good. Never shot any better than ninety at his club. Vince would shoot in the mid-seventies regularly, and had to give me strokes."

"And did he rub that in, too?"

"Oh yeah, he made a big deal out of giving me anything including advice."

"Did he ever cheat on his golf score?"

"Ummmm, not that I ever noticed. And if he did, I wouldn't dare mention it. There would be no peace in the family if I did something that foolish. But he was good, he didn't have to lie about his score. And, if you're about to ask me if I ever lied about mine, the answer is no, Vince kept count of my strokes, too. You couldn't get away with anything with him."

Nick was getting a pretty good picture of the relationship. Paul was a poor farm kid who became an art student. Married into a family with money. Then had to pay the price. It was a tough lesson for anyone, yet Paul managed to look the part, and hold his own fairly well. Nick gave him high marks for hanging in there the way he must have, under considerable pressure from Vince. And, he'd been concerned for Emily when Nick first arrived.

"Before we go, let me ask you one more unrelated question. Did you ever hear Vince mention anything about a franchise idea he might have had?"

"The only franchise idea I know about was a magazine he was thinking of starting. It had something to do with visitors coming into the Detroit area. The magazine would give the reader some insight into where the best places were to shop and eat. He wanted me to get some quotes on how much it would cost to produce it on a quarterly basis."

"Did he ever discuss that idea with Phil Freeman?"

"I don't know who he talked to. Maybe Mr. Freeman can tell you."

Phil Freeman was at the top of Nick's list of people to see. Paul had given him about all he could at the moment. Nick felt certain there was more, and he'd have to drag it out of him, in pieces . . . if this turned out to be something more than an accident. He'd have a more complete picture once he spoke to Ruth. For some strange reason, Nick was looking forward to meeting the lady with the big hooters.

Nick winked at the cute waitress as he was leaving. Paul was in front of him and didn't notice the waitress smile at them. Nick had left her a big tip. The coffee was good here, and the service was excellent. No doubt about it, he'd be back... soon.

CHAPTER 6

Phil Freeman lived in Bloomfield Hills, among the new rich crowd, where everyone was building a giant house on a small lot. The developers were getting top dollar for small parcels. And all the houses seemed to have circular drives with expensive and exotic cars on display. Living here, you would definitely have to keep up with the family next door, and it was very doubtful that their last name would be Smith, or Jones. Nick wanted to see where Phil Freeman lived. It took a little searching to get his unlisted home address, but Nick was resourceful.

The maid said Mr. Freeman was out of town, and not expected back until tomorrow night. He also learned that Mrs. Freeman was at the club playing tennis, and wouldn't be back until later. Nick was aware that most rich people liked to eat dinner late. It was 4:00 now, and close to the cocktail hour. Before leaving, he asked the maid what type car Mr. Freeman drove. She said it was a gold-colored Cadillac Seville. License plate was a vanity plate with 'Free-1' on it. Mrs. Freeman drove a white Buick Riviera with 'Free-2'. Perhaps there was an open marriage arrangement here. If so, then the name on the yacht didn't sound so strange after all. The stop wasn't wasted since the maid confirmed Phil had been out of town for the weekend. Perhaps she wasn't aware that he was back. Nick wondered if Mrs. Freeman was also unaware of his early arrival. And was there anything to make of that? Nick made a mental note to be sure to check out Phil's alibi for Saturday night. Maybe he was playing around and just didn't want his wife to know. Or maybe she didn't care. These days there were few real surprises when it came

59

to who was sleeping where, and with whom. Maybe it was because Nick had sex on his mind a lot lately that he saw that as an underlying motive to everything. And maybe it was distorting his perspective.

He thought about the cute waitress at the restaurant earlier. She was definitely interested. Might be worth a shot later in the week. First, he had a few loose ends he wanted to get tied up. Then he'd take care of his libido, in that order. Business first, that was one of Nick's rules, much to the annoyance of a few ex-female friends in his life. The problem with waitresses was, they were great one-nighters, but anything long term fizzled out quickly. Usually they had kids, they had to get up early, and their interest level always seemed to be narrowly focused. And here he was thinking about pussy all day. How narrowly focused was that? He laughed at his self-evaluation.

Paul Deckel indicated that Vince hung out at Chef Louie's Cafe, (commonly called Chez Lou's) and entertained clients there. It wasn't much out of his way, so Nick headed toward Woodward Ave. To kill a little time, he would drop in for a quick drink. The lounge had a reputation for drawing the chic and near-famous, plus a lot of the wealthy business trade. Food was the best anywhere in the area, with high prices to maintain that reputation. Nick pulled into Chez Lou's parking lot. It appeared to be almost full. Rather than leave his car with the valet, he drove slowly toward the rear of the building, looking for a vacant spot. And there it was, 'Free-1' sitting next to a bright red Corvette. Sometimes you just get lucky.

Inside, the place was as busy as the parking lot suggested. The bar had no open spaces. Nick stood for a few minutes, waiting for an opening, trying to catch the bartender's attention. He had plenty of time to take in the room. Mostly an over '50s crowd he decided. Lots of interesting attractive singles with a lot of gold showing, and a lot of smiling, bright white-capped teeth. It seemed that everyone was talking, smiling or nodding. He'd have to keep this place in mind for another time. An older black entertainer played a grand piano and sang cocktail-type love songs quietly so people could talk and still listen to the music. He was good. You could sit here for a few hours and get pleasantly smashed. The prospects were probably good for meeting someone nice, provided you had money. It was definitely the right atmosphere for getting lucky.

"Okay, you look like you're ready. What'll you have?" The bartender asked. His nametag said Peter.

"Make mine a Cutty & water with a twist, Pete. And, send over another drink to Phil Freeman will you?"

"Sure thing. I think he's drinking a vodka martini with Absolute." Nick was impressed. This was a good bartender.

When his drink arrived, he paid and kept his eye on Pete who had called a waitress over to take the martini to a corner booth, where three people were drinking. Nick followed the waitress with his drink in hand. It all looked so natural. One of the two men asked the waitress who had sent over the drink, just as Nick arrived.

"I sent over the drink, Phil. Name's Nick Alexander. We spoke on the phone a few hours ago, when you were getting ready for a dinner meeting in Orlando, remember?"

"Oh yes! Who told you where to find me?" Phil Freeman had a tan that contrasted nicely with his gray hair. Nick estimated that he was in his late 50s. He wore an expensive white linen dinner jacket, tan slacks and white loafers. The flowered sport shirt was tasteful, but more appropriate for Florida, where he was supposed to be. He looked concerned.

"That's the trouble with vanity plates. Sometimes they give you away. Mind if I join you?" The man and the woman seated in the curved booth had to move over. No introductions were offered. Phil Freeman was shaking his head slowly trying to think of something that might sound reasonable, but didn't say anything. He just sat there looking at Nick waiting for a question. Nick decided to wait, too, and took a sip of his drink, not taking his eyes off Phil. Finally Nick offered a very slight smile and turned to the two other people in the booth. They appeared nervous.

"Hi, I'm Nick Alexander. Most people just call me 'Lieutenant' since I rarely have much social conversation. You two can call me Nick. He gets to call me Lieutenant 'cause he's in big trouble with me." He nodded toward Phil. Nick gave him a plastic smile in return for the frown.

"Oh dear, what have you done now, Phil?" The blonde said forcing a smile that almost cracked her makeup. She too, was in her early 50s trying to look 40. Low cut dress with a big silicon front sticking out. Good job though. It was an expensive dress, showing a lot of leg. No wedding ring. She reminded Nick of a younger Carol Channing. Same type plastic smile Nick had used. He was fitting in already, he mused.

"Hey, Lieutenant you're really something, you know? I guess I didn't fool you. How did you know I wasn't calling from Orlando? Actually, I was there earlier. Got back sooner than I expected. I had a few things to clean up before going into the office tomorrow. No real crime in a white lie now is there? My turn to buy you a drink." It was a false friendliness, like introducing someone as your best friend, even though you hardly knew him.

"Well, since I'm off duty, and this isn't official, I'll have another Cutty & water, but only if these people here will join us."

"Actually, they were just about to leave. Fran why don't I catch up with you and Bill later, okay? This isn't anything too important, and it won't take long." Phil was trying to suggest they move by starting to slide out of the booth to stand up. Nick made no effort to move. He allowed Phil to negotiate the awkward departure of his friends, enjoying the moment.

"Phil, do you want me to call your lawyer for you?" Bill looked worried and kept staring at Nick like he didn't belong in this crowd.

"No, no, this won't take but a few minutes, right Lieutenant?"

"Whatever you say, Phil. You seem to have everything under control here." Nick watched them walk to the bar, looking back at Nick and Phil, still curious and a bit worried.

"So just what is it you want, Lieutenant?" Now, Phil sounded more annoyed than cordial. Probably an attempt to hide his concern over being tripped up, Nick decided.

"Some straight answers would be nice. When people go out of their way to blow smoke in my face, I usually go out of my way to let them know how much I appreciate it, know what I mean? You said you were in Orlando, when actually you were in Dearborn. Why did you feel that little ruse was necessary?"

"How did you find out I was in Dearborn? Who told you?"

"There must be something wrong with the way I ask questions lately. Every time I ask a question, people feel the need to answer me with a question. That's not the way it works, Phil. I'll ask you simple questions. If you don't understand, raise your right hand so I'll know, and I'll try to rephrase the question, or speak slowly. Got that?" Phil nodded that he understood. "It won't take much for me to learn everything there is to know about you, and that could be quite a lot." Nick finished his speech with a knowing grin. Then took a long sip from his drink.

"Okay so I called you from Dearborn. Actually, I stopped by the Fairlane Club so what?"

"That's a question, Phil, not an answer. You wanted me to believe you were out of town when you weren't. That's a very suspicious thing to do to a police officer investigating an accident that happened on your boat." Nick could see that Phil had perspiration forming on his forehead. He had a thin layer of hair combed across a balding area. Nick had a hunch that Phil probably wanted to take his handkerchief out and wipe his forehead, but was afraid that this would telegraph his nervousness. So he sat there playing nervously with his napkin instead.

"Look Lieutenant, I'm really sorry for that. It was a stupid thing to do. Learning about the accident had me upset. I was worried that I might be connected in some way. I don't know why Vince was there, or how he managed to get in. That's the truth."

"Uh huh." Nick stared into Phil's cold gray eyes. This was a man who lied a lot and got away with it by looking sincere. The word, truth shouldn't be in his vocabulary.

"And the only time I ever took Vince out on the boat was last month, when he and a few other friends of mine went fishing." Nick took particular notice that he said, 'fishing' and didn't mention anything about a presentation. Why hide something like that?

"Uh huh, catch anything that day?"

"What? Oh, yeah, Vince's son-in-law caught some Walleye. Vince brought him along. Kind of annoyed me. Trying to hustle some printing. He wasn't invited, either."

"Who else was along on that trip?"

"I don't know what possible difference that could make. You said Vince fell overboard. The two events don't have any connection whatsoever."

"Except it all happened on your boat. You keep a log of all your guests for tax purposes I would imagine."

"Yes, of course. I'll be happy to show you that log if you don't believe me."

"Good. I'd like to see it. Is everyone you invited that day listed in your log?"

"Of course! What are you suggesting, Lieutenant?"

"I'm not suggesting anything, just asking. Do you put down all the names, or just some of them, you know, like the people who are clients, not just friends?"

"I believe everyone is listed. I have no reason to leave anyone off. I only use the boat for business. It's one of several pieces of equipment my company owns and uses regularly."

"How about your wife, does she ever use the boat?"

"I don't think I like your line of questioning. And, I think you'd better call my office and make an appointment, if you want to talk to me any further. I'll make sure my lawyer is present. How's that for an answer, Lieutenant?"

"Sounded like a question to me, Phil. Maybe having your lawyer present is a good idea. By-the-way, did you happen to know Vince's assistant, Ruth?" Nick said this as he was getting up to leave. He watched for a slightly changed expression on Phil's face. It was almost undetectable, if you weren't watching closely. Nick felt sure Phil knew her, or at least knew who she was.

"I'm not answering anymore questions, Lieutenant unless I'm being charged with something."

"I can't imagine what I'd charge you with, Phil. But maybe I'll think of something before I call. Meanwhile, your boat is still under police custody. If you go out there, be sure to identify yourself to the officer guarding your boat. You won't be able to go anywhere until I finish my investigation. So the more cooperative you are, the sooner I'll be through, and the sooner you can have your boat back." Nick waved to the bartender as he left.

———   ———   ———

Nick decided to swing by the marina before going home. He wanted to be sure the boat was being guarded, and to alert the officer, that the owner would no doubt be coming around. If so, he was to accompany him onboard and stay with him until he left. The officer was to report everything that the owner did and said. Nick had a feeling that Phil might be coming out soon. And while reviewing his notes, he waited in his car in the parking lot. He didn't have a date, and there wasn't anyone back at his apartment waiting for him, not even a dog.

Monday night wasn't much of a party night at the marina he learned. He was about to turn on the radio when he remembered the stereo on the yacht. There had been music playing according to the security guard who discovered the body. Nick made a mental note to ask who turned off the stereo? And, there was that tape in the stereo, still on his desk. Not something anyone would normally wipe clean. Should be some prints there. He doubted that it belonged to the victim. Phil Freeman didn't appear to be the country-western type either.

The light beside the gate to the dock area was already on, even though it was still light outside. Nick waited and thought about his encounter with Phil Freeman. The man didn't volunteer any information and weighed his words carefully, only his eyes revealed any true reaction, or surprise. Phil's smile was more of a sneer. He was definitely a cold and calculating man. Hard to believe Vincent Blessing could bully Phil.

It took another hour for the evening to become fully established in darkness with twinkling lights coming on in various quadrants. Only a sliver of moon appeared now, as thin clouds drifted overhead. The effect would be very romantic under other circumstances. Once again he thought about the waitress and wondered just how interested she might be. His last brief romance had taught him a good lesson. There had to be some mutual interests beyond the sack. Looking at Phil's yacht, Nick decided that a night in the sack with a lively companion aboard, would be an exciting way to spend a night. Was that what Vince had in mind? If so, why had he drunk so much? Everyone knew alcohol could do a real job on your performance. So far, there wasn't any evidence of a romantic tryst. Eliminating that prospect, the meeting had to involve money. That seemed to be the basis for any relationship Phil Freeman would cultivate, and one of the few topics of interest to the victim.

Saturday night, or early Sunday morning had to have been similar to this evening. Not much activity, which really surprised Nick, since he would have thought this to be a more lively area for the fast crowd. Only a few cars in the parking lot, and most of the boats were dark. Low-level lights bordered the walkways and docks. Not the best location to murder someone, if you were planning it. Out on the open water would be much better, he surmised. Yet something fatal happened here. Why? Phil Freeman appeared sensitive when Nick asked about his wife. She knew Phil was out of town for the weekend. That gave her the opportunity to play around on the boat with a secret boyfriend. Nick made a note to explore that angle further.

Nick was just about to leave, when he saw Phil's gold Cadillac pull into the parking lot. He was alone. He went directly to the gate, unlocked it and walked down the pier to **The Other Woman**. Nick watched as the officer guarding the boat opened the door from inside. After a minute he let Phil enter. Lights came on below in the master stateroom. A few minutes later, the lights went out and Phil appeared on deck. The officer watched him leave and noted the time in his notebook. Phil returned to his car and drove off quickly, not noticing Nick parked between two other cars in the lot.

"Did he take anything?" Nick asked the officer watching the yacht.

"No sir. He said he wanted to check the fuel tanks, and make sure the phone was working. Didn't even look around much, or seem to care that I was here."

Nick asked which phone Phil had touched. Then he instructed the officer to place the unit in a plastic bag so it could be checked for fingerprints. There was always the possibility that Phil Freeman wasn't who he said he was. Phil didn't have to go into the master stateroom to check the phone, or the fuel.

"Did you follow him into the master stateroom when he went down there?"

"Ah, no sir, I just watched from the steps, but he didn't bring anything up with him."

"How can you be so certain? My orders were to watch him and I meant closely, not from a distance. The phone in the master stateroom is an extension. He didn't need to go down there to check the phone to see if it was working, he could do that from up here. And where do you suppose you check the fuel level?"

"Ah, I would imagine in the cockpit, sir."

"Right. And he didn't even bother to go there, or turn anything on, did he?"

"I'm sorry, sir. I'll be more careful next time. I really don't know anything about boats."

"Obviously. He might come back again, and you stick to him and report anything he says, or does, got that?" Nick was annoyed that they hadn't placed a more experienced man here. He was curious what it really was that Phil was looking for, or checking on. He hadn't stayed long. And, he hadn't bothered to check the railing where the victim did his exit. Perhaps he just wanted to be sure the yacht was okay, and that it was being guarded, as Nick had indicated. Phil Freeman was a man who used deception as a way of life. While he tested others, he couldn't be trusted. Nick wondered how much trust Vince had in him? An argument between the two of them would have been an interesting match to watch.

CHAPTER 7

At least a hundred people gathered at the cemetery. The line of cars was sufficient indication that an important person had passed away. Nick thought about how his funeral would be some day. Three cars maybe. And a few police cars in front, if he was still on the force then.

Nick wasn't prepared for Ruth Lambert. She wore a very stunning black dress and her black straw hat was a striking frame for her red hair. She stood just behind the family, yet a little separated from everyone else. Paul was right, she was beautiful. About 5' 7", and trim. It was difficult to judge her age. At the moment, it didn't matter. Nick didn't recognize any of the people attending the ceremony. Freeman wasn't there. Paul stood next to his wife and Emily. His wife was crying, and Nick was glad to see that someone had shed a tear for Vincent Blessing, even if he wasn't well liked. The man obviously had some friends, judging by the group here.

When it was over, Nick approached Paul and Emily and extended his condolences. Then he nodded to Ruth and extended his hand, introducing himself.

"This isn't a good time to talk, but I would appreciate a few minutes soon Miss Lambert. Here's my card. Where can I reach you?"

"I'll be at the Blessing's residence for the rest of the day to help Emily of course. And tomorrow, I'll work in the office, cleaning up some last-minute items that need some attention. You could stop by then I suppose." Her green eyes pierced him, and it took him a few seconds to compose his response. First, he had to regulate his breathing back to normal.

"Fine. I'll stop by tomorrow around ten thirty if that will

be convenient." He thought about asking her to lunch, but that could wait, and take its natural course later. Vince definitely had good taste in secretaries, or assistants, or whatever her title was. He hoped it wasn't mistress. With such an attractive person working in his office, why would the man want to fool around with anyone else? It was an amusing thought.

Paul's wife, Vincent's daughter, remained by the grave alone. Nick could respect this privacy and decided to wait for another time to talk to her. Death had first priority over anything else. And his questions could wait another day. He didn't expect that she could tell him very much. Paul seemed to have a good grasp of what was going on in the family.

———   ———   ———

Nick arrived at 10:30 precisely. Ruth greeted him at the door. Probably saw him drive up and was waiting. Once again, he was taken with her beauty and poise. He followed her into Vince's office. Everything appeared the same as it was Sunday when he was here.

"Would you like a cup of coffee, Lieutenant?"

"That would be great." He took a seat in a big high backed leather chair that was close to the matching sofa, and waited for her to return. Her perfume lingered in the air. He took a deep breath to capture it. While he was waiting, he looked at the magazines on the coffee table. He noticed that Vincent Blessing was listed as a Midwest Regional Manager in two of them. It seemed like a pretty fancy title for a salesman. When Ruth returned, she was carrying a tray with china cups, cream, sugar, napkins, a carafe of coffee and some delicious looking rolls with nuts on top.

"Thank you for seeing me like this. I know the family must be quite upset. But there are a few questions I have to ask, so that I can get a better picture of what actually happened."

"I'll be happy to help in any way I can, Lieutenant."

———

"It might be easier for both of us if I called you Ruth, and you called me Nick. I hope that's not a problem?"

"No, Nick, I prefer it." She lit a cigarette and sat down on the edge of the sofa close to him. She crossed her legs slowly enough to give him a partial look at her well-shaped legs and thighs. She was wearing a tan shirtdress with some expensive looking jewelry. She could easily be the owner of a women's fashion boutique. In fact, she could be a model. There was an understanding look in her eyes that said, she already knew the questions he was about to ask. Looking at her, Nick felt a dizzy moment pass. This was a most unusual experience for Nick, the man who was always in control of the situation.

"How long have you worked for Vince?"

"Let's see, just about two years now. I guess that's a record. Vince went through a few secretaries in a short period of time, before I came along."

"Why was that?" Nick liked the easy manner in which she answered him.

"Well, you had to know Vince. He was a big bully, until you really got to know him."

"In two years, you must have gotten to know him pretty well." It was more of a statement than a question, Nick realized after he said it.

"Yes, but not the way you're suggesting. What I meant was, he had a very kind side that he kept hidden from most people, except maybe his family. Outwardly, he was brash and bold and pushy. He said what he thought, and didn't care if you liked it, or not."

"That must have rubbed a few people the wrong way."

"Yes, it's true, he did annoy some of his customers. That's why he started using me more as his assistant. I know most of his customers and prospects fairly well now, and some of them actually prefer to talk to me, instead of Vince. Please don't take that the wrong way."

"I understand. How did Vince feel about that involvement?"

"Vince didn't mind at all. He rather liked the idea of me handling some of his accounts. It freed him up to do some of the other things he wanted to do."

"Such as?"

"Well, play golf for one thing. That takes up a little of your day, Nick. And when your Publisher wants a report, and a couple agencies want a media kit, well, I was able to handle all those things for him while he was out. He also followed the stock market closely. He and Emily have a lot of investments. He looked into many different opportunities. Money was important to Vince. He didn't waste it, or spend it foolishly."

"With you helping him, it seems to me that he had a good thing going."

"Actually, it worked out well for both of us. I was able to be more than just a secretary . . . he paid me very well. And, as you can see, this is a pleasant place to work."

"Yes, it's very comfortable. What did you do before you worked for Vince?"

"Oh, I worked for a small advertising agency here. I was Administrative Assistant to the President."

"Not just a secretary there, either, huh?"

Actually, I started out as a secretary, yes. Then I was given more duties. Soon I became involved in everything the agency was doing for its clients." She refilled Nick's cup as she spoke.

"Sounds like an interesting job. Why did you leave?"

"The President's wife was jealous of my working closely with her husband. She started making remarks, which weren't true, but caused trouble. So I started looking around for another job. When Vince came in one day and said he was looking for someone, I said I was available, and that's how it happened. Just like that."

"Was your former employer surprised that you left?"

"Yes, I think he was, but his wife was glad to see me leave." Ruth was smiling ever so slightly at Nick, knowing his questions had nothing to do with Vince's death.

"Well maybe he'll offer you your old job back now that Vince is gone."

"I sort of doubt that. He and Vince didn't get along very well. Anyway, is there anything else I can help you with?" Once again, the knowing smile appeared.

"I took his office calendar, which I'm returning." Nick placed it back where he found it. He was about to mention that one page was different from the rest, then decided not to say anything. "Did he keep a pocket appointment book as well?" As Nick leaned against the desk, Ruth stood close enough for Nick to inhale her perfume. He really liked it. He liked everything about this woman. She had confidence. She had poise. She had good taste in clothes. And she did have big hooters, just as Paul had reluctantly admitted. Nick tried hard not to stare at them.

"No, Vince just kept one appointment book. Keeping two was just too much trouble for him. If he forgot something, I would usually remind him."

"Did he play golf on weekends?"

"Yes, usually with his favorite clients. If he had a golf date, he'd always mark his tee time on the calendar." She flipped back a few weeks to show him an example. Nick already knew how Vincent kept his calendar, but he didn't interrupt her.

"Was he precise in keeping his golf tee-times marked on this calendar?" Nick was looking at Saturday again with the brief note to pick up something at the club. There was no tee time indicated for Saturday, so he must not have played. Nick flipped a few more pages trying not to show too much interest in that particular day. He'd already made a copy of the page.

73

"Golf was his passion. He could tell you his score three years ago on a given day."

"I see." Nick didn't doubt a word of what she said. " Do you happen to know Phil Freeman?"

"Only to talk to on the phone. He called here a few times for Vince. They talked mostly about investments. Mr. Freeman wasn't a client, just a business acquaintance."

"So he was more of a friend, huh?"

"I think more of an acquaintance than a friend. He had some ideas he was trying to interest Vince in. I'm not sure Vince was all that interested. I could be wrong."

"So it was just a casual relationship between them at best, is that it?"

"Yes, I suppose that's the best way to explain it."

"That being the case, I wonder why Vince would have been on his boat at that hour of the night? And with Mr. Freeman out of town, It doesn't seem to make any sense."

"I've been wondering the same thing. It's a mystery to me, Nick. And to Paul, too."

"And to me. Even though it's officially an accident, I'm curious, and there are too many unanswered questions for me to leave it alone. Probably take some time before I learn what actually happened."

"I can see you like what you do, and you're good at it, aren't you?"

"Modesty aside, yes I am." Nick smiled back at her.

"I can see that. Paul told me to be careful around you because you ask a lot of questions, and not always in a logical sequence. You jump around to throw people off."

"Paul said that, did he?" It amused Nick that Paul was that observant about his interviewing technique.

"Yes, I think he's a little intimidated by you."

"That right? Bet he was intimidated by Vince, too." And by you, Nick thought to himself. If Nick were Vince, he'd never leave the office... and to hell with playing golf.

"Oh, very much so. Poor Paul, he's such a nice young man. He's very bright and wanted so much to be accepted by Vince. Vince was always giving him advice. Pushing him to be successful. It was Vince that talked him into starting his own printing business, did you know that?"

"No, but it doesn't surprise me. It fits with all the other things I've learned so far. Did Vince lend Paul any money to get his business started?"

"I really don't know. I suppose he might have. That's one question you'll have to ask Paul."

"Did Vince have any real enemies that you know of? You know, people he might have pushed too far, or something."

"I suppose there are a few people who would fit that category. Vince had a low-level feud going with one advertising agency here in the Detroit area. And a few other agencies were on his low esteem list."

"Uh huh. And who was the agency he was feuding with?"

"He had a falling out with Jeremy Keller. He's President of Keller & King Advertising. Vince and Jeremy used to be pretty good friends, but the relationship turned sour a while back."

"Vince got too pushy in his selling efforts?"

"No. The agency was having financial difficulties. They were desperate for new clients. Jeremy knew that Vince had a lot of contacts, and asked him for some help."

"You mean Vince loaned this guy money?"

"No, not that kind of help. Vince introduced him to some of his more important friends from the club. Anyway, one of those introductions turned out to become an important piece of new business for the agency."

"So Vince was a hero. That should have solidified the friendship I would think."

"Yes, at first it did. They were grateful I suppose. But Vince never benefited from it."

"What did he expect to get?"

"I'm sorry. I keep forgetting that you really don't know about the agency business, or ad space sales. Vince played golf regularly with the President of a company here known as Replacement Parts, Inc. They make and distribute parts for lawn and garden equipment, and small engines. It's a growing company and they're now listed on the stock exchange. Anyway, one of the publications Vince represents, is a magazine called 'U-Do-It Digest'. It's for home handymen who like to fix and repair stuff, like lawn mowers."

"So Vince expected to get some advertising business, is that it?"

"Yes, precisely. The new ads were well suited to run in his publication. When he learned that the ad schedule was actually running in a competitive magazine instead, well . . . he was livid."

"So what did he do about it? Was there some sort of confrontation?"

"To say the least. Vince called Jeremy as soon as he saw the new ads in this other magazine. It was the first he knew that the program was already running. He had been told things were not finalized. Suddenly he learns that he's not even on the program, and his competitor got the business! Vince acted like a wild man around here. Jeremy wouldn't talk to him, and wasn't available. I can't remember exactly, but anyway, Vince wasn't able to get through to him. So he went over to their offices and barged right into a meeting, demanding an explanation."

"Doesn't sound like the best way to go about it, but then I've never been in sales, so I don't know how touchy situations like that are handled."

"I can't exactly blame Vince for being angry. The agency needed his help and got it. Then later, Jeremy forgot about his past help, and treated him like a stranger. The whole situation could have been handled more tactfully. Vince was in a rage and couldn't be reasoned with. He made some threats and stormed out."

"What kind of threats?"

"Oh, I think it was something like he'd make sure that the agency never got another new business lead, something like that."

"I don't know, that sounds pretty mild, considering what you've just told me. He didn't punch out this Jeremy did he?"

"He probably came pretty close. Vince was a big man and in good physical shape. Jeremy is much smaller. I doubt that it would be an even match of strength. Jeremy plays a lot of tennis, but he'd never be able to trade blows with Vince." She seemed to know a lot of details about the encounter. Nick wondered how it was she knew so much. It didn't sound like something Vince would brag about later.

"Now are we talking physical blows or verbal blows?"

"I'm talking muscle. Jeremy is very articulate and could no doubt handle most situations however heated. But that day, Vince just forced his way into the meeting and demanded to know what was going on. I believe he also said something like seeing to it that Replacement Parts found another agency soon. You know, if he could influence one shift, he could influence another. Something along those lines."

"Uh huh. And did he follow through with his threat?"

"Actually he did. First, he bought several thousand shares of stock in Replacement Parts. It was enough to become a significant voice at the annual stockholders' meeting. Then he went to the President and said he'd made a big mistake introducing him to Jeremy and wanted to apologize. I think Vince convinced him that he should be advertising in his publication, instead of the one the agency recommended."

"So he got some business after all?"

"Yes, he got it the hard way. He forced the President to insist on changing the schedule, which of course the agency did, but with some reluctance. It made the agency look foolish."

"I don't know, seems that Vince found an alternative solution to his problem after all. He probably should have gone to his friend first, and just forgot about the agency."

"That wasn't Vince's style. He went directly to the source of any problem in a straight line. He never avoided anyone, and never allowed anyone to avoid him. He operated on the theory that you did whatever it took to win. That's what made him so successful."

"So the bottom line was what? He kept the business and lost a friend at this agency Keller and something. How did that eventually turn out?"

"Well, the agency had the account for a few more months, then the client selected another agency, and Vince continued to get the business. Only he wasn't content to just win back their business, he wanted to put Jeremy out of business!"

"Oh. So he was vindictive?" Nick was paying close attention, because it now appeared that a grudge match was surfacing. He wondered how many more similar incidents there might have been to this one.

"Very much so. He became a one-man crusade to get even with Jeremy. Even told him that he would eventually destroy his business personally."

"Now that's a strong threat! What you told me earlier sounded mild. This is different. How far did he go to put the agency out of business?"

"Well, every time Vince learned that Keller & King was pitching a new account, Vince would somehow make it known that the agency wasn't the best selection. He'd spread rumors that the agency was gouging on printing prices, things like that."

"That's malicious. He could have been sued."

"Yes, and Jeremy threatened to do just that, but didn't. Maybe because some of what Vince hinted at was true. Paul bid on some of their work, and came in with some very low prices and didn't get the jobs."

"I guess not. Didn't Jeremy know that Paul was Vince's son-in-law?"

"No. Vince never told anyone that Paul was a relative. He kept that a secret, so Paul wouldn't be harmed by any of Vince's entanglements."

"So is this Jeremy still in business?"

"Yes. They took on a new partner though. Sarah Katz became a money partner and insisted on having her name as part of the firm. It's now Keller, Katz & King. Vince had a field day with that. He called them the KKK of Detroit."

"Guess we should add slander to malice. How did Vince manage to keep from getting sued by these people?"

"I think the feud finally evaporated. Vince hasn't even mentioned that agency in months. He refused to do any business with them, or call there."

"Do you suppose this Jeremy might have been friends with Phil Freeman by any chance?"

"I really don't know. What are you suggesting, Nick? You think Jeremy had something to do with Vince's death?"

"Oh I doubt it. Just thinking out loud. Two more quick questions and I'll let you get back to work." Nick could have kept up his questioning for another hour at least, maybe longer, but he wanted a reason to contact her again.

"Okay . . . ." Once again she smiled knowingly as she lit another cigarette. Every motion was sexy.

"First, are you engaged, seeing anyone? Divorced, what?" It hadn't come out as he had planned. He wanted to slide into this question subtle like. Now he was sounding like a Rookie.

"What has that to do with your investigation?" She continued to smile at him. It was a warm, inviting smile. She wasn't upset, she was playing with him, teasing him.

"Nothing. Just curious because it hinges on my next question."

"And what's your second question?"

"What are you doing for dinner tonight?" It was a bold question to ask, and he felt bold. This was a woman worth all the time it took to get to know her. And he wanted to know a lot more about her . . . personally. Also, the advertising business was something Nick knew nothing about, yet he found it fascinating. Yes, they'd have lots to talk about.

"And if I say I'm divorced, but busy tonight, you'll get a warrant, right?" She was smiling at him. Her eyes looked directly into his and he felt she was reading his lascivious thoughts without blushing. This woman had a lot of experience handling men. Vince had to be a piece of cake for her. And poor Paul was just out of his league.

"Something like that. I'm not as pushy as Vince was, but I don't like being put off, either. And I don't take no easily, so maybe old Vince and I have something in common."

"Okay. Where would you like to meet?"

"How about your place around seven?" He wanted her address and phone number anyway.

"Can we make it seven-thirty?"

"Fine. Now I need an address so I can be at the right place at seven-thirty." She already had it written down. She gave him the information on a memo page.

"First date for me in a while . . . ." Nick started for the door, looking at his watch and having a hard time believing he'd been there so long.

"Really? I thought it was a summons." Then she laughed, proving she had a good sense of humor as well. He liked that... and everything else about her.

"Oh, one more thing. Any chance there's a file on this agency Keller & King around? You know, like letters and any notes Vince might have made and kept."

"Boy, promise dinner and they want favors. And I haven't even been fed yet." She winked at him as she pulled out a file folder from the cabinet against the wall. He took it along with the slip of paper from Vince's memo pad with her address and phone number on it.

Nick decided he needed a haircut. While looking for a convenient parking spot, he spotted a florist and thought he might as well go all out this time. Ruth would no doubt tease him for buying flowers, and that was just fine. He liked the way she teased. He had the flowers delivered, so he wouldn't have to carry them into his office, or leave them in the car to wilt.

Vince's file on Keller & King advertising agency was fairly thick. There were copies of letters to various people, suggesting they investigate Keller & King for future consideration. Obviously Vince had gone out of his way to get Jeremy some business. Then he spotted one of Vince's memos with a notation . . . *Find Jeremy's weak spot.* No date appeared on the paper. It must have been written as a reminder. Nick wondered what Jeremy's weak spot might be? There was something else about the note that bothered him. He couldn't quite grab it. However, Nick knew that his mind would continue to work on whatever it was, and sometime later, it would surface. It would probably come to him while he was shaving, or during his morning run.

Nick returned to his office. The Chief wanted to see him. The Chief was getting close to retirement. That always surprised Nick, when it came up in conversation. He and the Chief had been friends for the past 15 years. Nick thought of him more like an Uncle, than a superior to whom he had to report.

"Nick, you're spending a lot of time on this Blessing drowning. Have you come up with anything interesting yet, to warrant a continued investigation?"

"Chief, the case looks like a simple accident on the surface, but the more I dig into it, there could be some motives for knocking the guy off. If it was murder, it wasn't very well planned. It might have been a spur of the moment thing. You know, right time, right place, just give the guy a big push and end it."

"Well give me something concrete pretty soon, or we'll have to write it off as an accident. I'm getting a few calls from the media, asking why we're so interested in this one."

"Yeah, they want you to tell them we're not satisfied, so they can start building a story. For now, I'd say we call it an accident still under investigation."

"Easy for you to say, Nick. Next call I get, I'll have it transferred to you. You tell 'em. I see you got a haircut, must have a new girl friend. Who is she?"

"Nice of you to notice. Actually, it's been a month since I've been to the barber, so I stopped on the way back from an interview with the victim's assistant."

"Must be pretty nice, if that reminded you to get a haircut." The Chief knew him well.

"And people accuse me of being the suspicious one in the department. They should talk to you more. Truth is, I haven't had time to think about women, or my love life for several weeks now. I've been too busy."

"Nick, don't try to kid me, okay? I'm the last guy in the world you ever want to lie to. I can smell your lies even before you start to tell me. That's how well I know you and the way you are around good-looking women. You sure can catch 'em, but you never seem to keep 'em. Must be something like fishing, eh? Maybe you need a bigger hook." The Chief seemed to think that was funny. He'd been around Sergeant Gary Mitchell too long.

"Ha, ha, hah. There's nothing wrong with my hook. Just need better bait. Do we still have the victim's car?"

"Yeah, nobody's tried to claim it yet. Probably haven't even noticed it missing."

Ruth had mentioned that Vince was a very neat person. He kept all his files and papers in an orderly fashion. Yet the files and papers in the trunk of his car looked like they had been gone through hastily. So maybe someone had been searching for the envelope that Nick found earlier. Nick had noticed that Vince printed all his appointments . . . except the notation on Saturday. That was the item that bothered him earlier. And the note about Keller was written, too. He compared the two written items, the appointment page and the note on Keller. The handwriting didn't match. It wasn't even close. Nick wasn't sure what that proved, except that Vince hadn't written both. Once again, there were more questions than answers. If Vince didn't write the note, about finding Keller's weak spot, then who did? And why?

20-STAN

CHAPTER 8

Nick examined the contents of the envelope from the golf bag. He found a proposal for a new pizza franchise. He also discovered another envelope. This one was from New Horizons Publishing Co. The address was a P. O. Box in Birmingham, MI. No phone number. The proposal was to establish a local magazine to be known as **DETROIT VISITOR**. There was a sample layout of the cover, and a detailed outline of how the magazine would be distributed at local motels, hotels, better restaurants and through the convention bureau. **DETROIT VISITOR** would serve as the pilot model for similar editions in other major metro cities like Chicago, Cincinnati, and Cleveland.

Vincent Blessing seemed to be interested in a variety of investment opportunities. The Pizza franchise proposal was not on any letterhead. It had been prepared in a different typeface, and on different paper. There was a note paper-clipped to the inside page of the Pizza franchise proposal that Nick had missed earlier.

Vince,
Be careful with this information
It may have contributed to
Sal's mysterious death in Florida
H.G.

H.G. were the initials for Mr. Harrison Giles, whom Vince apparently met at his club on Saturday. This had been noted on the victim's desk calendar. Gary was able to confirm that Mr. Giles had given Vince an envelope containing information he felt Vince should have, on Saturday. Gary had been by the victim's car when Nick found the envelope in Vince's golf bag. Since Vince was picking up his clubs that day, he must have stuffed the envelope into the side pocket and left it there, not actually trying to hide it from anyone. Was this information that valuable? Apparently Mr. Giles thought so. Either he or Gary would have to have another talk with Mr. Giles to find out the meaning of the attached note he'd just discovered. Vincent seemed to be surrounded by mysterious events.

Another item that bothered Nick, there were no tee times indicated on Vince's appointment calendar for Sunday morning, yet there had been a call from a golfing buddy who was waiting for him. So, he was expected somewhere. So why wasn't that noted? All his other golf dates were. It was a small detail that Nick noticed. And, if Vince picked up his golf clubs and bag from his locker at the country club on Saturday, then he no doubt planned to play elsewhere on Sunday. Otherwise, why pick up his clubs? Vince had consistent habits like neatness, and printing appointments on his calendar. Therefore, a handwritten note on the calendar for Saturday, was a glaring inconsistency. Also, the note about finding Keller's weak spot was in a different handwriting than the hand written notation on the calendar.

Nick arrived at Ruth's townhouse in Birmingham promptly at 7:30. He'd made dinner reservations at Chez Lou's. He wasn't sure how that would go, he'd play it as he went along. Maybe they'd run into Phil Freeman again. And maybe old Phil would recognize Ruth. Then again, maybe Ruth would see through his ploy and become annoyed. Either way, he was hungry, and eager to see Ruth again. For once, the mystery of the case was second to the mystery of the woman.

"Hi, come on in," she said with a smile, standing aside for him to enter. She lived in a 2-story townhouse on a quiet street a few blocks east of Woodward. As he entered, he noticed that everything in the room seemed perfect. It was difficult for Nick to imagine anyone actually living here. It looked

85

more like a model suite, nothing out of place. It was quite a contrast to his apartment. The room was comfortable and well suited to Ruth's good taste in furnishings.

"Very nice." Nick took in the interior quickly. Light walls, large abstract prints with small spotlights hanging overhead, giving them a subtle emphasis.

"I'm glad you like it. Thanks for the flowers, that was very thoughtful of you, Nick. I guess this isn't all police business after all."

"Some of it is, some of it isn't. I thought maybe we could mix the two if you don't mind."

"I had a feeling you'd say that. Of course it's okay."

"Want a drink before we go, or are you starved?" Ruth asked.

"If I have a drink and sit down on that couch, I may never want to leave."

"Well in that case, sit down and I'll bring you something that will hold you 'till we eat. What would you like to drink?"

"I think something light. Maybe a vodka tonic if you have it."

"Two vodka tonics coming up. There's a typed list of all the calls and appointments Vince made in the last month on the table. You didn't ask for it yet, but I assumed you would sooner or later. Also some names of people that didn't have fond feelings toward Vince, in case you wanted it."

"Thanks." He was pleased and also curious how she could have anticipated him. She was back quickly with a tray with 2 tall glasses and a bowl of mixed nuts. The mixed nuts also surprised him. He would have guessed cheese and crackers.

"You don't think Vince's death was an accident, do you?" she asked.

"Well, I keep saying, it's a little early to draw any firm conclusions on that. I need to know as much as possible about the man and his habits. Also more about the people he tangled with. It seems to me that his death hasn't posed too many problems for anyone . . . except maybe you."

"You won't believe this, but Vince's Publisher called me today and asked if I would continue as their temporary sales representative, until they could get someone. He also hinted that they might not try too hard to find someone else . . . ."

"Good for you. Well then, everyone seems to have benefited from Vince's death. Emily will no doubt receive a sizeable insurance settlement. I doubt suicide will ever be suspected. And Paul will be out from under the critical pressure Vince must have exerted. If he owed any money to Vince, I'm sure Emily will forgive the debt. Did Emily ever mention how much insurance Vince carried?"

"No, but Vince did. One time when he was bragging about his success, he mentioned that when he died, he'd leave Emily and Susan a sizeable inheritance. He was insured for five million dollars." She lit a cigarette and leaned forward looking directly into his eyes. He was fascinated by her stare and couldn't allow his gaze to explore lower.

"Hey, now that's some serious money! Why so much? I gathered Emily's family had money. I wouldn't think she'd need that much."

"I really think that was the point. For once, his money might be more than hers. And, he wanted to be sure Susan could live comfortably, too."

"Paul won't have to worry about keeping Susan in the lifestyle she's used to then will he?" It wasn't meant as a question, just a statement. "What I can't understand is, why he was on that yacht, and at that hour? My hunch is, Vince was invited by someone. Maybe a business related meeting, but it sure was an odd time for that. It suggests discretion. Did he fool around?"

"I seriously doubt it. He never made a pass at me, and he had more than enough opportunity with both of us working in the same office. And I don't recall his ever getting any personal calls from women. No, I don't think Vince was a skirt chaser. If he was, he was extremely discrete."

"That's my point. If he was meeting some lady friend, he was doing it in a very discrete manner, where he wasn't likely to be seen." Maybe if Phil Freeman was in Orlando, Vince was seeing his wife. That picture was beginning to make some sense. After all, it was Phil's boat.

"Okay, I see where you're going. It's true, he and Emily had a rather distant affection for one another. I think I only saw Vince kiss her once, and that was on the cheek. Well, if you need any help, I'm more than willing. I mean that."

"Thank you. I know you do. And I appreciate what you've done already. I'd also appreciate it, if you'd keep this conversation completely confidential. I don't usually discuss any of my investigations, or even my personal opinions on a case, with anyone outside the department." Nick realized that this was the first time he'd ever broken his own rule.

"My turn to say thanks... for the trust. I'm getting hungry, shall we go? Or would you rather we stayed here? I can throw something together for us."

"Ruth, I made reservations at Chez Lou's." He made them with a dual purpose in mind, but liked the idea of having dinner here. "Dinner here sounds like a better idea. How about ordering a pizza, you up for that?"

"I love pizza. Tell you what, you call, and I'll make a salad. You want wine, or beer with your meal? "

"Wine would be nice." Nick was glad they weren't going anywhere

"Good. The number for pizza is next to the wall phone in the kitchen." She left the room without another word. 10 minutes later she emerged wearing a white jumpsuit. She had changed from the black cocktail dress she had on. Nick had to admit she looked equally stunning in both outfits and showed his appreciation with a big smile. He had 2 glasses ready with a Rose wine he found in the refrigerator.

"Want me to make the salad?" Nick had taken close notice of all the refrigerator contents. He could see that this lady liked to cook. It was well stocked with vegetables and a variety of cheese. There were a few hard-boiled eggs, and a red pepper, which was like storing gold at the current prices. He was overdue to show off his culinary expertise in the kitchen.

"And the man likes to cook, too. You're full of surprises, Nick." She sipped her wine and sat on a kitchen stool watching as he prepared a giant salad.

"It's the least I could do under the circumstances. After all, you just saved me at least a hundred bucks on dinner."

"Obviously you haven't eaten at Chez Lou's lately. It would have been much more than that, I can assure you." She smiled and refilled both their glasses. "We can save it for another time."

His salad was a winner. Together, they finished off the large pizza, most of the salad, and the bottle of wine. He couldn't remember when he'd eaten so much. Nick was in the kitchen preparing to clean up. The papers he'd found in Vince's golf bag were still on his mind.

"Do you know anything about a magazine that Vince might have been considering working for, or buying? I think the name was **DETROIT VISITOR**, or something like that."

"I recall seeing a file in the office on **DETROIT VISITOR**. I think someone had an idea for starting a new magazine locally. I think Vince was considering it as a possible new venture. I'm not sure it was his idea. How is it that you know about that idea? Did Paul mention it?"

"Actually, I found some documents about it in his car." Nick decided not to mention exactly where he found the envelope, or its contents.

"Hmmm. That idea hasn't surfaced for several months. I thought he'd forgotten about it, or decided not to go ahead with it. There are several other similar publications."

"I think it would take a considerable investment to start a magazine, even a local one like that." Ruth mentioned Paul, so perhaps he knew something about the magazine proposal.

"I guess. I'm not sure what Vince planned to do with it." She switched the conversation. "I'd offer you another drink, but I don't want you driving home with too much alcohol, even if you didn't get a ticket, if you were stopped."

"Sounds like a good reason for spending the night here. But you're right, I've had enough to drink and it would be really embarrassing to get stopped. Besides, I have a full day that starts very early tomorrow."

"I wasn't suggesting that you leave right away. Stay and have a cup of coffee. You haven't told me much about yourself, or is this interrogation still going?"

"Truce. I'd love a cup of coffee. Talking about myself isn't something I'm very good at. And, there's really not that much to tell."

"So try me. I'm a good listener." He'd already discovered that.

"Well, I'm divorced. Like a lot of cops, my wife left me, because she felt left out, and to some extent, she was. My son, Nickie Jr. is a good kid, and we do things together when we can. He's going to college in September, so I'll only see him about once a month, when he comes home to borrow some money, and do some laundry. And get fed! Right now, he's away for the month at a summer camp, working as a counselor to the younger kids there. He's teaching swimming. How about you? Any kids?" It was a very brief summation of his life. Not one you'd give to an attractive lady you just met and might be trying to impress.

"Divorced, no kids. I was married to a doctor who liked to make house calls and play house at the same time. When one of his patients sued him, it all came out in the papers. In fact, that's when I learned he'd been cheating on me. At first, I didn't believe it. Then when he admitted it was true, I filed for divorce. The lawsuit and the lawyers took most of what we had, so I had to start over. No more club life, and long lunches with the girls. To tell you the truth, it was a boring way to live. I wouldn't do it again if I had the chance. I really enjoy working and keeping busy. And, I like the advertising business. It's fun, but it does have its difficult moments."

"I can see that. I'm glad things are working out for you. Now you'll be selling advertising. Vince's Publisher made a wise decision to ask you to stay on. Will you continue to use Vince's office, or will you move?"

"I don't know. Emily and I have become good friends. I don't know how she'd feel about my remaining there. We haven't discussed it yet. I won't make any decisions about that for a while. If she's agrees to have me stay, then I think I will. After all, it's still Vince's business, not mine actually."

"Sounds like it will all work out okay, given some time. Emily is certainly an unusual lady. I think I like her, but I don't understand her at all. Is she in touch with reality? She didn't seem to be too upset by her husband's death." Nick thought maybe it was her quixotic manner and had been willing to accept her on those terms.

"Oh she's a very quiet, very private person. And very strong in a way you wouldn't notice. She has definite opinions, yet she's guarded about expressing them, except in closed circles. Her family had money, so she never had to worry about finances. Vince became successful in recent years. I don't think his family was rich. He had to fight for everything he ever got. At least that's the way he always told it. Emily never corrected him. Then again, she wouldn't. She allowed Vince to make most of the decisions."

"Did they ever fight or argue?"

"I suppose they did, but never in front of me or within my hearing. Emily went along with whatever Vince wanted."

"Did they do much entertaining together?"

"I don't think so. Vince used the club for most of his business entertaining. Emily preferred to remain home with her music and her garden. She's not the least bit interested in an outside social life."

"I guess my next question is . . . ."

"Did they have separate bedrooms? Yes. I've had tea with Emily in her room a few times. It's very lovely; very feminine. She claims Vince snored so loud that she couldn't sleep. So a few years ago, they agreed it was the best solution for both of them."

"So Vince could be out late. He could even come home and not be seen, or heard, arriving late." Nick had already determined that was why the family didn't realize he was missing on Sunday morning.

"I suppose so. We never discussed it. Emily trusted Vince, and I doubt that he ever gave her any reason not to."

"It's just my suspicious nature to link facts and events together into what I call a logical progression." So far, this case didn't seem to have any logic to it.

"And I'm not trying to be vague, Nick. I'm just giving you my interpretation of what Emily and Vince are like, or seemed to be. I'm sure there are many things about Vince that I don't know, and might be shocked to learn."

"How is it you knew about his blow up with Jeremy Keller in such detail? You told me about it almost as if you were there when it all happened."

"Sooner or later, I knew you'd ask me about that. You really don't miss much do you? That's the agency where I used to work. I was Jeremy's assistant before coming to work for Vince. I still have some friends there who were present when Vince made his big scene and they told me about it. All nine yards."

"I see. Did your leaving and joining Vince add some grease to the fire?"

"Probably. I learned a lot about the agency side of advertising while working there, and it's been a big help to me since then. Now, I talk to a lot of agency people, and I understand what they're going through with their clients."

"This Jeremy Keller, did he make any passes?"

"Yes. There were opportunities, but I was never interested. He's married for one thing, and I'm not about to get involved with another woman's problem, or make it mine. And, I wanted to be recognized for the work I did at the agency, not for sleeping with the boss."

"Did anyone?"

"I'm not sure, but I think so. Jeremy wants to be liked by everyone. He has a friendly way that he uses to get what he wants. He uses it with his clients, and on those who work for him. I saw through it pretty early, so I never fell for his act."

"But he did make some advances?"

"Oh sure. He's not shy, just smooth. And his wife doesn't trust him out of her sight. She's not so smooth. She says whatever it is she has on her mind. And she doesn't care who hears it. Cassandra is part of Jeremy's problem."

"She and Vince sound a lot alike."

"Well . . . they're both outspoken. I don't think she ever liked Vince very much. Then again, she never seemed to like anyone who worked in the agency, either. She treated us all as though we were underlings who could be ordered around, when Jeremy wasn't there."

"Really? Another Queen of Mean? She must have been pleased when you left."

"Oh Cassandra was. Jeremy wasn't. He offered me a raise if I'd stay."

"In your opinion, is he a good businessman?"

"He's fairly good at what he does. He's creative. But, he gets in trouble regularly. Several of the publications he advertises in, bill the client direct. That's because he owes them money, and is on an overdue basis. If his clients knew that, he'd lose some of that billing. And all the printers around

---

town have him on C.O.D. with an advance, before they'll touch any of his assignments."

"Is that a normal practice?"

"Yes, with printers and some publications. They don't like it when the client has paid the agency, and the agency uses the money, instead of paying them. He'd get calls fairly often asking when he was sending a check. Jeremy was a master at stalling them. I never knew anyone who could make up so many excuses."

"So now he has a new partner, and it's a woman I believe you said."

"Yes, and I'm sure that creates a new problem for him, and particularly his wife. Sarah and Cassandra are cut out of the same pelt of fur. Both come from money, and both have expensive taste. I doubt they'll get along."

"So this Jeremy is a smooth talker, and a high roller who doesn't seem to be able to pay his bills. Was he ever late paying his staff?"

"Twice he was late with me. The second time I told him I wouldn't be coming in the next day, unless my check was there. He got the picture. I'm very practical when it comes to money. I've had to be. That's something Vince and I had in common."

"So when things started to get tough, that's when he turned to Vince and asked him for some help, by introducing some of his friends to the agency, right?"

"Yes. Vince figured that if he steered some business into Jeremy's agency, he'd get the advertising space. I don't know if it was ever openly agreed to on that basis, or if it was just assumed on Vince's part. But it never turned out that way, and you know the rest of the story."

"It seems to me Vince taught old Jeremy an expensive lesson in business relationships, as well as in a friendship that soured as a result."

"Yes, they were never friends after that."

"It seems to me that Vince got more than even. He got you. He got the business back, and he got some personal satisfaction."

"Could that be a motive for murder?" That was the second time the suggestion had been voiced, first by Paul, now by Ruth.

"Maybe. I'll know a lot more after I talk to Jeremy Keller." Nick liked having all this extra background information before the interview. It gave him a decided edge. Ruth had been a big help there.

"I'd sure like to be a mouse in the room for that session. Will you tell me how it goes, or shouldn't I ask?"

"I guess it depends on how it goes." He'd already violated one of his personal rules not to discuss police business outside the store. Nick stood up to leave. He didn't want to leave, and he wasn't sure that Ruth wanted him to go, either. His second rule was not to jump into the sack with anyone on a first date that he truly cared about. He didn't want Ruth to be a one-night stand. And here he was contemplating breaking that rule, too.

"I know you have to go. Next time, I'll fix dinner. Your salad was very good . . . ."

Nick held her, and kissed her lightly. And seeing a smile on her face, he knew there would be a next time. He smiled, and kissed her again . . . longer this time. He wanted to press against her in a tight embrace. With his passion growing, and her intoxicating perfume, it took all his will power to break it off and leave.

"I'll call you tomorrow." He waved goodbye and drove off feeling like he was 25 again. He was horny, and happy at the same time. For Nick, it was a strange paradox.

Saying goodnight always seemed awkward to him. Tonight was different. He'd enjoyed the evening. And, he'd learned a little more about Vince, Emily and Jeremy. And Ruth, she was a classy lady. He had sensed that the first time he'd met her. Driving home, he ran back through all the comments Ruth had made that evening. He was pretty sure now that Ruth and Vince had never been lovers, and he was glad about that.

CHAPTER 9

Nick's secret weapon was his vast network of contacts. Over a 20-year period, he had made numerous friends at several county court houses, at the state capital in Lansing, the license bureau and at Detroit Metro Police Dept. At Detroit Metro, Nick's buddy was Devereaux Washington, whose nickname was 'Wizard' because he knew so much about computer programs and how to get access to sensitive information. Wizard had direct links into the FBI, Dept. of Transportation (DOT), DEA, ATF and a host of other groups with similar alphabetic IDs. He had the ability to go in the front door, or hack into a database through the back door, when necessary. Devereaux was the man who knew just about everything and everybody worth watching. Part of his daily routine was to input and retrieve criminal intelligence on the Mafia and Detroit area gangs.

Because he was frustrated with the way this case was moving, Nick called Wizard for some confidential help. He wanted background checks, credit information, recent IRS reports and vehicle registrations for Vincent Blessing, Phil Freeman and Jeremy Keller. He also asked for the last real estate tax appraisal for all property listed in their respective names. Some of this information wasn't necessary, but sometimes when you put everything together, it gave you a more complete picture of whom you were dealing with.

Wizard knew from past experience how Nick used this data, so he always tried to get more, rather than less than what he was asked for. Dev liked being a behind-the-scenes detective. And unlike some of the other officers he helped, Nick kept him current on why he wanted this data, and where he was going with it. That helped Wizard a lot when tapping all his resources for input. Credit reports were easy, but you had to know how to interpret them. The same was true with criminal background checks. What you saw wasn't always the complete picture. You looked for patterns. Working with Internal Affairs, Wizard had honed his skills. He knew not to reveal anymore than what was necessary when making an inquiry. And, he knew to ask who else was also interested in that same information recently. Those were just some of his many tricks.

"Nick, can you fill me in on what you've got so far on this drowning at the marina? I hate to be the media's main focus on a slow news day," the Chief asked.

"What have I got so far? Just bits and pieces. The victim had a ton of insurance, so the widow stands to gain big bucks, even though it doesn't look like she needs it. There are a few hate candidates I'm checking out now. The more I learn about the victim, the more I'm discovering that he wasn't shy about confrontations. Pissed off a lot of people apparently,"

"That doesn't sound like much to go on. You talk to the owner of the yacht yet?"

"Briefly. He's a real dancer if I ever met one. He seems to be trying to avoid me, and that just makes him look like a good suspect. I'm also working on a possibility that it was Freeman's wife who was on that boat with the victim. Freeman was supposed to be in Orlando. Flew back early, so maybe he was checking up on his wife. I'm exploring every angle. So far, no motive, but several people have actually gained by his death."

"Yeah, well wrap this one up fast. You've got several other cases that need attention. I'm just afraid that we're wasting our time on this one. Talk to the owner, get some kind of logical reason why the victim was there, and bag it. Did you see the Medical Examiner's report?"

"Yep, sure did. Victim died from drowning and had an

unusually high blood-alcohol level, so he was drunk. The final toxicology report will no doubt confirm the ME's conclusion. Pitched his cookies, slipped, hit his head on a piling, which probably knocked him out, and took a big drink of bad water. He wasn't in his underwear. Beds weren't messed up, and he wasn't capable of doing anything, including driving home. If he hadn't bought the farm at the marina, he might have been killed in his car, driving home. It was just a matter of where it would happen."

"It has all the ingredients for an accident. Satisfy the basic questions and move on. By-the-way, you get any yet from your new sweetie?" There was that smirk on the Chief's face.

"You wouldn't believe anything I told you, so why should I bother? For the record, she's not my sweetie, so it should follow that we are not doing the horizontal cha-cha." Nick knew that there would be a new rumor floating around about him soon. At this point, he didn't care.

"You're absolutely right, I don't believe it. But if you want to deny it, and have egg all over your face later, that's okay by me."

Wizard was on the line, when Nick walked out of the Chief's office. Time was running out. Intuition told him there was much more to this case than he'd uncovered so far, but it may remain an unsolved mystery, if he didn't find a few answers quickly.

"Hey Nick, just finished talking with a brother in the Coast Guard. That bad boat you're looking at has a hot background, man. Seems it was stolen by modern-day pirates down in the Caribbean a few years ago. DEA confiscated it after a drug raid in Fort Lauderdale. They put it up for auction about a year and a half ago. It was bought by a guy named Calvin Justine. The same guy bought a lot of other stuff, too. A twin-engine plane, and three limos. He got the whole enchilada for a half mil. Not bad, huh?"

"So where does Freeman fit into the picture?"

"Just getting to that. This Calvin Justine sold everything to Freeman Enterprises shortly after he bought it all. Boat was in Boca Raton for a while, then moved to Port Clinton. That's it's last known whereabouts. I'll have more for you later. Want me to fax it over?"

"Okay, but call me first so I know it's coming. No need for everyone around here to see what we're looking at. And thanks." The boat had a colorful past. Apparently used for running drugs, so maybe there were some hidden compartments. And just maybe, that was what Phil Freeman was checking, when he went back onboard the other night. Nick could have missed a secret compartment. Only the DEA people were good at that.

——— ——— ———

Phil Freeman was on the top of Nick's hit list. When Nick called Freeman Enterprises, he was told that Mr. Freeman was tied up in a meeting all day, and wasn't available to see anyone. At least Nick knew where he was. That was good enough. Freeman's office was in downtown Birmingham. Nick could be there in a half hour, using the freeway. The nice thing about the trip across town was that Jeremy Keller's agency was also in Birmingham. Jeremy was number two on the hit list of people to see. So Nick hoped he could see both today, then maybe have dinner with Ruth. She would certainly want to know how his session went with Keller.

Nick saw the familiar 'FREE-1' parked in a reserved space under the overhanging section of the 3-story office building. Freeman Enterprises was on the 3rd floor.

"I'm sorry, sir. Mr. Freeman isn't seeing anyone today," said the receptionist. She was about 25 and very attractive. Nick couldn't fault Phil for having good taste. The reception area was nicely done, with expensive looking landscapes and seascapes on the walls. Couch and chairs were all soft brown leather.

———

"That's okay. I'm sure he'll want to see me. Please give him a message that I'm here to see him on his turf. But, if he prefers, we can do it on my turf. His choice. Be sure you give him the message exactly that way." Nick sat down, picked up the current issue of FORTUNE and waited while the young lady rewrote the note. Then she quickly disappeared behind the double doors. And just as quickly returned.

"Mr. Freeman said he'll be with you in just a few minutes, if you don't mind waiting."

"That won't be a problem." Nick smiled at her and continued to read about how rich people were buying condos in The Cayman Islands. So, if Castro is having a hard time financing his government, now that Russia had pulled out, why doesn't he invade The Cayman Islands? Lots of money there, Nick mused. He was still smiling when Phil Freeman came out to meet him.

"Hello, Lieutenant. Sorry you had to wait. Come on into my office." Nick followed Phil through the double doors. He winked at the frowning receptionist as he passed by her desk.

It was a large paneled office. Large desk with a big curved overhang on the visitor side. There were several marble sculptures on pedestals at various points in the room. One wall was all windows. Thin drapes diffused the light and the view. Today, Phil Freeman was wearing a charcoal gray pinstripe suit. Quite a contrast from the casual outfit he was wearing last time they met. Neither of them had attempted to shake hands. Phil motioned for Nick to have a seat, and rather than sit next to him in an informal manner, he chose to sit behind his desk. It was his power center. The body language spoke clearly to Nick. Next would come the tent positioning of both hands, fingers touching. As if on command, it happened and Nick smiled. Some motions and expressions could be anticipated. It was another way to dance around the current subject or problem, in Phil's case.

"I appreciate you letting me interrupt your meeting." As

Nick said this, he was also aware that another person had quietly entered the room from another entrance.

"Lieutenant, this is Nelson Hoffman. He's in charge of our Charter Division. He's also our Chief Pilot. He and I flew down to Orlando together this last weekend." Nelson didn't attempt to shake hands either. He had a very casual air about the way he sat down on the white leather couch opposite Nick. He was tall, almost 6 feet, tanned with sun-bleached blond hair. He could easily pass for a tennis pro. He was wearing a sport shirt, open at the collar revealing a gold chain. Expensive tan slacks, and alligator loafers that had to cost $500. Nelson just nodded to acknowledge the introduction, then examined his manicured nails. The man exuded confidence. Nick was sure it would take a lot to intimidate him, if that was possible.

"So you fly the company plane. Do you also skipper the yacht?" Nick was pretty sure of the answer, but waited to hear it. Nelson took his time.

"Occasionally, if I'm not busy. Have you learned anything about why that guy was on our yacht?" Nelson crossed his legs and put one arm across the back of the sofa in a relaxed position that was almost a pose. The man never took his eyes from Nick. It was a cold stare.

"I was just about to ask the Lieutenant that same question," Phil interjected. Nelson held up his hand, indicating he didn't want Phil to interrupt. The motion didn't escape Nick's notice.

"No, that's the primary focus of my investigation. I've looked into Vincent Blessing's background, and I'm fairly convinced, that he was invited there by someone. It appears to have been some sort of meeting. Since both of you were out of town, do you have any idea who he would have been with?"

"So you don't know anything yet. We have no idea what he was doing there, or how he even got onboard. Is there anything else we need to discuss?" All this was coming from Nelson, not Phil Freeman. It was almost as if Nelson was in charge.

"Yes. Mind telling me what your relationship is with Calvin Justine?" Nick addressed his question to Phil and saw his eyebrows arch.

"He's an associate with the firm," Nelson responded quickly.

"He's a senior partner actually," Phil added.

"I see. And how do I contact Mr. Justine?" Nick looked from Phil to Nelson, not sure which one would answer.

"You don't. He spends most of his time at our West Palm Beach office. We talk to him about once a week." Again, it was Nelson who was doing all the speaking.

"And do you have a phone number for Mr. Justine?"

"We do, but we prefer not to give out that information. Calvin is very guarded about talking to anyone outside our firm. We handle all the details here. There's really no need for you to speak with Calvin." Yes, it did appear that Nelson was in charge here, regardless of the big impressive office Phil occupied. "In fact, I believe he's in Europe right now."

"Tell me, Phil, just what does Freeman Enterprises do?" Nick decided to ignore Nelson for the moment.

"We are a multi-faceted company, privately held by a few stock holders. Our primary mission is investments. We try to acquire promising companies that require capital to grow. We also have a Charter Division that allows clients to travel at their convenience, in whatever style suits them. And we own the travel agency that you might have seen on the first floor of the building." Phil said this like he was giving a formal presentation.

"I see. How long have you been in business?"

"I don't know where this conversation is going, but you'll have to excuse us. We have a client waiting, and we've answered your questions relating to the accident. We've con-

103

tacted our insurance company, so if the victim's family wants any information, they can contact United Mutual Assurance. We don't anticipate a claim, since it's our position the man was trespassing on private property." Nelson was in charge. He stood up to indicate the meeting was over. It was obvious that Phil was annoyed at the abrupt ending and walked Nick to the door.

"Does Mrs. Freeman have access to your yacht, Phil?" Nick saw the concerned look.

"No, she does not. And I don't think I like where you're going with that."

"And she was home alone, while you were in Orlando, right?"

"Of course she was. I spoke with her on the phone late Saturday evening."

As Nick backed out of the parking space, all he could think about was money laundering. Nelson was Phil's alibi, and Phil was Nelson's. Flying in a company owned plane killed any chance for seeing a plane ticket as proof of the trip. However, there were other ways of checking. Wizard could check FAA records to see if a flight plan had been filed. That still wouldn't prove that Phil Freeman was on that flight, so the weak alibi still had a few holes.

Nick made a note to have Wizard check out Nelson Hoffman. Nick was sure the man was every bit as dangerous as he appeared Nelson's cold blue eyes did not sparkle. They pierced into you. If he hadn't been out of town with Phil, Nick would have listed him as a number one candidate for throwing Vincent overboard. Only he would probably have taken the boat out into the lake and done it there. And poor Vincent would no doubt have a couple of concrete blocks tied around his ankles, to keep him from being discovered. Yes, that would be more Nelson's style, Nick decided. Nelson was no doubt one of the private share holders as well since he pre-empted Phil and elected to end the meeting abruptly without any objections from Phil. Once again, the face-to-face meeting, however short, gave Nick much more insight than a phone conversation. Body language and surroundings could tell you a lot if you took the time to notice. Now that Nelson entered the picture, Nick took special notice of the other cars parked in the reserved section. He spotted a metallic gold Mercedes-Benz Convertible and guessed that it would be the kind of car Nelson would prefer to drive. Nick jotted down the license number. One more item to check out on L.E.I.N. (Law Enforcement Information Network) Nick could get this on his terminal at work, but Wizard could get FBI and DEA information not listed. Having the right contacts, and years of experience was the big difference between Nick and hundreds of other officers still coming up through the ranks. If Nick hadn't been the Duty Officer on call Sunday morning, this whole affair would be written off as an accident and Nick wouldn't be involved now. He wondered, as he often did, how many other similar incidents had suspicious circumstances that never got investigated completely, and were chalked up as accidents to keep the record looking good? The political side of police work was the Chief's area of expertise.

CHAPTER 10

Jeremy Keller was expecting Nick. Nick had called to say that he'd like to talk to him about his relationship with Vincent Blessing, and had made an appointment for 10:30. That Gave Nick plenty of time to find Keller Katz & King's offices, one block off Woodward Avenue.

"Mr. Keller will be with you in just a few minutes, Lieutenant. He knows you're here. He's on an overseas call with a client that shouldn't take too long." The secretary was polite and perhaps a little curious as to his presence here, or perhaps she suspected. The lobby area was interesting with ads displayed in frames along with an assortment of awards. Dozens of magazines were displayed on the coffee table. It was a different assortment than he'd seen in Freeman's office.

"Sorry you had to wait, Lieutenant," Jeremy Keller came out of his office to meet Nick. He wasn't wearing a jacket, so his red suspenders became an obvious part of his attire. He also wore round wire rim glasses to give the scholarly look that was currently popular. He was shorter than Nick, about 5' 7". He had a mop of curly hair that looked like a Brillo pad.

Nick accepted a cup of coffee and waited until Jeremy cleared a few papers from his desk before he began. Jeremy sat in a high back, black leather chair behind a huge cluttered desk. Nick detected a slight nervousness in Jeremy's manner, even though the man wanted to appear cool and in control. Nick just looked at him without giving any hint of approval or undo interest in the office. It generally produced the effect he wanted before starting an interview with someone he felt might be difficult. So far, Ruth had described him well.

"When was the last time you saw Vincent Blessing?" No preliminaries with this guy.

"Get right to it, don't you? You haven't even asked me if I knew him, Lieutenant, or what our relationship was." Jeremy was posturing. He pressed the tips of his fingers together into a tent. It must have been what Jeremy considered as an executive pose. The man would make a good actor. He was no doubt a good presenter, which Ruth said was necessary when an agency pitched a new client.

"I assumed you were a busy man, Mr. Keller, so I decided to save some time and cut right to the main points. I don't have much patience with people who play games, so let's not start, okay?" Normally Nick wasn't this blunt, but once again his hunches were working overtime. This man would dance around the edges with him, if left unchecked.

"I appreciate your directness, Lieutenant. And please just call me Jeremy. You're Nick, right? Or do you prefer Nicholas?"

"Lieutenant is just fine. The last time you saw Vince was when?" Nick still remained standing knowing full well this had to annoy Keller who wanted to be at eye level. Jeremy had motioned for him to sit when he first entered the office.

"That's not easy to answer. It's been a while. He was a space salesman, so his normal contact here at the agency would have been with Wilma, our Media Buyer. I'll have to ask her when Vince was in last." He started to turn to the intercom.

"My question was when you last saw him, not someone on your staff."

"Well, like I said, not recently, so a date just doesn't stick out in my memory . . . ." Jeremy was trying to stay cool.

"Then let me put it differently. When was the last time you two had an argument?"

"I can see you've been talking to a few people in the business. So, you must know Vince wasn't an easy guy to do business with. He was a bullshit artist. Never gave you a straight answer . . . ."

"So why don't you try giving me a straight answer. Then I'll know you're not a bullshit artist."

"Ouch. Sorry if you think I'm being deliberately vague, I assure you I'm not. I'm trying to be helpful and polite. I thought you wanted to discuss Vince and my relationship with him, which by-the-way, wasn't much. Won't you have a seat? You look uncomfortable standing there."

"Uh huh. So you rarely saw him, and he concentrated on your media person for his contacts here, is that right?" Nick decided it was time to sit down.

"Yeah, pretty much. Oh I'd see him in the lobby and say 'hello' and ask him how he was doing, things like that. But we didn't get into deep discussions about his magazines. That's Wilma's department. She selects the magazines we use for our clients."

"And you go by whatever she recommends, is that it?"

"Yeah, it's her job. That's what she gets paid to do. I'm busy enough working on the creative stuff. If I took the time to see all the space reps that stop by here, I'd never get anything accomplished. Most of those guys just want to chat you up and get friendly, hoping you'll throw some business their way."

"I see. Do you ever make changes to her media recommendations?"

"Of course I do. Sometimes the client wants us to use a particular magazine that we haven't recommended, and if it has merit, we'll go along with it. After all, the client is the one who foots the bill. It's important to keep the client happy."

"I really don't know much about the advertising agency business, so my questions will seem very naive to you, Mr. Keller." Nick picked at some imaginary lint on his sleeve.

"Jeremy, please. Go on."

"As I was saying. Suppose you recommended a publication

to a client, and you learned that the client decided not to go along with that recommendation. Then you learned that some space salesman for another publication had influenced that decision, that wouldn't set too well with you, would it?" Nick smiled slightly to show he knew more than he was letting on.

"It all depends. What you've just outlined sometimes happens. Some hotshot sales rep. gets to the client with a story that seems to make sense, so the client buys it. Then we have to do a lot of homework to prove to the client that our recommendation was actually the better way to go. Usually the client doesn't have all the facts, or as much as we have here. They're sometimes influenced by personalities. Vince for example was a good golfer. I understand he entertained a lot of important people at his club. That could influence a client to throw some business his way. In fact, that's the way Vince sold most of his space ... on friendship, not facts. He relied a lot on favors."

"Uh huh." Nick wasn't taking any notes.

"So, under those circumstances, a client may become impressed and make promises to run some space. Then we get the rotten task of having to be the bad guys and tell the rep. he really isn't going to get any business, after we've done a complete analysis of the circulation and all that."

"I see. So you do go out of your way to support your recommendations to a client?"

"Absolutely!" Jeremy was toying with a cuff link and hoping Nick might notice how expensive they looked.

"And you'd resent it then, when someone suggests another publication not on your media recommendation."

"No, I can't go along with you on that. What I said was, we do our homework. More than most clients would. So we're in a better position to evaluate the magazines. For the most part, our clients accept our recommendations. Hell, that's part of the package. They pay us to do that. It's a little like asking your lawyer for advice, then not taking it."

"Uh huh. And Vince, did he ever get any of those media recommendations changed in his favor after you did all that homework?" Jeremy was playing with a letter opener now and not looking directly at Nick. He knew where this was leading.

"Just what is it you're looking for here, Lieutenant? I didn't have any reason to justify a media recommendation to any of our clients, where Vince was concerned."

"I see. So you and Vince were only casual acquaintances and you didn't have any reason to discuss media with him, is that right?" Nick had already caught him in a lie.

"Oh, a few years ago, before we had a media department, I saw all the space reps. that called here, including Vince. I don't want you to hang me on a technicality. I was aware of the books Vince represented. Unfortunately, we didn't use any of them in the past year or so."

"Any particular reason for that?"

"Sure. Vince had a lot of competition. And some of those competitors had better prices. We try to negotiate the best possible deal for all our clients. With Vince, there was no negotiating. So he lost some business. It happens."

"So you were looking for a deal, and he wouldn't meet you half way, huh?"

"Well, in a manner of speaking. It's a little more complicated than that. These magazines use rate cards, but will offer you a special deal sometimes. And, we're always interested in a good position for the ads we place. Some magazines will work with you on that, others won't. So, it's not as clear cut a process as it might appear on the surface."

"And all this transpires with Wilma, not you, correct?"

"Look Lieutenant, I really don't see the point to all these questions. Vince had an accident and died. I'm sorry that happened. I don't see how his accident has anything to do with me, or the way I do business with my clients. We seem to be discussing history, and I fail to get the drift of it all. Is this going somewhere?" Jeremy was being very animated with his hands.

"To make it easier for you to understand, Jeremy, I'll try to use some of your expressions. I'll run this by you, and you can try it on for size. First, you and Vince were close friends at one time, but you tell me he was a bullshit artist, and that you only knew him casually. I find that quite interesting. You once asked him for his help and he came through for you, only you forgot to return the favor, when it came time to placing ad space. You ran a program with one of his direct competitors instead. I imagine that must have pissed him off pretty good. And, from the profile I get on Vince, he wasn't shy about displaying his feelings. So it's a pretty good guess he confronted you about your recommendation to your client. I doubt he wasted his time with Wilma, he came directly to you, didn't pass go, and didn't collect a thank you along the way. The relationship might have been tense, but it was anything but casual. Vince was so pissed, he probably made some threats. And that in turn must have made you angry. Maybe you made some counter threats. How am I doing so far?"

"You must have been talking with Ruth. Is she the one who told you about that little argument? It was no big deal. And it was some time ago, not recently."

"Never-the-less, you had a heated exchange. You still have that client?"

"No, we don't as a matter of fact. They went with another agency." Jeremy's face was getting red. He took off his glasses and carefully started to clean them.

"And did Vince have anything to do with that switch?"

"I really don't know, and I guess I don't care if he did, or not. Like I said, it's history. Part of the agency business is getting new clients. Sometimes you lose one. You can't waste a lot of time pissing and moaning about it. You move on."

"Come on, Jeremy, you were upset. You really expect

me to swallow all that? Vince got to your client, the same guy he originally introduced you to, and convinced him to make a change. That had to get you steamed. I know it would me. Vince doesn't seem like the kind of guy I'd care much for." Nick gave him a slight smile.

"Okay, so he managed to get to the client. So what? They were golfing buddies. I was a little upset for a while. But all that happened two years ago. Are you suggesting that there was a lingering grudge going on?"

"Maybe. From what I've learned so far about Vincent Blessing, he was quite successful, and he had a bad temper. And, he used his influence to any advantage. A person like that can be dangerous. My mission is to learn all the facts surrounding Vince's death, including any incidents that could be relevant. Or any enemies he might have made. Which leads me to the big question, where were you last Saturday night?"

"Hey, you telling me I'm a suspect in a murder? Come on, you can't be serious."

"I don't recall saying anything about murder."

"I guess maybe this friendly conversation had better be put on hold until I call my lawyer. Don't you need a warrant or something to ask me questions like that?" Keller was now standing beside his desk. His left hand flexed in an uncontrolled manner.

"Suit yourself. Call your attorney and have him meet me along with his client in my office and we'll do this again with a tape recorder. Better rehearse your presentation very carefully 'cause if I catch you slipping up again, you'll look bad in front of witnesses and the camera." Nick got up.

"What camera?"

"You know, the one on the other side of the mirror you always see on TV in that poorly lit, dismal interrogation room with just a table and a few hard chairs. Bring your own cigarettes. We don't furnish them at today's prices."

———

"You're kidding me! Okay, okay. Look, there's no need to make this a federal issue. I don't see any reason, I mean, I don't have any reason to call my lawyer. Hell, his field is tax law anyway, not criminal. I don't have any reason not to tell you where I was, but it must remain confidential, you understand?" Jeremy ran his hand through his hair and slumped into his seat.

"Does this have a happy ending, or is it going to be another dance?" Nick asked.

"I was with someone, okay? In fact, I was supposed to be with a client, but I spent the day with a special friend. We were together most of the day, and Saturday night."

"Uh huh." Everyone seemed to be someplace away from their home base lately. Keller loosened his tie, unaware of the body language he was exhibiting.

"That's the truth, so help me."

"This special friend was a woman, right?"

"Yeah, sure. Do I look gay? But I can't give you her name 'cause she's married, and that would cause a problem. A very big problem right now!"

"Aren't you married, too?"

"Of course, but you know what I mean. It's a delicate situation that could cause a lot of embarrassment for both of us, if anyone found out. We've been seeing each other off and on for about a year now. It's kind of complicated, with both of us being married. A divorce would be inconvenient at the moment, so we're being discreet about it, okay?"

"Uh huh. And just who is this special friend you were being discreet with?"

"Believe me, I'd like to tell you, but I can't."

"I think you'd better make that call to your lawyer. My patience is getting pretty thin."

"Shit. Look, promise me you'll keep all this out of any of your records. I can't afford any scandal right now. It's a sensitive situation."

113

"It seems to me you have a problem with priorities. You have problems, and then you have potential problems on top of that. Right now, what you should be doing is resolving the big problem I represent, which is bigger than those other problems ... that may, or may not surface later." It sounded like the kind of doublespeak Jeremy would use.

"You should have gone into advertising, Lieutenant. You have a real knack with words. But, you like to push people into corners, and don't allow any options."

"Not true. I don't push anyone. I listen and wonder why everyone feels the need for so much bullshit to simple questions. Most people create tension for themselves, like you. You still have the option of calling your lawyer, or telling me whom you were holding hands with. I have to check anything you tell me, so until you do, it remains a question unanswered. As such, it will get asked again, either here privately, or at the police station, where the reporters all hang out. They love to see new faces coming in with their lawyers, and get those 'no comment' responses when you leave, as they take your picture for the six o'clock news."

"Okay. I get the picture. You've made your point, and I don't need that aggravation. Her name is Sarah. Sarah King, and she's my partner here at the agency. She's not here today, she's out, but when she returns, she can tell you that we were together Saturday evening."

"Uh huh. And Sunday morning, too?"

No. Sunday morning I was home ... with my wife, and the kids, of course. Don't tell me you need to check that out, too."

"I'll get back to you."

"Where did you pick up all that agency lingo?"

"On TV, where else?" Nick didn't shake Jeremy's offered hand. He looked directly at him noting the perspiration on Jeremy's face and turned without any comment. As he was leaving, the door opened almost hitting him, forcing him to step back.

114

"Jerry, you had better talk to that little prick in the service department. They won't release my car! They want cash, or a certified check. Who ever heard of that shit! You had better take care of it right now!" She was yelling, ignoring Nick.

"Excuse me, I was just leaving," Nick smiled. He guessed this was Cassandra Keller. She wore a lot of make up and expensive looking jewelry. It was actually out of place for anyone working in an office, and he doubted that she worked at anything, except giving other people a hard time. She didn't seem to care that Jeremy had a visitor. Nick could have been a client. If this was Jeremy's wife, and he was fooling around with his new partner, the man had a death wish. Nick didn't envy his problems.

Nick drove by the restaurant where he'd met Paul Deckel. He needed a cup of good coffee and hoped the friendly waitress with the cute ass was working. He found an empty booth. She found him, just as he was starting to make a few notes on his yellow pad.

"Well hi there. I was wondering when you'd stop back," she gave him the biggest smile he'd seen all day.

"I guess you missed me, too. I'll just have a black coffee and as many smiles as you care to flash my way." It came out without thinking. Because he was alone and she didn't appear to be busy, he took a long moment to look at her from the top down. If anyone had noticed, they would have guessed that he was undressing her in public, while she willingly modeled for him.

"You're a cop, right?" Nick nodded with a slight smile. He'd done this scene before, several times in fact. "One of the other waitresses told me about you. She said she saw your picture in the paper a while ago, about some robbery, where you caught the guy."

"Yeah, that was me, a public servant just doing my job, protecting the public from the bad guys," Nick said this with a big grin. "Any protecting I can do for you, just ask, okay?"

115

"Honey, you'd be all the protection any girl would need. Can I bring you a piece of pie with that coffee?" She half-turned so he could admire her profile. She knew what she was doing, and just how to do it. She already knew Nick was a good tipper.

"Ooooh, I'd better not. All those calories, but you're tempting me. Bring me something that's not too sweet, I'll trust your judgment."

The waitress was back before Nick could start making notes. She took off her apron and slid into the booth facing him. She said she was taking her break and took out a cigarette and lit it, without asking Nick if he cared. She watched Nick eat the coconut custard pie. She told Nick her name was Mavis, she was divorced, had a daughter who was five, and her mother babysat the child when needed. Mavis indicated that she didn't have a boyfriend, wasn't currently seeing anyone, and she got off at 3:30... in case he was interested. Nick nodded while finishing the last bite, while Mavis turned his pad around and wrote her name, and phone number. Then she drew a happy face and wrote, 'call me'. Never before had Nick obtained so much information, from anyone so fast. In return, he gave her one of his cards. She hadn't bothered to ask him if he was married, so he didn't supply that extra bit of information. He did however arrange to take her to dinner Friday night. Mavis said her mother would keep her daughter overnight, so there wouldn't be any problems. Also, there was no check. She refused to let him pay anything. So, he left a three-dollar tip.

Totally distracted, Nick left the restaurant smiling. It all happened in less than a half hour. Their next meeting would be a true clash of hormones, he was sure of it. What they'd talk about later, was another question.

It took Nick a few minutes to shift back to the present. Phil Freeman said he was in Orlando. Jeremy Keller had also been away. Now his girl friend, Sarah was not available. Summer was a tough time to try to reach people, Nick decided. Nick found a shady side street where he could park and make a few notes, while everything was still fresh.

Check on Nelson Hoffman!

Why did Nelson jump in and the answer the questions Phil Freeman was asked? Afraid what he might say?

Check on Phil's & Nelson's alibi/Orlando area.

Check out Calvin Justine/West Palm Beach, Florida. Find him!

Check on Keller's alibi/with partner (Sarah King).

Check Keller's credit report. Financial trouble there?

Check Mrs. Freeman's alibi for Sat. night.

Does Mrs. Freeman have access to yacht?

Check records for Phil's phone call home from somewhere in the Orlando area

CHAPTER 11

Susan Deckel had agreed to see Nick at her parent's home in Birmingham. Vincent's car had been returned, it was parked in the driveway when Nick arrived. Susan opened the door before Nick could ring the bell. That seemed to happen frequently here. She appeared to be very nervous. When they entered the living room, Emily wasn't there. Somehow it seemed much colder in here than his last visit.

"So how is your investigation going, Mr. Alexander?" She didn't call him Lieutenant.

"Well, it's definitely keeping me busy. If you want, you can call me Nick, everyone does."

Susan Deckel was about 25 or 26 and a very attractive brunette. She was a few inches taller than Emily, making her about 5' 7". She wore just a hint of make up. Nick thought she could easily pass for a model. She sat on the one sofa with her hands folded and legs crossed. It was a learned position showing grace and style, Nick suspected. Other times she probably slouched.

"I'm sorry if I seem upset, I've never spoken with a detective before. And everyone seems to think my father's death may not have been an accident. Why would anyone want to kill my father?"

"Mrs. Deckel, we're not sure that your father's death wasn't an accident. It's just that the circumstances surrounding his drowning leave a lot of unanswered questions. It's my job to find those answers."

"Paul says you're treating it like a murder investigation. Do you have any suspects?"

"Well Paul is free to think whatever he wants. Why anyone

would want your father dead is a tough question. Perhaps you can help me with that."

"I can't. I really can't. My father was the dearest man in the whole world. He helped a lot of people, and he was very well liked . . . ."

"I'm sure he was. Did he discuss his business activity with you?"

"No, I didn't know much about his work. He talked to my husband about it, though. Daddy helped Paul get started, that's the kind of person he was."

"But you didn't know his business acquaintances then? So, he could have made some enemies that you never knew about isn't that true?"

"I don't know. Paul would have told me, if anyone was mad at daddy. Besides, he was a very important man in this community. He knew a lot of people, and he had a lot of friends. If there was ever a problem, all he would have to do, was pick up the phone and call someone to help him."

"Was there ever a time when he needed help?"

"I don't think so. Oh, wait, yes there was a time when I got a speeding ticket. He took that down to the police station and talked to someone there who took care of it."

"Uh huh. He never had to borrow any money, or go to his friends for any serious help?"

"Goodness no! If daddy ever needed any money, all he would have to do is ask Grandmother. And I don't think he ever had to do that. It's not like we're exactly poor you know." This really was a spoiled, rich kid.

"No, of course you're not. That's very evident. You're aware that your father had trouble keeping a secretary until Ruth Lambert arrived? Why do you suppose that was?"

"Mr. Alexander, I already told you that my father's business affairs didn't concern me. That also included his temporary help. I think Ruth lasted because she got on well with my mother. She's not exactly like the rest of them. She doesn't have to work." ———

119

"You don't work, either do you?"

"I do some volunteer work at the hospital, and I give tennis lessons at the club, that is I use to."

"I see. Would you happen to know Jeremy Keller? I understand he's a pretty good tennis player."

"Yes, I know him. He's not a member of our club, but I've played tennis with him a few times. Not recently. He's pretty good, or at least he was."

"Was he ever a guest here?"

"No, and I don't see what it is you're driving at? My father did most of his entertaining at the club, not here. My mother wouldn't allow it. Daddy kept business friends and social friends separate. Was there anything else Mr. Alexander?"

"No. Thank you, Mrs. Deckel. I appreciate your time. Oh, just so I can keep everything in order, you and Paul were home Saturday night?"

"Yes we were. We were here for dinner, then we went home. You don't suspect us do you?"

"No, of course not. It's just police procedure Mrs. Deckel. Thank you for your time."

<hr/>

At 4:00 that afternoon, Nick received a phone call from an investigative reporter from one of the network TV stations asking if he was investigating the Vincent Blessing murder? And if so, why were the police still officially calling it an accident? Nick replied that there were some unanswered questions surrounding the accident. There was no proof that a crime had been committed, just questionable circumstances. So, even though he was busy with a heavy caseload, Nick was trying to find some additional answers. When asked what specific questions remained unanswered, Nick said he didn't want to hinder the investigation, but he was still wondering what

the victim was doing on a yacht that belonged to a casual acquaintance, who was out of town at the time of the accident? Also, there was evidence that at least one other person was there, and had left. That person might be able to shed some light on the events leading up to the "accident". Nick didn't mention who the owner of the yacht was, or the fact that fingerprints had been wiped clean from all the normal places. It was enough to satisfy the reporter.

The 5:30 news carried Vince's suspected murder as their lead item. Nick called Ruth and asked if her VCR was working, and would she tape the news program for him? His VCR was being repaired. Then, almost as an afterthought, he offered dinner, if she was interested.

"Give me a call when you're ready to leave your office and I'll have everything ready when you get here. What do you think, thirty minutes to drive it in traffic?"

"Depends on what you're planning for dinner. I could use the siren and lights and make it in twenty minutes . . . regardless of traffic."

"If I know you at all, you'd never do such a thing. And, I'm not sure you could shave ten minutes in traffic, even with your siren. People just don't get out of the way any more, even for ambulances. It's disgusting. I'll plan on a thirty-minute warning."

Nick arrived a little after 6:00. The news was still on and some of it was a repeat of the 5:30 version. Ruth handed him a vodka tonic when he entered, and kissed him on the cheek. It was if they had known each other a long time and seemed very natural.

"Did you win the war today... against the bad guys?"

"Hard to tell who the bad guys are anymore, but yeah, I made some progress."

"Wait until you see who they are interviewing about Vince's murder."

"Yeah, I know. They called me earlier this afternoon."

"Well you're in for a big surprise, sweetie pie. I won't spoil it for you. Sit down and relax. Dinner won't be ready for a while yet. And I have the whole program being taped so you won't miss anything." She had actually said, 'sweetie pie' just as the Chief had.

"Thanks." Nick sat hunched over his drink while he waited for the reporter to return after a commercial.

" . . . And now, live from Birmingham, Angie is with one of the people the police are questioning about the possible murder of a local prominent businessman earlier reported as an accident. Angie . . . ."

"Thanks, Bert. I'm standing here with Jeremy Keller, President of a local advertising agency, Keller, Katz and King. Mr. Keller, you said the police have been here asking you questions about Vincent Blessing who drowned last weekend. Are you a suspect in his murder?"

Jeremy had his jacket on. He was standing outside his building in the parking lot holding a briefcase in an executive pose. He nervously adjusted the knot of his tie as the camera zoomed in on him. "Actually, I don't believe I'm a suspect. There's no reason for me to be, but they're treating me like one. My lawyer says that he'll be present when I talk to them next time. If there is a next time."

"Just what kinds of questions are the police asking?"

"Well, they want to know my whereabouts the night he was killed, ah I mean had his accident. I just can't understand how they can go to such extremes searching for a motive."

"You said you were out of town the night of the accident, so why would you be a suspect?" The reporter pushed the microphone in front of him blocking his full view of the camera. Jeremy pushed it aside enough so the camera had a full shot of his face and smile.

"Well, the victim and I had an argument about two years ago. It wasn't much of an argument, but it has since been blown out of proportion. I guess based on that, I'm a suspect. At least that's how they're treating me. They come here when I'm busy with clients and interrupt my schedule to ask me silly questions about something that happened years ago. I can't even remember the last time I saw, or talked to Vince, it's been that long. I guess my not being able to remember the exact time and date makes me appear suspicious."

"It appears the police have very little to go on at this time. I called Lieutenant Nick Alexander, who is handling the investigation, earlier this afternoon, and he said that the case is still being considered an accident. He also said that there were a few unanswered questions surrounding the event, like what was Mr. Blessing doing on that yacht that late at night when the owner was away on a business trip? That hardly qualifies as a reason to suspect murder, so maybe the police don't have enough other crimes to investigate. If that's the case, we can suggest a few they should take a look at, like the increasing drug problem here in the city. Back to you, Bert. . . ."

"He's a smooth bastard. I pushed him into a corner today, and thought he was going to cooperate. Instead, he pulls a phony press conference so he can get some free publicity at our expense. Now when I call him again, he'll scream harassment and have his attorney there." Nick was caught off guard by this sudden turn of events. The Chief would not be happy about this.

"I knew you'd be surprised. Just how did it go with Jeremy?" Ruth sat on the arm of the couch with a glass of wine and listened to him recap his earlier interview, nodding in agreement with his observations.

"Jeremy is a man who lives on the edge all the time. He loves a challenge. He's a fierce competitor on the tennis court. And, when he pitches for a new client, he's a great actor. He'd have you believe he was President of a very large ad agency. Did you see how he moved that mike when it was in his face? He knows how to face a camera, and present his best profile."

"Yes. You certainly called it right on this character. He thinks he's off the hook now, and that I'll take it easy on him, but he's in for a big surprise. He pulled an unusual stunt, I'll give him credit for that, but it was also risky. If I can prove that he's seen and talked with Vince in the last few weeks or months, then I have him nailed as a liar, with TV coverage on tape to prove it. It could backfire on him."

"He wouldn't have done this unless he's scared. There's something he's trying to hide, I just feel it," Ruth said this as she patted Nick's arm and got up to check on dinner.

"Oh I think I know what he's trying to hide. He's playing house with his new partner, and she's married. Old foxy Jeremy doesn't want his wife to find out because it could cost him a divorce, and a bundle of dough no doubt."

"I don't think that's it. Jeremy has fooled around before and she's caught him a few times. If she was going to call it quits with him, she would have done it sooner. She likes spending his money. In fact, without her around, Jeremy's financial situation might improve."

"Now that's interesting. His wife is the big drain on his financial situation? So a divorce wouldn't be so bad if it happened. Must be King's husband that's the problem then. She's his alibi, and he doesn't want me to talk to her about that night. He acted a little worried."

"That's the key word, acted. He wanted you to think he was worried. I'm telling you the man loves to act. When he was younger, he starred in a few little theatre productions, you probably wouldn't know that to look at him."

"Well, if he was acting earlier today, he did a terrific job, and convinced me. Either way, I'm not through with Mr. Keller." Nick finished his drink and followed Ruth into the kitchen.

Dinner was a terrific tossed salad with a special light oil and vinegar. Hot rolls and chili with grated cheese and onions on top, just the way he liked it. Without making too much fuss over the meal, Ruth knew he enjoyed it by the way he ate everything. When they were finished, he made coffee and cleared the table, while she stacked the dishes into the dishwasher.

"What would you like to do now," she asked with a knowing smile.

"Well I accused Jeremy of not having his priorities in order today, now I'm having difficulty with mine. Part of me wants to jump in the sack with you, while part of me wants to review that tape again . . . ." Nick glanced at the VCR, struggling with his decision.

"Ah hah, a true detective. Allowing sex to take a back seat to catching the villain. Probably something your wife never appreciated in you." The moment she said it, she wished she hadn't. They hadn't discussed sex, or their relationship, if indeed there even was one. And here she was making light of a serious subject that could be a sensitive zone. She looked at Nick with some apprehension.

Nick saw her expression before it changed. He laughed so the moment would pass easily. Ruth had hit on the real reason he had not been a satisfying partner. When he had a problem to solve, it stayed up front in his mind and worked overtime. It took first priority over any emotions or feelings that he might normally have. Ruth had been quick to recognize the problem, which they hadn't discussed. Maybe it was ESP. They both laughed as they sat on the floor in front of the VCR and waited for the tape to rewind. Coffee was on a tray beside them on the floor. This was the kind of extended foreplay he'd been missing.

With the surprise element eliminated, Nick could concentrate on the tape closely. He watched Jeremy's eyes as he listened to the audio. Ruth was right, the man was an actor. He was enjoying this interview. It was a game, a risky game, but still a game of wits, and a subtle challenge to Nick. Jeremy was almost saying, 'try to get me now and I'll fix your wagon good'. Nick could see how Vince and Jeremy must have clashed. Two big egos, two big bull shitters going at each other with threats. And as the hatred continued to build, each was encouraged to strike harder. Ruth had indicated that even after Vince got the business, he wasn't satisfied. He had wanted to put Jeremy out of business, crush him. And the note in the file that said, 'Find Jerry's weak spot'. Now Nick was also wondering what that weak spot might be? He also wondered if perhaps Vince had discovered it, and maybe paid a high price as a result? Attractive women could be Jeremy's weak spot, or his lack of money to stay solvent. Or, was it his need to be important? All were strong motivators. And Keller was beginning to look like a dangerous dancer!

"Nick, is there any way I can help you with your investigation? I'd really like to, you know." Ruth was sitting with her back against the base of the sofa, her knees up, revealing perfectly tanned legs and thighs. He could also see a little lace trim on her panties and he became excited. She made no attempt to pull her skirt down over her knees. She reached over and held his hand, knowing where his mind was.

"Since I've already violated a personal rule and discussed this case with you, which I shouldn't have done, I'll say yes. I need proof positive that Vince and Jeremy met or talked to each other recently. Go back through his calendar and any files you can find that might be a clue. Even go back through his expenses. He might have something noted. You have his phone charges, anything that might give me a handle." It was a poor word choice. She smiled knowing he was having difficulty hiding the bulge in his pants.

"Calls from the office to Keller's would be local and wouldn't show up on the bill. Couldn't you get a list of all the outgoing calls from Vince's office?"

"Yes, I can get that from the telephone company, but not without some authority. And, a call record from one office to another wouldn't be proof that Vince actually talked to Jeremy, only a suggestion that they might have spoken to one another. What I need is a witness, like somebody at the club or at a bar, or something."

"They wouldn't have met socially. They hated each other. There wouldn't be a reason."

"I suppose not, but let's give it a try anyway. Good detectives win their cases based on long hours of boring work digging through mundane records and asking hundreds of people the same questions over and over."

"Doesn't sound very glamorous when you put it that way."

"It really isn't. TV makes it seem like every cop fires a hundred bullets every week when in truth, most never fire their guns except on a qualifying range. If you check, you'll find that most FBI agents have accounting degrees or law degrees. That's because they're trained to investigate records and look for discrepancies."

"Here I thought I had met an interesting man who loved his work and was good at it. Now you tell me that it's really a job of looking into waste baskets for clues."

"Sometimes it seems that way. Let's go over to Chez Lou's and have a drink. I want to talk to the bartender over there. You can come along and see real police work in action."

"Are you sure you want to do that now, or later?" She stood up and smoothed her wrinkled skirt. She was giving him an open invitation.

"I think... we'd better go." It was difficult to make that decision. Right now, Nick had two conflicts going, and he had to keep his priorities straight, or he was no better than Keller. There was plenty of time to take care of his sexual needs, after all, he'd gone six weeks so far. That was almost a record for Nick. And, he was pretty sure that an all-nighter was available on Friday with the cute waitress, Mavis. Paul

Deckel had mentioned that Ruth had a boyfriend, yet she hadn't made any mention of that, even when he had asked her earlier. So there was plenty of time to sample some of her sweet surprises. A quickie now wouldn't be good enough, and right now his mind was racing in several directions at the same time.

"Okay. Give me a minute to check my face and hair before we go."

"I thought all women just powdered their noses."

"See, and you thought you knew everything. There are still a few surprises waiting for you, Lieutenant. Oh, and the file on **DETROIT VISITOR** is on the side table over there, I almost forgot to mention it in all the sudden excitement."

"Thanks." He picked up the file, but didn't read it. Instead, he was reading between the lines of her last comment. Ruth had made it clear enough that she was interested and available. And he planned to take full advantage of that invitation very soon.

For the first time in a long while, Nick was uncertain whether or not he was doing the right thing. Discussing the case with Ruth had seemed so natural. And it did help him put some of his thoughts in order. She confirmed some of his suspicions, and added some insight into Jeremy's character that he might not have noticed. Now he was taking her along while he did some additional checking and it seemed quite natural. That bothered him. She was easy to be with and he liked that, yet it scared him at the same time. "Nick, old sock, you might not be in complete control, even if you think you are," he could hear a voice in his head say. Judging by his erection, the voice may be right, he wasn't in complete control right now.

"What the hell, you can only die once," he said in answer to that voice.

"Nick, did you say something?" Ruth entered the room checking her earring.

"Yeah, I was just issuing a challenge to old Jeremy, that I plan to nail his ass to the wall. He's a real dancer."

"Dancer? I don't think I understand . . ."

"That's a guy who tries to evade direct questions. Dances around the issue, asks a question, instead of giving you an answer, that sort of thing."

"Oh. And do you like to dance?"

"As a matter of fact, I do."

"I thought so. You mentioned something earlier about the cha-cha." She giggled.

"That was the horizontal cha-cha, and that's a different dance entirely."

"I know. My ex-husband used to call it belly rubbing. He was a terrible dancer."

"Which, on the dance floor, or in bed?"

"Would you believe both?" She gave him a teasing smile.

Nick continued to be amazed at how easy it was to talk to this woman about sex and anything else. She didn't show any signs of indignation about how crude it was to discuss sex, or one's past sexual experiences. It just all came out in a very natural way. He liked it. This was a classy lady who had been around. She exuded warmth and charm, and a lot of polish. She also excited him and he wanted to react to some of her slightly flirty suggestions and yet at the same time, he wanted to prolong this flirtation and savor it. Like foreplay, it was probably more important to the experience than the actual sex act itself. And he wanted it to last as long as possible. He'd never felt this way with any other woman, which made her very special. His last romantic relationship seemed to be a long time ago, even though it had only ended six weeks earlier. For once, he was not classifying sex and romance together. All his recent exploits had been solely for sex, there hadn't been any romance or real flirtation. The realization was just now hitting him.

——— ——— ———

Peter, the bartender was on duty. He didn't seem to recognize Nick. The lounge was busy and the noise level was moderately high with music in the background and everyone seemed to be in conversation. It reminded Nick of a continuous tape that never ended.

"Mr. Freeman here tonight, Pete?" Nick noticed the corner booth was empty.

"No sir, haven't seen him. What will you and the lady have tonight?"

"Two vodka tonics. And when you get a few minutes free, I want to ask you a few questions." Nick displayed his badge in a subtle manner so it wasn't obvious to anyone else sitting at the bar. It looked like he was taking money out of his wallet.

"Yes, sir. I suggest that maybe if you went down to the end of the bar, I could take your drinks down to you there."

Nick liked the way this young man handled the situation. He was a good bartender and nothing seemed to annoy, or surprise him. Obviously Nick wasn't the first police officer who wanted to ask him questions, and he knew just how to handle it without anyone taking special notice. Nick and Ruth moved to the far end and waited for a vacant stool. Pete appeared with their drinks and leaned over and whispered something into the man's ear who was sitting directly in front of Nick. The man nodded and got up giving his seat to Ruth without any comment. He just evaporated. A big tip was in the making here.

"Did Vincent Blessing come in very often?" Nick asked the question and assumed that Vince was a regular customer.

"I know who he is, but he didn't come in, you know, like every evening. Once in a while, and only to meet a friend, not to pick up anybody." Obviously Peter knew he was dead.

"Uh huh. You happen to know who that friend was?"

———

"Usually it was to speak to Mr. Freeman in his corner booth over there. That's where Mr. Freeman sees most of his friends." It was the same booth where Nick had met Phil Freeman.

"Sounds more like his office."

"Yeah, I think he meets with a lot of people there. He's some kind of financial consultant or something, and I think a lot of people ask his advice."

"Popular guy, huh?"

"Yeah, pretty popular. Tips well enough, too." The suggestion wasn't missed and Nick handed him $ 10.

"Thanks, Pete. I appreciate your comments. I may need some more information later. If so, is there a number where I can reach you?"

"Uh, I'm staying at my girlfriend's place right now. I think it would be better if you just called me here, if that's okay."

"Sure. And thanks again."

"So, did we learn anything?" Ruth asked. She'd been quiet and listened to Nick as he had asked his questions.

"I'm not sure. Phil Freeman conducts some of his business in that booth. Since it's empty, let's go over and have our drinks there." They had no more than sat down when a waitress appeared.

"I'm sorry, this booth is reserved. Can I take your drinks to another table?"

"Oh, that's okay. We're waiting for Phil Freeman and I understand this is his booth. I guess we're a bit early."

"I see. Well in that case, just let me know if there's anything you need." She walked away, accepting Nick's comment as if it were a frequent occurrence.

"You really do think fast, Nick. First you get a fix on this guy from the bartender, then you take that information and use it. Do you suppose this Mr. Freeman will show up tonight?"

"Don't know. If not, we'll just enjoy his booth knowing

0-STAN

that nobody is going to bother us." With that he moved a little closer to Ruth, put his arm around the back of the booth and smiled at her. Then he did a poor imitation of Bogart, picking up his drink, "Here's looking at you, kiddo."

"The man has a sense of humor after all." She laughed at his attempt, and put a hand on his thigh and patted it. She left it there, knowing the effect it would have.

A tall blond, well-built, well-tanned man wearing an expensive blazer and silk sport shirt open at the collar to show some hair, walked toward their booth. He walked with a purpose and didn't look around. Nick estimated his age at maybe 30 or 31. On closer inspection, Nick could see thick neck muscles, indicating the man worked out regularly. Nick could see a faint outline of sunglasses. He approached the booth and didn't smile. He had a cold stare that signaled caution. The man looked like he could handle himself in any situation. It was a confident attitude some men had, and it showed on this fellow, like a neon sign.

"I understand you're waiting for Mr. Freeman. Do you have an appointment with him?" The man was speaking to Nick but looking at Ruth, undressing her. He didn't appear to care that Nick was aware of his admiration. He was an animal who had smelled the musk and came looking.

"That depends. Who are you, his personal secretary?" Nick didn't disguise his growing annoyance.

"No, I'm an assistant to Mr. Freeman. And he isn't planning on being here this evening. Was there something you wanted?" Still no smile. Dressed differently, the man could have passed for a waiter taking an order, standing there beside the table. However, this man was wearing expensive loafers and a very expensive aviator's chronograph. Phil Freeman apparently paid all his young associates very well. They seemed to be cast from the same mold. This man wasn't as polished as Nelson, but otherwise, there were similarities.

"Yeah, well since Phil isn't planning to show up tonight,

132

maybe we'll just sit here and have a few drinks and catch him another time."

"Sorry. This is a reserved booth. I suggest you move to a table or another vacant booth."

"Nick, maybe we should leave," Ruth whispered, sensing a confrontation.

"Reserved for Mr. Freeman, who isn't planning on being here. So what's your problem?" Nick asked the younger man, looking directly at him as he took a sip from his drink. It was Nick's way of letting him know he wasn't being intimidated.

"Look buddy, this is Mr. Freeman's booth all the time, whether or not he's here, or someplace else. And right now, it would be in your best interest to move someplace else, and not give me a hard time about it. You understand what I'm saying?"

"Sure I get the message. You mind bringing the Manager over here, so we can settle this in a friendly manner? I'd ask you to join us, but we're having a private conversation and right now, you're the one who isn't needed, do you understand what I'm saying?" Nick tried to use the same inflection the young man had used.

"If it's trouble you want, buddy, you'll get more than you bargained for. I was asking you nice. Now, I'm telling you. Leave and you won't get hurt. Stay, and you'll wish you had left, so don't play silly games with me to impress the lady." The younger man nodded toward Ruth.

"So, you're Mr. Freeman's muscle as well as his personal secretary. He must pay you pretty well. Nice shirt you got on sonny boy. I'd hate to have you get it wrinkled, or even stained. Believe me, bloodstains don't wash out easily. I know. We'll just finish our drinks and then we'll leave. However, you can still get the Manager over here. I'd like a few words with him before we go." Nick could feel the adrenalin beginning to take over.

"Just drink up and beat it. I'm nobody's errand boy. And

---

don't push your luck." The young man leaned on the table with both hands flat on the surface. He was face to face with Nick staring with cold, gray eyes that didn't blink. Nick was close enough to smell his cologne. It was expensive like his clothes. Fingernails were manicured, too.

It happened so fast that Ruth wasn't sure how Nick had managed to finish his drink and slam the edge of his heavy glass down on the man's right hand below the wrist. It was a smashing blow that caused the man to scream and grab his hand with his left, while glaring at Nick in disbelief. Before anyone could move, Nick had pushed the table away and was trying to get to his feet. The man blocked his way, so Nick fell back toward Ruth and at the same time, swiftly lifted his right leg to the height of the table catching the man just below his fly, causing him to double over onto the table in agony. Nick grabbed him by his blond hair and lifted his face by snapping his head back sharply. The man was kneeling on the floor with his chin on the table. His eyes telegraphed pain . . . and hatred.

"Sonny boy, I could hurt you a lot worse than that. I don't like being told what to do. And I don't like being interrupted when I'm talking with a beautiful lady. You forgot your manners. And a good looking outfit isn't enough to get you accepted, even if you do work for Phil. Now I suggest you beat it before I get angry. That's your only warning."

Nick wasn't able to finish his lecture because the Manager and a waiter had arrived at the table. The man got to his feet and was attempting to adjust his clothes and smooth his hair. His right hand was swelling, and he was trying hard not to favor it. His face was red with anger.

"What's going on here? I'm calling the police if you don't leave at once."

"Mr. Freeman invited us to meet him here for a drink. Then sonny boy here decided we didn't have an appointment, and tried to show us the door, before we were ready to leave.

I didn't realize he worked for you. What is he, a part-time bouncer?"

Peter, the bartender had seen it all. He came around the bar and whispered into the Manager's ear. Probably that Nick was a cop, and to take it easy.

"Its time you learned Neil, that this isn't Mr. Freeman's property, nor is it his office." The Manager turned to Nick looking apologetic, "I'm sorry if there's been a problem. This gentleman is Mr. Freeman's assistant. I assure you he doesn't work for this establishment. Can I send over another round on the house?" The tense mood disappeared. Mr. Muscle was applying an icepack to his injured hand, while glaring at Nick.

"No thanks, we were just about to leave when we learned that Phil wasn't going to be here tonight." Nick and Ruth were both standing. Nick turned to Neil, who now had a name, "I'd say no hard feelings, but I wouldn't mean it. You might lift weights, but you wouldn't last two minutes in an alley. Take my advice, and stay out of alleys, Neil. And, if you happen to see me in here again, which is possible . . . smile. But do it from a distance, okay? You have bad breath!" Nick took Ruth's arm and together they walked slowly to the door. Nick could feel Neil's angry stare burning into his back, and felt certain they would meet again. Nick wasn't looking forward to it.

"Wow, that was exciting! For a moment there, I thought you were backing down to that guy." They were in the parking lot and Nick was searching for his keys while trying to hide his trembling hands.

"Yeah, he thought so, too. It's always a mistake to think you know what the other guy is going to do. He sort of had me in a bad position there, I couldn't get up."

"So you kicked him in the jewels, so he'd move?" Ruth was almost laughing.

"No, I kicked him in the jewels so he'd bend over. And that way, I could talk to him face to face." He winked at her as he said it. It was like something he's seen once in a Bogart movie.

"And you said investigating was a boring job. Seems to have a certain amount of excitement in it."

"Yeah, I have to do that now and then to keep from falling asleep on the job." He felt good and also a little foolish for showing off in front of her.

"So how come you didn't tell that man you were a police officer? He probably wouldn't have bothered us and just went away, leaving us alone."

"I think Peter told the manager who I was, since he turned nice so suddenly. As for Neil, let him learn a lesson the hard way. I hate pushy guys who like to throw their muscle around. And, we learned something tonight."

"We did?" Ruth was sitting close to him.

"Yes. Mr. Freeman has a bodyguard. That's what he uses Neil for. And if my guess is right, Phil Freeman is a high-class moneylender. He's an investment consultant, but that can be a fancy title for a loan shark."

"Do you really think so? What would Vince be doing around someone like that? Vince didn't need to borrow any money, he had plenty of his own."

"Well, he could have been a future resource for funds in case Mr. Freeman needed money to lend. I don't know, I'm just letting my mind run a little wild. The only people I know who need muscle men for bodyguards are celebrities and crooks. It's just one more piece of the puzzle, and it makes Mr. Freeman all the more interesting. I wonder where Neil was, when Phil was in Orlando? I'll have to remember to ask him that next time we meet."

"And you're planning on doing that face to face with him I suppose."

"It's the only way to ask important questions. You want to watch their expression while they're giving you the answer. Sometimes the expression is the answer." Nick had never had this much discussion with another woman about the work he did, or how he went about it.

He drove Ruth back to her town house and opened her door for her, helping her out, leaving the engine running. "Want to come back in for a nightcap, or some cha-cha lessons?"

"You know I do. Rain check?"

"Oh yes, you have a rain check. You're an interesting man, Nick Alexander. I feel as though I've known you for some time, even though we've just recently met. And, I want to get to know you better, much better. Thanks for an interesting evening."

I know. I feel the same way, Ruth. That's why I'm not rushing it. I'm not looking for a quick roll in the hay, and I guess I'm trying to prove that to you."

"Okay, the point has already been made. And I assure you that my bed is more comfortable than any hay you've been rolling around in lately." She kissed him lightly and then she kissed him again, this time longer, teasing him with her tongue, all the while pressing hard against him. Then, she abruptly turned and went inside without waving, or watching him drive away.

Nick knew he had to get his thoughts organized, and wanted to do it now. He had just passed up a great opportunity and regretted it. They had both teased each other, knowing the final conclusion would erupt soon enough. Back at his apartment, he drank a glass of orange juice at the kitchen table, while he made notes. If he could answer the question about why Vince was on Phil Freeman's yacht, he might unravel the rest of the puzzle that had developed. He felt more certain now that Vince's accident may have been helped along. The motive was still elusive, but it too, would surface when he could locate the reason for Vince's presence on that yacht at that late hour. Somehow money was the common element that seemed to link everyone together. Money laun-

137

dering was looking like a good reason for Phil Freeman to be hiding something. Had Vince stumbled onto it? Or, was he part of it?

Get background info on Neil (need a last name).
Where was Neil Sat. night?
Why would Freeman need a bodyguard?
Why did Keller feel the need to play games?
Did Vince know about Keller's girl friend?
Who is Ruth Lambert's boyfriend???

CHAPTER 12

Wizard called Nick with additional information. A flight plan had been filed for a twin-engine Beechcraft King Air, from Pontiac Airport direct to Orlando's Executive Airport. The pilot's name was N. Hoffman. The flight plan listed 3 souls on board, but didn't show the passengers' names. It could have been Phil, or it could have been someone else. The flight departed on Saturday, at 7:30 A.M. It was a 5 1/2 hour non-stop flight. The owner of the plane was Freeman Enterprises.

IRS records showed that Phil Freeman claimed an income of only $150,000. per. year. The house he owned was valued at $850,000. Freeman Enterprises was a privately held corporation with assets listed at $4 million. Nick thought the company's assets would have been much higher. The yacht and the plane would total that much. Calvin Justine was listed as a Senior Partner in the company. Nelson Hoffman was also listed as a Senior Partner. So he was much more than hired help. That also explained why he felt so confident to answer the questions Nick had directed to Phil Freeman. Still, there was the question of who was really running the show, Nelson or Phil?

Vincent Blessing reported an income of $325,000. per. year. His house was valued at $650,000. It appeared that Vincent was indeed a successful salesman. Neither Blessing, nor Freeman had a mortgages on their property. Freeman didn't own the building he occupied for Freeman Enterprises. The owner was listed as Horizon Properties in Palm Beach, Florida. Nick found that particular item very interesting since Calvin Justine also lived nearby in West Palm Beach. Was that just a coincidence?

Jeremy Keller was a different story. He claimed an annual income of $75,000. He owed some back taxes. His home was valued at $360,000. And, there was a mortgage. His wife, Cassandra owned the building the agency occupied, and it was valued at $500,000 and had recently been refinanced. He had a dozen credit cards, all with high balances. It appeared the man was living beyond his means. He was carrying a lot of debt and trying to remain in the fast lane.

Blessing had no criminal record. Keller had several speeding tickets and 4 overdue parking fines. Freeman was a different story. He had been acquitted of extortion charges 4 years ago in Miami. He was currently being investigated by the DEA because of his recent ownership of **The Other Woman**, which previously had a different name. It had been listed as **Tide Me Over** when it was confiscated. That name would have been more appropriate for Keller, Nick thought.

Wizard was unable to find anything at all on a Calvin Justine. The man did not exist as far as the IRS was concerned. So how was it that he was able to bid on, and purchase the yacht for half a million? Perhaps Freeman Enterprises put up the money, and that would explain why title was quickly transferred. Calvin Justine may have been the front man for the transaction. Nick had the distinct impression that Nelson Hoffman did not want him talking to Calvin. And, neither Nelson, nor Phil had offered an address or phone number in West Palm Beach. Without a court order, Nick couldn't force them to supply any information. His only option was to continue to dig deeper. Somewhere he'd find the answer to all his nagging questions. He also needed a last name for Neil, just in case he had a rap sheet.

"Nick, I'm suggesting that you close the case on Vincent Blessing. We'll go by the ME's report that it was an accident, even though the circumstances provoke some questions. And certainly you've spent enough time searching for those answers already. Since we can't find a witness, we don't have a solid suspect, and a motive hasn't emerged, so we have no reason to keep that yacht under our watch. I've released it. I realize that little escapade on TV was a poor excuse for publicity at our expense, but what the hell. It happens all the time. Have I accurately summed up our position on this?" The Chief knew that Nick wasn't happy about releasing the yacht.

"It sums up your position very well. And while I can't argue with what you've just said, I think there's a lot to be uncovered yet. I think Blessing stumbled onto something that was more than he bargained for, and it got him killed. I don't think the vendetta with Keller was sufficient reason, but the guy hasn't been straight with me. And neither has Freeman. You'd think he'd be more concerned that someone died on his boat. Something stinks, I just need more time to sort it all out." Nick wanted to go back and examine the yacht closely, look for secret compartments, but that was no longer an option.

"Well you don't have any more time. The case is closed. We move on to other business. I have Sergeant Mitchell talking to witnesses on that hold-up at the Seven-Eleven. I'd like you to review his notes and see if we can make an arrest. By-the-way, Mr. Freeman didn't appreciate your busting his associate's hand, just to impress your new girlfriend."

"That his comment, or yours?"

"Actually it was his, but I think there's some truth to it. They are not pressing charges, but think about it, Nick. It was a stupid thing to do. It's not like you to do something like that. And that's what I told Mr. Freeman on the phone. I said something had to provoke you to act like that. You want to explain it to me?"

"Not really, but I will. Phil's got this Mr. Muscle for his bodyguard. That should tell you something about Phil. Anyway, Phil seems to own this corner booth at Chef Louie's. That's where he holds court with customers. When he's not there, no one is allowed to sit at that booth. However, I didn't know that until Mr. Muscle showed up. He pissed me off."

"I heard this guy asked you nicely to move, but you refused. Why not just go along with it? There were other tables available weren't there? Why make a scene?"

"Chief, you had to be there. The guy got nasty, and I lost it. You're right, it shouldn't have happened. It won't happen again, unless Mr. Muscle wants to make an issue out of it, then I don't know." Secretly, Nick hoped Neil was hurting, but didn't look forward to a return engagement with him. Without the surprise element, Nick wasn't sure what the outcome would be. Neil could hurt someone without much effort, even with a broken paw.

"Consider yourself lucky. Did your sweetie pie get all excited and wet her panties when you showed her your muscle?" The Chief had that snickering look again.

"No, she's a tough lady. I think she's seen it all at one time, or another. She'd be hard to impress." As Nick thought about it again, it was that look that Neil had, when he was mentally undressing Ruth, that had triggered Nick's anger. It wasn't what was said, it was the look.

———   ———   ———

Out of curiosity, Nick drove to the marina and discovered that **The Other Woman** was gone. He wasn't entirely surprised. He wished the Chief hadn't acted so quickly and released it before he could make one more complete inspection of the yacht. He felt sure it held a few hidden secrets that had been overlooked. The Chief considered the case closed, Nick didn't. Now, he'd have to be careful how he spent his time. He had some vacation time available, and a trip to West Palm Beach had some appeal. Maybe he could locate the mysterious Calvin Justine. And maybe, he could talk Ruth into going along. The case didn't intrigue him as much as Ruth did. Now that the case was closed, he didn't have to worry about their relationship, or talking about the

———

case. Nick had another strong reason for flying down to West Palm Beach. He had a standing invitation to go fishing with his old friend, Ben Wheeler. Ben was a Sergeant with the Palm Beach County Sheriff's Dept. Nick met Ben at a police seminar in Chicago several years ago. Fishing and crime were the two common activities that brought them together. Since then, Ben had sent several reminders to Nick. Now was the perfect time to accept.

When Nick returned to his desk, he had several phone messages. Jeremy Keller had called to say that he may be unavailable for the next few days, because he had a business trip to make. Nick hadn't told him not to leave town, so this was a subtle dig. The second message was from his ex-girlfriend, Gloria. She wanted to know if Nick had found a missing gold earring? She thought it may be in his apartment, and would he look for it? The last call was from Ruth. No message. He decided to return Ruth's call first.

"Hi, how's your day going?" he asked when she answered.

"Pretty good so far. I'm sorry if I bothered you at work. I didn't really have anything special to say, but I was wondering if you felt like going to a movie, or something tonight? Just to take your mind off work for a few hours."

"Ummm, the 'or something' sounds really interesting. Yeah, a movie is okay with me. Anything special you want to see?" He was pleased that this woman felt like asking him out, rather than waiting for his call. It was the kind of thing people did when they were comfortable with each another. And this time, his priorities wouldn't interfere with getting laid. It would be at the top of his things to do list tonight.

"Why don't we decide over dinner? You up for that?"

"Ruth, I love it when you talk dirty. With you, I'm up for anything you want to do right now. Tell you what, if you don't mind the drive over here, why don't we meet at Jack's On The Pier, do you know where it is?" Jack's seafood restaurant was adjacent to the marina where Vincent had his accident. And, it was just 2 blocks from Nick's apartment. It was quite possible they wouldn't make it to a movie.

"Of course I do. That sounds great. Is six too early?"

"See you there at six. I'll be at the bar waiting." If he left work early, he would have time to take a shower and straighten up his apartment. Then he'd walk over to Jack's. That way, Ruth could drive him home... and maybe drive him crazy. That last thought lingered while he tried to connect it with something else on the back of his mind.

"Excuse me, Nick, you looked like you were a thousand miles away just now," Sergeant Mitchell said, interrupting Nick's intimate thoughts.

"Actually, it was just fifteen miles. What's up?"

Mitchell didn't know yet that the Chief had closed the file on Vincent Blessing. He had been over to the Golden Oaks Country Club talking with a Harrison Giles, who confirmed that he'd met with Vincent last Saturday around noon. The purpose of that meeting was to give Vince an envelope that contained a proposal for a pizza franchise. A friend of Giles', named Sal Del Vecchio had an idea for a new chain of pizza parlors he wanted to franchise. The name would be Pizzano Pizza. About three years ago, Giles had introduced Sal to Vince, thinking Vince might be interested in investing in the idea. Vince thought there were too many pizza franchises already and didn't show any interest.

The date of the proposal Sal gave to Vince on Saturday was February 15, 1996. Giles found a copy in Sal's locker at the club. Apparently Sal located an investor who was interested, and flew down to Florida to see him. While there, he had an automobile accident and died. Giles forgot about the proposal until a few months ago, when he was in Texas on a business trip. While there, Giles saw a TV commercial for Pizzano Pizza. In the commercial, a young man wearing an obviously false mustache and chef's cap, hands a pizza to the customer and says, 'Ciao Piazzan', the implication being that everyone was a little bit Italian when you ate Pizzano Pizza.

Giles was surprised to see his friend's idea had materialized after all. He was also curious enough to check with the store manager, who in turn gave him the owner's phone number. The franchisee reported to Giles that he had bought the franchise for $ 250,000. from a company in West Palm Beach, Florida. The man he dealt with was a Calvin Justine. The company provided very little support and later sold out to a company in Atlanta. All this took place after Sal's accident. Giles mentioned all this to Vincent upon his return. Vincent became very interested in the events, once he heard Calvin Justine's name mentioned, since he'd met the man. Giles warned Vince to be careful because it was possible that Vince's idea to franchise a new magazine could take a similar twist. That suggested that maybe Sal Del Vecchio's death was no accident.

"Hmmm. Maybe we do have a motive for murder after all." Nick had listened to Mitchell's report. Then Nick told him the latest news, that the case was closed.

"So what appears to have been an accidental drowning was actually a murder," Mitchell shook his head in wonder. Nick had been correct all along in not assuming it was an accident, until they had investigated it completely. Score one for Mr. Serious.

"We still don't know that for sure, but it has that certain smell about it. The problem now is they've moved the yacht. I don't have a clue where it is, but I doubt we'll see it for a while. And if there was any important evidence left behind, you can bet it's not there now."

"If they wanted to get rid of Blessing, why didn't they just take the boat out into the lake and dump him overboard out there? Then they wouldn't have to worry about anyone showing up to check their boat. Who would know?" Mitchell was just speculating.

"It's a good point, Gary. Maybe that was the plan, and something went wrong. I've had this thought for a while that whatever happened, it was hasty and unplanned. Somebody panicked and didn't want it known they were there with him. Whoever that person is, holds the answer to all the questions. Vincent may have been there on a sniffing mission, or he may have tried to blackmail them. Either way, he didn't know who he was dealing with, that's for sure." Nick tried to conjure up his earlier thought just before Mitchell arrived, but it escaped him again.

Nick rummaged through his desk drawer looking for Ben Wheeler's phone number. It was time to do some fishing. And Calvin Justine was where he planned to start. Maybe he could get Ben Wheeler's help. Ben's friends actually called him 'Bubba' because he looked so much like the Deputy in the TV series, IN THE HEAT OF THE NIGHT, one of Nick's favorite programs when it was still running.

CHAPTER 13

Nick was able to reach Ben Wheeler at his office in West Palm Beach. Ben said that he could get at least 2 days off so they could go fishing together. He was looking forward to Nick's visit. Feeling a little guilty, Nick decided to explain that he also had a second reason for coming. He needed Ben's help searching for Calvin Justine. There wasn't any listing for him in the phone book, or with Directory Assistance. When he called the West Palm Beach offices of Freeman Associates, he got a recorded announcement. Wizard was also digging for information on the elusive Calvin.

"Hey, if he's living here, we'll find him, Partner," Ben said.

"One other item, you might be interested in looking into. There was an auto accident about two years ago. It involved a Sal Del Vecchio. There seems to be some doubt that it was an accident. Any chance you could take a look at the file?"

"Does this have anything to do with this Calvin Justine fella you're interested in?" Ben wasn't sure how much fishing they would be able to cram into just 2 days, if they were also looking into mysteries, but he didn't mind.

"As a matter of fact, it does. Del Vecchio flew down there to meet our Mister Calvin about a year and a half ago. There is some reason to believe they met, but that's all I have to go on."

When Nick finished with Ben, he glanced at the clock on his desk. It read 5:15. He could make it to his apartment in less than 5 minutes, but he'd have to hurry, if he wanted to do some last minute cleaning and change the sheets on the bed.

Ruth was sitting at the bar with a Bloody Mary when Nick arrived. She knew how to fit in with the boating crowd. She was wearing white shorts, a flowered tee shirt and sandals. Her long, tan legs complimented her casual outfit. Nick walked over to her, put his arm around her waist and kissed her on the cheek. It was so natural that anyone watching would have thought they were old friends. In Nick's mind, this was their third date. So far, he'd been the perfect gentleman.

"Sorry I'm a few minutes late. I wanted to stop by my apartment for a few minutes before walking over here." He hoped she heard the message. Her smile told him she did.

"I didn't realize you lived that close. So you're on the water then?"

"Yeah, I can see the lake from my living room. The nice part of living around here is that I can also walk to the office whenever I feel like it."

They had drinks and dinner on the patio outside. They were able to watch a variety of boats pass by. None were the size of **THE OTHER WOMAN** and Nick found himself wondering where the yacht might be at the moment, and who was on it? He'd call around Port Clinton tomorrow. Nick told Ruth about the case being officially labeled an accident, even though he still had some doubts.

"So, the interrogation phase of our relationship is over, is that what you're telling me?" Ruth teased.

"I never considered it to be an interrogation where you were concerned," he replied. He wanted to ask Ruth about the boyfriend Paul Deckel mentioned, but he was afraid to spoil the pleasant mood. He'd save that question for another time.

"I'm thinking about taking a few days vacation and flying down to Palm Beach, to do some fishing with an old buddy of mine. Why don't you come along?" He was trying to be casual.

"Thank you for the invitation. I'd like to, but I can't. There's so much catching up I have to do now. And, to be honest, Florida in July isn't the best place in the world to be taking a vacation, Nick. I know, I used to live down there." Nick knew she was right about the heat in Florida this time of the year. He didn't remember her mentioning that she lived there. He realized that she had asked him questions about the case and himself, but hadn't really told him a lot about her earlier life, just a brief mention of her divorce.

"When you were married, where did you live in Florida?"

"We lived in Fort Lauderdale. And earlier, we lived in Miami. Actually it was Coral Gables, but that's still Miami, or at least it was when we lived there. Talking about it stirs up some bad memories." She patted his hand, smiled and lit a cigarette. "So, what other cases are you working on now?"

"The usual stuff. I have a pretty good lead on a robbery suspect. We're looking for him now. However, I'm not entirely satisfied with the Blessing case. I think I'll do a little sniffing around while I'm down in Florida."

"Tell me something, Nick. Is that really a good idea? I mean, if you have some vacation time coming, shouldn't you just go, relax and have some fun with your friends? I think Emily and Susan will be happy to know that it's listed as an accident. I know Paul will be. He's been terribly upset ever since you talked to him last."

"Really? Now that surprises me. I got the impression that he wasn't very close to his father-in-law, and sort of resented some of the advice. Susan, on the other hand, I could understand being upset. Vincent spoiled her didn't he?"

"Yes he did. Emily wasn't too thrilled that he bought her that Porsche since she drives with a lead foot. She's had three tickets, and now Daddy isn't here to bail her out of all those annoying little problems."

"I take it you and Susan didn't get along very well. Was it because you worked for Vincent, or because you get along well with Emily?"

"I think it's a little of both. Emily tells me things. That

probably makes Susan feel she's being left out. She was very close to her father, and she gets whatever she wants... even if Emily objects. That might change now."

"Well, maybe things will be easier for Paul. He can do things his way and not have to worry about what Vincent thinks."

"I hope you're right. He's been helping me in the office, and Susan has been on him about it. I feel a little sorry for him, everyone always telling him what to do. First it was Vince, now it's Susan. He desperately wants to be his own person."

Ruth's observations coincided with Nick's. He was glad to learn that Emily had made a fuss about the car. Maybe another ticket and Susan would have to face reality. Anyone driving a Porsche, or a Corvette drew attention, even when they weren't speeding.

They finished dinner and lingered over a second round of drinks. Neither was in any hurry to leave. There was a pleasant breeze coming off the lake and the music inside provided a relaxing atmosphere. When they left, there was a line of people waiting for tables. Nick tipped the valet, then got into the passenger side of Ruth's Red Mustang convertible. She had the top down. It was only 2 blocks to Nick's apartment complex, so she drove slowly. She found a vacant parking spot, and followed Nick to his front door without any hesitation. They had both been waiting for this magic moment.

Nick unlocked the front door and immediately knew something was wrong. The sliding patio door was open allowing a breeze to blow the vertical blinds. Several cabinet doors were open. Nick cautiously walked to his bedroom and peeked inside. Dresser drawers were left open, the light in his closet was on, and all the jewelry in his cuff link box was gone, including an expensive gold Seiko watch his ex-wife had given to him. The mattress was hanging halfway off the bed. Nick stood in the middle of the room and made a circle sweep of the mess. Whoever had done this was looking for small objects, money and jewelry. They left his stereo and TV. He checked the closet, reached into the dirty clothes hamper and found his gun. He kept it in a leather clip holster, loaded. While the apartment had been ransacked, it wasn't trashed. For that he was grateful.

"Nick, are you planning to call anyone about this break in? I realize you're the police, but you still have to report this don't you?" Ruth asked. She sat down on the sofa watching as Nick took a quick inventory.

"Whoever it was, didn't break in. They had a key. They left the patio door open so I'd think they came in that way, but they didn't. I'm going to report it now, but I'm pretty sure I know who did this." He had $300 stashed away in an envelope taped behind his dresser. It was gone, along with 2 ties from the closet. His ex-girlfriend, Gloria, had given him those ties. She had called him earlier, and he had never bothered to return her call, so perhaps she decided to pay a visit. It was very unlikely the woman he knew. Why would she do it? Maybe she was on drugs. Nick tried to think back, he didn't recall ever giving her a key. He went into the kitchen and checked for the spare, it was missing. Nick couldn't recall when he'd seen it last, so maybe Gloria took it before she left. All this couldn't have happened at a worse time. The romantic evening he had planned would have to wait for another time. The bottle of wine he'd left in the refrigerator to chill was also gone.

———— ———— ————

One of the on-duty officers came by and wrote a report of the home invasion. None of the neighbors saw anything, or heard anything. Nick was glad his gun hadn't been taken. The 2 missing ties, and the hidden money were enough for

151

Nick to know that Gloria was somehow connected to all this. He was able to straighten up the apartment in less than a half hour. Ruth left when the officer arrived. Their third date ended with disappointment.

Nick called the number Gloria had left earlier. A gruff voice answered the phone.

"Who's calling, and what d'ya want?"

"I'm returning Gloria's call. Is she there?"

"She ain't here right now, who wants to know?" Nick examined the number on the paper. It had been 6 weeks since she walked out. The number she had left for him to return her call didn't look familiar.

"Just give her a message. Tell her Nick called, and I hope she found the earring she was looking for." He hung up before the man could reply.

Nick searched through his briefcase behind the sofa and found his address book with an assortment of names and numbers. Gloria's number was different from the one he'd just called. He dialed the number listed in his book; it had been disconnected. So she's moved, he surmised. Tomorrow he'd find out an address to match the new number. No, she'd ruined his evening, now it was his turn to ruin hers. He called the phone company, gave them his ID and wrote down an address that was on the east side of Detroit, in a bad area.

Driving alone in this section of Detroit, wasn't a smart thing to do. Doing it after dark wasn't a good idea either, even for a policeman. There were a few vacant lots where houses once stood, and had since been torn or burned down. Skeletons of stripped cars sat in the street. People didn't sit out on their front porch in the evening in this neighborhood. Prior to the riots in '67, it was a very nice place to live. Now it was a place where the desperate people existed. It was the next step before becoming homeless. Garbage cans remained on the sidewalk overflowing and adding an unpleasant stench to the night. It was the smell of the hopeless. It mellowed

Nick's anger. If Gloria was living around here, she was in deep trouble. Just 6 weeks ago, she was still a nurse, working at a walk-in clinic. He wondered what could have happened in that short time span.

Nick found the house, there was a light on inside. He was beginning to have second thoughts about how smart this was to come alone, but he didn't want to wait. The man who opened the door wasn't wearing a shirt, just a pair of dirty shorts. He needed a shave and a haircut, which made it difficult to determine how old he was. He could have been 28, or he could have been 38. He was missing a few teeth and had tattoos on both arms. People like this remained south of 8 Mile Rd., the boundary for Detroit and its surrounding affluent suburbs.

"You must be the asshole who called earlier. She ain't here. I haven't seen her all day, so she didn't get your message." He stood in the open doorway. He sounded worse on the phone than in person.

Nick pushed his way inside and wasn't surprised to find it filthy. Another man lay on the torn couch sleeping. Junk was strewn everywhere. The man at the door came at Nick with a baseball bat. Nick turned and ducked just in time. He hated to add to the man's already miserable life, but self-defense was necessary. He hit him 3 times quickly. The man went down like a sack of potatoes. The idea of looking any further was too disgusting, so Nick left. Gloria could have everything she had taken. He no longer wanted any of it. He didn't even want to touch those things she'd handled, if she was living here now.

Tomorrow he'd have the locks changed. And, he'd call the clinic where she worked, though he was certain she was no longer there. Something very sad had happened to her. Nick wondered if maybe Gloria was doing drugs when they had met, and while they were dating? If so, why hadn't he noticed? He remembered she'd had some mood swings that left him perplexed a few times. And, she had a bad temper. When she left him, Nick naturally assumed it was because he'd had to work later than expected again.

The clinic confirmed what he suspected. Gloria was let go 5 weeks ago, soon after she walked out on him. They wouldn't tell Nick why she was fired, but he could guess. She probably took some stuff from the clinic's medicine cabinet. Nick was having a hard time trying to remember what it was he liked about her. She was rapidly becoming a blur, a very sad blur.

Wizard called to report that **THE OTHER WOMAN** was back in Port Clinton. The DEA investigators had a tracking device hidden on the yacht so they could track it, after it was sold at auction. Nick wondered if the plane Freeman bought also had a similar device. If so, maybe the folks at the DEA could corroborate Phil Freeman's trip to Orlando. The idea struck him as humorous. Wizard also located a Calvin Justine with a Lantana address. Lantana was a community just south of West Palm Beach. Calvin had used the Freeman Associates address at the DEA auction.

Nick informed the Chief he was taking a few days off to go fishing. He didn't mention where he was going, but promised to check in periodically. It was short notice, and the Chief wasn't too happy about this sudden change to his schedule.

"Be careful, Nick. Let me know if you find anything on this Calvin Justine," the Chief smiled knowingly. Without being told, he knew Nick well enough to know he'd continue to explore loose leads until he was satisfied.

Nick stopped by the cleaners to pick up some shirts he'd left. As he was packing, he suddenly remembered that he had a date Friday night with Mavis. He called her at work, told her he was being called away on an important case that he couldn't discuss. He promised to call her again sometime, and maybe they'd get together. Ruth now occupied all his sexual attention. Then he made it to the bank just before it closed. He had reservations for a late, non-stop flight from Detroit metro to Orlando. He'd reserved a car in Orlando and planned to drive to West Palm Beach. He would return to Detroit from there. Now, he was ready to go fishing.

CHAPTER 14

Nick picked up his ticket at a nearby travel agency. Then, because it was still the cocktail hour, he decided to swing by Chez Lou's for a quick drink. Maybe he'd spot Phil, or his bodyguard, Neil. He and Neil were destined for a second round. To avoid a surprise encounter, Nick thought maybe an apology would work to some benefit. It might even precipitate some worthwhile conversation. What he didn't want was reciprocal broken bones, which wasn't likely, now that Neil knew who he was. Then again, it still paid to be prepared for the unexpected. Nick gave that lecture more than once to Sergeant Mitchell, and others. Now, he needed to heed his own advice.

It was early enough to find an empty seat at the bar. The lady seated two stools away looked familiar. Then he realized it was Cassandra Keller. She hadn't noticed him. She was talking with the younger man seated to her left. When she took out a cigarette, Nick leaned over with a light, she turned toward him with a slight flicker of recognition and a big smile.

"Thanks. You're not one of the regulars here," she didn't put it in the form of a question.

"No, but I'm beginning to be." He nodded to Peter behind the bar and was surprised when Peter produced a vodka tonic before he ordered it. Pete did indeed have a good memory for what people liked to drink.

"It really has become sort of a local's place. Most everyone who comes here knows everyone else," she said as she shot him a wink. Cassandra appeared to have had a few, and was feeling flirty. She was showing a lot of leg, and not being too careful about it.

"I just stopped in to see if Phil Freeman was here, or his associate, Nelson." Looking around, Nick didn't see any sign of Neil either.

"Really? You know Phil?"

"Doesn't everyone?" Nick decided to see how far he could take this before she realized who he was. Perhaps she didn't care, considering her present mellow condition.

"Be careful with Phil. Dealing with him can cost you big bucks. You don't look like one of his regular clients." She was appraising him more carefully now.

"So, do you know his associate, Nelson? He's in here regularly, too," Nick asked sipping his drink, acting as though he was making small talk to kill time.

"Of course! Nelson is some hunk, Honey. Lots of ladies around here would drop their panties for that one." She signaled Peter to bring her another drink. As several more people approached the bar to sit, Nick moved over so they wouldn't be separated. The young man on her other side didn't seem to care, and Nick noticed that Cassandra had her own tab going. So, for the present, she was alone. And, she knew Phil Freeman and Nelson. That suggested that Jeremy no doubt knew them as well. And just what would be the connection there? If Keller was having financial problems, maybe he'd turn to Phil. It was a possibility.

"Is that right? I can see where he might be a real lady's man. Then again, he might be gay, you can never tell these days," he laughed, all the while wondering if she knew him well enough.

"Oh I doubt it. He's a bit of a mystery though. Phil seems to rely heavily on him. He's originally from Florida and he's never lost his tan. Say, are you sure that we haven't met someplace?"

"Yes, I believe we have. You're Cassandra Keller, and we met briefly in your husband's office, just as I was leaving."

"We did? Are you a client?" She reached out and touched his arm.

"No." Nick wasn't sure how much he wanted to say at this point.

"Don't tell me, Jerry owes you money."

"No." He owes me more than money, Nick thought about the brief television coverage.

"So what were you doing at the office?" She looked at him over the rim of her glass.

"Trying to establish where he was last weekend." Nick couldn't stall any longer.

"He was probably screwing that whore, Sarah Shithead! That's what he does on weekends lately. And every evening, when her husband isn't around. They're like a couple of horny rabbits."

"You mean he's married to you and seeing someone else?" He lit another cigarette for her. This time she held his wrist lightly drawing the match to her. She hadn't asked him why he wanted to know where Jeremy was last weekend. Had she been more sober, and less interested in flirting, she would have asked.

"Not seeing, Honey, sleeping with and banging. I hate to use that fucking f word. Say, you never told me your name?

"Name's Nick, as in Nicholas."

"Oh yeah? As in Saint Nicholas, huh? You don't look like any Santa Claus to me, but I'll let you buy me another drink and promise to be a bad little girl. I won't even hang up my stockings, I'll just leave them on the floor for the maid. Ha, ha hah. When I was a little girl, I used to sit on Santa's lap and wiggle. And we didn't even celebrate Christmas, since my family is Jewish." She obviously thought she was teasing. Nick decided to play along for a while longer, hoping he could learn anything worthwhile about Jeremy. That's what Vince had been interested in, according to the note he had found.

"Well, maybe you remember that old saying about good girls go to heaven, and bad girls go anywhere they want to go." They both laughed.

———

"Cute. It reminds me this girl has to go to the ladies room and pee. Don't go away, Santa, I'll be right back."

"Don't forget to powder your nose."

"Don't be a smart ass, Nicholas. I was just beginning to like you. She touched the backs of several chairs as she passed them to steady her walk. She did it casually, but Nick could tell she was pretty well gone, or would be soon. Cassandra had all the practiced moves of an alcoholic.

While Cassandra was gone, Nick took advantage of her absence to ask Peter, the bartender if Phil Freeman or Nelson had been in? Neither had been there since Nick's brief altercation at the corner booth. Then he casually asked what Neil's last name was. Nick said he wanted to apologize to him for breaking his hand. Nick hadn't seen him anywhere and tried to be as casual as possible in scanning the room.

"I only know him as Neil. Never heard a last name mentioned," Peter said.

Nick ordered a tonic water, and had a light ready when Cassandra returned. The young man on her left had since moved, replaced by an older man, his back half turned to them. It was as much privacy as they would get, unless they moved to a table and Nick wasn't planning on staying much longer.

"So, old Jeremy is fooling around. You don't seem overly upset about it. Why don't you divorce him?"

"That bastard has been chasing pussy for a long time. Now he only chases the ones with money. I'm just waiting until he gets rich, so I can teach him an expensive lesson."

"This Sarah, is that his new partner?"

"Loosely speaking. She's married to some rich old geezer about twenty years older than her. Probably can't get it up any more, or lost interest. He supplies the money, and Jerry supplies the sex. Want to know something funny?"

"Sure, tell me something funny. Is it about Jerry?" Nick took a quick look at his watch.

"The little creep. I really don't know what Sarah Shithead sees in him. He's got a little bitty pecker, and he doesn't even use it all that well. I ought to know, I'm the one who had to live with it all these years. It's guys like Jerry that boost the sales of vibrators, isn't that hilarious? Ha, ha, Hah!" She said this rather loudly and Nick looked around, a little embarrassed.

"Well maybe all your passion scared him away. Couldn't measure up to your standards, something like that."

"Nicholas, all woman have passion. Some more than others maybe, but it's there to be discovered by the right man. As for measuring up, right now I'd settle for a good stiff six inches, and a half hour of dirty pillow talk. What turns you on, Nicholas? You into kinky?"

"Yeah, I can handle kinky, what exactly are we talking about?" Nick didn't have to think about that very long. If he hadn't met Ruth, and considering the 6-week dry spell he'd suffered through, he'd be feeling horny right now, but he wasn't. Rubbing knees, talking dirty, and seeing a lot of tanned thigh just wasn't enough to get him excited here. And fooling around with drunks was stupid. They either passed out, or puked all over you. He thought about Ruth and made a mental note to call her from the airport.

"Ever do it while eating Chinese food? I mean at the same time?" She was trying to look coy and failed. The idea didn't even appeal to him.

"No, but I'll have to keep that one in mind if I ever run out of kinky things to do." He wanted to get off sex and back to Jeremy. "So, are you and Jeremy still living together?"

"What's with all the questions about Jerry? You a cop or something?"

"I've been called worse. Would it bother you if I was?"

"No shit? And you'd like to handcuff me and show me your big six shooter, right? Or is it one of those little jobs like Jerry's?"

"Nope. You wouldn't find it all that interesting." Nick was fully aware of where this could lead, and he had to be careful. While they had been talking, Cassandra had very casually put her hand on his upper leg, rubbing it gently.

"Why don't you let me be the judge of that?" Her lipstick was smeared giving her an angry appearance.

"I guess I wouldn't want to get Jeremy angry at me. He looks like he could cause real trouble."

"He's a wimp! He talks big, but it's all bullshit. You've got nothing to worry about."

"Well, you're still married to him and living with him."

"Married, yes. Not living with him. He moved into an apartment about a month ago so he could play house with his new bangeroo. I don't give a shit. If he wants to play around, then two can play that game. And I'll tell you a little secret, I'm better at it than he is. How about you, you're married I suppose?"

"Yep." He'd learned all he was going to learn.

"So what are you doing hanging around here then? You should be home banging your wife, or playing with the kids."

"I guess you're right."

"Damn right I am. I know all the regulars here, and who's available. I know who they meet, and what they drink. I even know who's screwing who. And I knew you weren't a regular right away." Her voice was getting loud.

"The bartender could probably say the same thing." Nick hadn't meant to voice his thought. He was just trying to leave quietly without too much attention.

"Maybe, but he doesn't know as much about them as I do. Are you going to buy me another drink, or am I buying you one?"

"Tell you what, why don't you let me give you a lift home? Or at least get you a cab. I've had my limit." And she was way past hers.

"So, you are still interested after all. I was just getting ready to brush you off. You really a cop?"

"Yep." Nick pulled out a $ 20 bill and left it on the bar.

161

"Let's have one more drink, then you can follow me . . . . I don't live that far from here."

"Won't Jeremy be stopping by to check on you?"

"Fuck him, who cares? I threw him out over a month ago. There's no reason for him to show up. Want to do it in the sauna? Fast way to get all sweaty."

"I'll bet. Sounds like a real work out." Nick was trying to leave.

"Yeah, it keeps me looking young and desirable. You coming over, or not?"

"No, I think I'll pass. I better go home and play with the kids, you're making me feel guilty." It was the best way Nick could think of to end this and leave politely.

"So what was all this about then? You just like to get off being teased so you can go home and bang wifey-poo? I know your type. You're no cop, and you're no stud, either. Get fucking lost!"

"I wish you wouldn't use that fucking f word so much, Cassandra, it's unbecoming of your feminine qualities." He waved to Peter, smiling as he left. Old Jeremy's alibi had a big hole in it. So did his head.

Nick tried calling Ruth. First time the line was busy. Second and third tries got her answering machine. It was nice just to hear her recorded voice. He wondered if maybe she had a date? Paul mentioned that she had a boyfriend, although Nick hadn't seen any evidence of him at her place. No pictures, and she hadn't brought it up. It had been a long, long time since Nick had experienced any jealous feelings. He was having them now, like leg cramps. It hurt.

His flight was boarding in a few minutes. Nick decided to try calling Ruth again. This time she answered and he felt better instantly. "Hi, its your friendly travel agent calling to inform you that you've just won a free trip to Orlando, but there's a catch . . . ." If she changed her mind, they could still take a later flight together.

"Ha, ha, hah. That's funny. I thought you would have left by now. Are you at the airport?"

"Yep. Aren't you interested in the catch?"

"Okay, what's the catch?" She sounded sleepy.

"You have to be ready to leave in two hours or less. There's another flight, and we could take if . . . ."

"Nick, that's sweet. I really wish I could, but we've already discussed it, and I just can't get away right now."

"Okay, but I thought I'd try one more time, just in case you missed me, and had second thoughts. I wanted to give you a chance to change your mind. I can see you're dedicated to your job. I'm becoming a little less dedicated to mine, does that tell you anything?"

"If you were less dedicated, you wouldn't be chasing down to Florida on your own time to find some guy you've never met, and don't know anything about. Your job is also your hobby, Nick. Nick?"

"Yeah?" Right now she was saying things he didn't want to hear . . . again. He was changing, and she was the reason he was trying to change. For a second, he thought about canceling this trip and spending the night with Ruth instead. He could catch an early flight tomorrow . . . . Damn, this woman had him going crazy, just like that tape he'd found on the yacht, which he remembered, still needed to be checked for prints. With all that was going on, he'd forgotten about it.

"Be careful!" It was almost a whisper.

"I'm always careful. Besides, this is just a routine check on an alibi, and a check on a mysterious partner. It probably won't be that much of a trip anyway since you're not coming along." He wasn't looking forward to it any longer.

"Don't you plan to see your buddy down there and go fishing?" She had sensed his mood change.

"Yes, we probably will. I'll call you tomorrow night."

"Call me late, okay? Then we can talk sexy on the phone and I'll know you miss me."

163

STAN

"I miss you already. And we can talk sexy on the phone right now . . . ."

"No we can't. I'm not in bed, and you're standing in a public phone area with lots of people around. It has to be quiet, and private."

For the next half hour, Nick was smiling just thinking about what he'd say to Ruth when he called. One minute she was poised and looking very professional. Then, without much prompting, she could change into a wild and sensuous woman. Almost like two different people. Nick liked both of them, although he wasn't sure he understood either of them.

CHAPTER 15

The two and a half hour flight to Orlando went smoothly. Nick declined the in-flight snack hoping to get something after he picked up his rental car. It seemed to get dark in Orlando earlier than it did in Detroit, even though it was the same time zone. And it was steamy. Not the best time of year to be visiting Florida, as Ruth had already cautioned. The heat and humidity made his hunger vanish.

Nick had requested a Ford Crown Victoria, which was what he drove at work, and also owned. He liked driving the same make car because he always knew where the horn was, and the light switch. Being a native of Detroit, he liked Ford automobiles. When he arrived at the rent-a-car counter, he had to settle for a Thunderbird. It didn't take much time for him to decide that he liked it. He looked for a place to eat and found that many were closed. He settled for a hamburger and fries at a Steak and Shake on Colonial. It had been a while since Nick had been to Orlando. Last time was when Nickie Jr. was twelve, and they all went to Disney World.

The airport, and the city had changed considerably from the way he remembered the area. The traffic was almost as bad as it was at home. He remembered that he liked getting up early in Florida before the heat arrived and running a few miles, listening to all the birds and feeling the sun working on his body. He also remembered the late afternoon showers were predictable.

It was too late to visit the repair facility at Orlando Executive Airport. Supposedly this was the place where Freeman came to get an estimate on repairs for the plane. This was formerly called Herndon, and as he drove by the en-

165

trance, he noticed the restaurant they had visited seven years ago. It was an old French farmhouse surrounded by World War I relics. Nickie Jr. had gotten really excited over that place. For no special reason, Nick waited for the traffic to thin, then turned around and pulled into the parking lot passing an old guard shack called, "Check Point Charlie". Everything looked real, and Nick was sure that his father would have been able to point out a lot of small details that escaped anyone who wasn't in the big war. Nick sat in the parking lot for a few minutes and thought about the last visit. It was a time when he was happily married, and they had had a fun vacation. He had enjoyed Disney World as much as Nickie Jr. If Ruth had come along, he would have taken her there. The thought of Ruth brought him back to the present and he pulled out onto Colonial Blvd. and started looking for a motel close by. He needed sleep. He thought about calling Ruth and decided to wait a day.

After a good night's sleep, a good 3-mile run and a big breakfast, Nick was ready to begin checking Phil's alibi. Executive Aviation appeared to be a first class operation. Nick pulled into the visitor parking area and walked over to the canopied entrance. At least a hundred twin-engine planes and jets were parked on the blacktop area facing him. Everything was spotlessly clean. An attractive clerk, in a smart looking uniform, looking somewhat like a stewardess behind the counter, directed him to the Service Manager's office down the hall from the pilot's lounge. Passing through the area, Nick observed several well-dressed men sitting around watching TV and looking at maps. He decided they were corporate pilots waiting for their passengers for business flights to other cities. Seeing them there reminded Nick of earlier days when he dreamt of becoming a pilot. It had been one of his fantasies for many years.

Free coffee was available, so Nick helped himself to a cup on his way, nodding to one of the men using the special direct-line phone to get a weather briefing. Must be nice to be able to do this, he thought to himself. It was another world to him, but he acted like he was comfortable with it.

Buzz Thomas, the Service Manager, was much younger than Nick expected. The man appeared to be in his early 30s. Nick noticed his clean uniform and knew Buzz had a desk job. No grease, and no dirty fingernails. Haircut had to have cost him $30. Nick identified himself and sat down still holding his cup of coffee.

"Are you familiar with a twin Beechcraft owned and operated by Freeman Enterprises?"

"Sounds familiar. Where are they based?" Buzz asked.

"I believe it's based in Pontiac, Michigan. It makes numerous trips down here. They've been talking to you about an engine overhaul . . . ."

"Oh sure, now I know the plane." He checked the computer on his desk. " We're scheduled to start on it this week. Should be ready in about ten days. Like all our customers, they're in a hurry and need it yesterday."

"I'd like to know when it arrived, and who you talked to about the repairs."

"Well, let's see what we have here." Buzz returned to his terminal and punched up the entire record. "Here we are. They have an older model King Air with high time engines. We're replacing both turbines, on an exchange basis, and overhauling the props, which are also due for overhaul. We might do a periodic inspection while it's here." He faced the terminal as he spoke and Nick tried to follow all this. Like advertising, aviation was truly another world with its own jargon. Buzz was assuming Nick knew something about aviation repairs.

"Sounds about right. How much money does that involve?" Nick was just curious.

"Oh, close to three hundred and fifty thousand, before we're done. It depends on what else they might need. Usually they ask for a regular hundred-hour inspection while it's in the shop and opened up. It's a good time to do it, and saves them a few bucks."

"So the plane will be tied up for about two weeks?"

"Well again, it depends. Those are Pratt & Whitney engines and we swap the engines for rebuilt ones. That takes a week. The props are already ordered and will be here this week. We could have it out of here by then, unless we run into something unexpected. You just never know with older aircraft."

"Who authorized the work?"

"Let's see, Mr. Phillip Freeman came in with his company pilot, Nelson Hoffman. They were in here last Saturday and left the aircraft."

"Did you speak with both of them when they were here?"

"No, I spoke to the pilot earlier, I wasn't here on Saturday when they came in. My assistant was here, but we were expecting them, and we already quoted on the work earlier, so it really wasn't necessary for me to see them."

"So what you're saying is they just dropped off the aircraft and left?"

"Pretty much. Jim, my assistant, didn't mention anything out of the ordinary. If there was a problem, he would have told me about it, or left me a note. We log everything into the job order here in the computer. Even phone calls. That way we can document everything, in case there's a problem, or the FAA wants to examine our records, which they do fairly often."

"You have a phone number and address listed for Freeman Enterprises here in Florida?"

"Yes sir, there's a number in West Palm Beach, do you want it?" It was the same number Nick already had.

Nick showed the young man the picture taken by Paul on the boat and asked him if he could identify anyone in the picture. The Service Manager picked out Nelson as the pilot with whom he had spoken several times. He did not point out Phil Freeman since he wasn't here when Freeman supposedly arrived. Nick asked if Jim, the Assistant Service Manager, was available. He was, and Nick went through the same routine again. This time, Jim identified Phil Freeman as the other man who had arrived. So far, the alibis were holding up. However, Phil or Nelson could have flown back in time for a meeting with Vince later that same day. Only question was, how did they get back? The plane was here!

On his way out, Nick spoke to the cute counter girl, and she also identified Nelson as someone she recognized as coming in regularly. She was working last Saturday when they arrived. and mentioned she had gas receipts for both planes.

"I remember the pilot because he reminds me of some movie star, who's name is on the tip of my tongue. He signed the fuel slips for both planes."

Nick almost missed what he was hearing. "Both planes?"

"Yes sir, the Piper Aerostar was left here for several days and refueled. It left, let's see, last Saturday afternoon." She showed Nick the fueling order. He noted the aircraft N number which was similar to an auto license plate. All U.S. registered aircraft had a registration number that carried the prefix N, followed by a series of numbers and often letters. She was unable to tell him the actual time the Aerostar had left, or how many people left in it. The second fueling slip was for the Beechcraft King Air that was getting new rubber bands installed. Same pilot had signed both slips, N. Hoffman.

If Freeman Enterprises had another aircraft waiting at Orlando, why didn't Nelson and Phil Freeman just fly back in that plane? And, why did Phil Freeman bother to fly down here at all? It appeared that this trip wasn't necessary, based on what he'd learned from the Service Manager. The repair arrangements had already been made. Maybe Phil had other reasons for being in Florida, or maybe he was just trying to establish an alibi as far from Detroit as possible.

His next stop was to the FAA Flight Service office in the next building over on the second floor. This was where pilots could check weather, get a briefing on what to expect the conditions to be at various altitudes, and file a flight plan so their progress could be monitored along the route of flight. The agent at the counter was able to confirm that Freeman's Aerostar, N600FE did depart on Saturday at 14:30 hours for Palm Beach International airport. Route was Victor 159 to Vero Beach, then Victor 3 direct to Palm Beach. Estimated time en route was 40 minutes for the 150-mile trip. Driving would have taken at least 3 hours, which is what Nick was now facing.

Before leaving Orlando, Nick stopped at the Marriott Hotel where Phil indicated he stayed. The desk clerk referred Nick to the Manager who checked the records and confirmed that a Phillip Freeman had checked in on Saturday, and had left on Sunday. Neither the Manager nor the clerk could identify Phil Freeman. So, anyone could have checked in using Phil's name and credit card and posed as Phil, for his alibi. The receipt wasn't enough evidence to convince Nick. He didn't have the names of any of Phil's friends that he supposedly met. So now the question was, did Phil Freeman remain in Orlando overnight, or did he leave for West Palm Beach with Nelson? And, how did he get back to Detroit?

Nick called his office and spoke with Gary Mitchell. Nothing was going on that required Nick's attention. Wizard had left a message for him, that Nelson Hoffman was originally from Fort Lauderdale and worked as a charter boat captain for 5 years. This was just prior to joining Freeman Enterprises, so he had stepped up in the world. He also held a Commercial Pilot's license for the past 7 years, and held several additional type ratings for twin-engine aircraft. The DEA people had shown a little interest in him, while he was operating in Florida, but no arrests. What was interesting, was that Nelson owned a Ferrari in addition to the Mercedes-Benz Nick had seen. So the man was apparently well paid for his services.

Drugs were a distinct possibility now, along with money laundering. Reason enough for Phil to have a bodyguard, and use him as an enforcer and debt collector. If that was true, then Phil was more dangerous than Nick had speculated. Nelson didn't look like he needed a bodyguard.

Nick had Ben Wheeler's home phone number and work number. After 2 tries, he was able to reach him. Nick declined the invitation to stay with Ben and his family, saying he preferred a motel. Ben understood and agreed to meet him later for a drink, once Nick had arrived and found a place to stay. It wouldn't be difficult finding a vacancy in July.

Listening to a Country & Western station, Nick drove the Florida Turnpike south to West Palm Beach. He wondered if Ruth liked Country & Western music, too. He'd call her as soon as he checked into a motel. The drive took longer than the 3 hours he had anticipated. There were two exits for West Palm Beach. Nick took the first one and drove east to A1A. He had his pick of places to stay. Since he was traveling on his own money, he selected a modest motel that advertised color TV and waterbeds. His room didn't have a waterbed, but it was clean and reasonable. His room was on the first floor and he could park in front of the room. There wasn't a second floor, so he wouldn't have to listen to someone above him moving around.

With the air conditioner turned to high, he took a quick shower, put on a pair of jeans and called Ruth. It was still early, too early for her to be in bed. He waited while the phone rang, trying to think of something witty to say as a follow up to their last phone conversation. He wasn't prepared for her answering machine when it clicked in after the fourth ring. Wasn't she expecting him to call? He listened to her recorded message. Once again, he was reminded that she did indeed have a sexy voice. Maybe she'd pick up after he started to speak.

"Hi Ruth, it's Nick. I'm in West Palm Beach staying at

the Pink Sands motel. I'll try you again later." He forgot to leave the phone number with her, but he could do that when he spoke with her later. It shouldn't have surprised him that she wasn't home, but it did. Maybe she was in the shower.

He called Ben. They agreed to meet at a local joint called Pokey Joe's Bar. It was one of Ben's regular hangouts. Nick followed Ben's directions and arrived fifteen minutes later. Ben was waiting for him at the bar.

It had been several years since he had actually seen Ben and that was in Atlanta, where they met. They had been attending a seminar on lie detector tests and became friendly spending a few evenings touring the city's bar scene. Ben was a few years younger than Nick, close to 40 by now. And at least 40 lbs. heavier, and 3 inches taller than Nick. He was a big man. Ben was married with 3 kids. Like Nick, he liked to fish and that was a common subject between them whenever they dropped each other a note on a Christmas card. Ben had a naturally easy going, laid back nature. He was someone strangers felt comfortable talking to. As a result, he was also a very good police officer. He could get people to tell him what he wanted to know just by smiling. That was his way. No one in their right mind would even consider giving this man trouble. When they shook hands, Nick was once again surprised how much bigger Ben's paw was than his.

"Hey, Nick, you finally made it! Took you long enough to get your scrawny ass down here." Ben hadn't changed much from what Nick remembered.

"Good to see you, Ben. You don't look any different, maybe a few pounds heavier."

"Well you look the same. How do you manage to stay so skinny anyway?"

"Eat two meals a day, and lots of exercise.."

"So tell me, how's your love life these days? Find a steady lady to shack up with?" Ben was always direct and never too subtle when asking a question Nick recalled.

"Ladies . . . I've had a few temporary situations, but they never seem to last very long. Guess the job gets in the way too much. That might be changing, though." Nick went on to tell Ben about meeting Ruth, and how she was completely different from the other women in his life. He also mentioned the episode with Gloria, and how sadly that seemed to end.

"Hey, listen up Pardner. When you get home, you gotta switch guns, know what I mean? Put the old six-shooter in the dresser drawer, and warm up the old two-shooter."

"Maybe that's my problem. Mine's a one-shot, and it doesn't always go bang the way it use to." Nick laughed at his own joke. For the past year he had been aware that his sexual inclination was strong, however his ability to perform had diminished somewhat. It bothered him because he knew he was healthy and too young to start taking Viagra. With Ruth, he was sure his problem would vanish.

"Not to worry. Old Doc Ben here is gonna fix you up. Down here, even the rusty guns get a work out. We got more horny women needin' attention, and not enough guns to go around. Hell, you may not want to go back up to Detroit after you've been here awhile. How long you plannin' on stayin'?"

"Couple of days." Then Nick told Ben about his investigation. It took four beers and an hour and a half to get it all out. "It's really a strange case, Ben. No apparent motive, a couple of suspects, and a lot of alibis with big holes. Everyone was supposedly out of town except his wife, his daughter and son-in-law. And they have no reason to want him dead. I guess I don't want this one to turn out to be an accident because I've already put too much time into it. I'll really look foolish, since I've been neglecting a few other cases to concentrate on this one."

"Got to meet some interesting people though didn't you?"

"Yeah, I got to admit, meeting Ruth just might make a big difference in my social life." Nick was back talking about

Ruth. "One minute she's this sophisticated lady, the next minute, she's sort of wild, wicked and wonderful."

"Hey, that's beginning to sound a bit serious, Pardner. You think maybe you're falling in love with this lady?"

"It might turn out that way. Hell, I haven't flirted with anyone since I left Detroit. I think about her a lot, and that's something I haven't done it years, particularly when I'm working. Hard to keep focused sometimes."

"Well give it some time, see how it works out. You don't have to be in any hurry to do anything serious."

"I know. I haven't thought about getting married again until now. But it has crossed my mind a few times."

"C'mon Pardner, don't do anything foolish like that until you got the old two-shooter workin' regularly. You know what they say about marriage. That's when the fun stops and the bills begin. You ain't ready for that again are you? Why not just enjoy the ride for as long as it runs?"

"I don't know what I'm ready for. I'm taking it one day at a time right now. The woman makes me horny just thinking about her."

"Well, we can take care of that problem real easy . . . ."

When they walked out into the parking lot, Nick realized how much the four beers had hit him. Then he remembered that he hadn't bothered to eat anything since lunch. That explained why he felt those drinks so much. Ben seemed sober enough. Being so big, he could hold a lot more.

"So what's your plans for tomorrow?"

"I thought I'd try to get some information from the Post Office on who owns that box . . . ."

"Already tried. They won't give us anything except the name. That's your Calvin Justine you're lookin' for."

"Well then, I'll see how often he checks his box, get some idea of when the mail gets picked up, and stake it out for as long as it takes."

"Shit Nick, that could take a few days, or a week!"

───

174

"You got a better idea?"

"Yeah, I'll put a guy on it, and we can go fishin'."

"I don't think so. I have his picture and I know what he looks like. I'd like to meet him personally if he shows."

"And what if he doesn't show. What then?"

"Well, I got two other things I can still check on while I'm down here. Freeman Enterprises owns some equipment that was purchased by Calvin Justine at an auction in Miami. I want to talk to someone down there about it. Maybe they know this Calvin, and where I might find him. Freeman Enterprises charters their boats and planes under the name Halcyon Charters . . . ."

"Boy, that name sure rings a bell. You got that picture with you of this guy?"

"I got it back at my motel room. I'll stop by your office tomorrow with it. And, I want to check on an accident that happened down here in 1996."

"Does it have anything to do with this investigation?"

"It might. Like I said, it's a strange case with a lot of loose ends."

"Okay, I'll see you tomorrow. You packin' any iron?" Ben asked.

"No. There wasn't any reason to bring a gun along."

"Want to borrow one of mine while you're here?"

"Thanks, Ben, but there's no need." Nick knew that Ben could get into trouble doing that. Because this trip was part vacation, Nick hadn't bothered to bring his cell phone, or his gun, just his badge in case he was stopped driving.

Nick drove slowly back to his motel. He didn't want to get stopped for drunk driving. It was late, and he was in a strange town. He made a wrong turn, got confused and had to circle around several blocks before he saw a sign for A1A. When he finally pulled into the motel, he was aware of how dark it was. There were just a few cars. The "No Vacancy" sign was lit out in front, so the Night Manager was no doubt sleeping and didn't want to be bothered with any late arrivals.

He fumbled with the door key in the lock and suddenly realized it was open. Had he forgotten to lock the door? He was pretty sure he had locked it. Nick reached for the light switch, and saw his open suitcase still on the bed. The heat and all the beers were taking effect. After a quick visit to the toilet, he sat on the edge of the bed, taking off his shoes. Then he lay back on the bed and fell into a sound, drunken sleep.

In no time Nick was dreaming. He dreamt that he and Ben were in a bar together drinking and listening to a Country and Western band playing. Ruth was on stage, singing. She sounded just like Patsy Cline, the famous Country singer on the tape he had found. Nick was fascinated by her voice and the way she sang love songs. She seemed to be singing them just for him. The song she was singing was "Sweet Dreams". She kept blowing kisses to Nick, and he'd blow them back.

CHAPTER 16

Nick woke to the phone ringing. He looked at his watch, it was 7:30 in the morning. He'd slept despite the pain in his head. He had a terrible hangover. The heat didn't help.

"Nick? Did I wake you?" It was Ruth.

"Hi. Yeah, I'm awake now, but just barely. Good thing you called, or I probably would have slept another hour."

"Are you okay?"

"Yeah, sure. I was out with Ben until about one thirty. I guess I didn't get a lot of sleep. It was a long drive over here." He needed a drink of water, his mouth was dry. His head was still pounding. Coffee and some aspirin might get him through the next few hours.

"You sound groggy. How is your vacation so far?"

"Believe it, or not, I forgot that this trip was a vacation. It's sure hot, though. I called you last night and left a message. I guess you got that, or you wouldn't be calling now." It sounded somewhat like a question.

"Actually I was home. I had the phone turned off earlier, and didn't realize it was still off, so when you called, you got my recording and I didn't hear the phone. Sorry. I called you back. I had to get the number from information."

"I'm sorry, I should have left it. I planned on calling you again sometime today." Nick stretched out of habit and immediately regretted the added movement. He ached from sleeping on his side, in his clothes. Something he hadn't done in years.

"So, any progress on your secret investigation?"

"Yeah, a little. I think Phil Freeman is blowing a lot of smoke around. He was down here with Nelson, but either of them, or both could have flown back earlier. Phil seems to have taken some precautions in establishing an alibi, but it's thin. And Nelson remains a big question mark. I'll know more about him later, since he supposedly flew over here after he left Phil in Orlando. Maybe he has a lady friend here. He might, if he spends enough time in this area. Whatever he's up to, I'll find out about it before I get back." Nick looked over at the air conditioner. He thought it should be working, but it wasn't. No wonder it was so warm.

"Well don't forget to do some fishing with your buddy, Ben."

"Yeah, maybe tomorrow. We've got a few things to check out first. I'll call you tonight."

"Okay, Nick. Have fun, and be careful. I miss you."

"Miss you, too. Bye."

As soon as he hung up, Nick knew something was wrong. The air conditioner was working when he went out last night. He remembered turning the temperature control down to 65 so the room would be cool when he returned. That way, he'd be able to sleep comfortably. He bent down and turned the unit on. It started blasting cooler air immediately. He needed a shower, a shave and something to eat. For once, he didn't feel like running to start his morning. He unpacked the strewn contents of his suitcase. He searched for the photos he'd brought along and couldn't find them. Maybe he left them in the car. He checked the car and still couldn't find them. He had them yesterday when he was in Orlando. He had shown them to the cute young lady at the counter at Executive Aviation. He was sure he hadn't left them there. It was annoying to wake up like he had, with a headache, upset stomach, and then not being able to remember where he had put something. Something important! Then he realized that his notes were also missing, along with the copy of the fuel slip he'd picked up in Orlando. He searched everywhere. They were gone. He had to get some replacements quickly.

Nick explained the motel incident to Ben as they drove over to the Post Office together.

"If you're onto something big, Pardner, and someone is getting nervous about what you might find out, then you could have someone watching you. Ever think about that?"

"I didn't notice anyone following me."

"Yeah, but were you lookin' to see if anyone was following you? You were probably thinkin' about fishin', or your new girlfriend, Ruth right?"

"Not really." Nick had to admit he'd been preoccupied working on this case. Ruth had warned him to be careful, and now it appeared that he should have taken her advice seriously. His awareness level was usually much higher. It annoyed him to think he had been so careless. It wouldn't happen again. He would be on full alert from now on.

"So who knows you're down here, and what you're doin'?"

"Only the Chief, a Sergeant I work with . . . and Ruth."

"Then it doesn't make much sense, does it?"

"No. Right from the very beginning, this investigation hasn't made any sense. That's the only consistent element."

A clerk at the Post Office told them that someone picked up the mail in that box every day, sometime after the noon mail was sorted. But never in the mornings. That meant Nick had to come back later to watch the box.

In the car Nick mentioned the car accident that killed Sal Del Vecchio back in 1996. Nick wanted to see the accident report. They returned to Ben's office and found the accident report. It had happened on State Route 21, outside the city, in a remote area. Apparently it had been raining and the roads were wet. There were skid marks indicating that the victim's car went out of control at the top of a small rise where a culvert passed under the road. There was a ditch on both sides of the road. The car left the two-lane blacktop road and

179

rolled on its right side in the ditch. Sole occupant was the driver, Sal Del Vecchio. He hadn't been wearing a seat belt and was thrown into the windshield and steering wheel with sufficient force to kill him. No witnesses to the accident. A passing motorist noticed the car in the ditch and reported it to the Sheriff's office. Time of the accident wasn't known. Victim's driver's license indicated he was from Michigan and his wife was contacted. The rental car was towed to one of their lots for the insurance company to evaluate the damage.

"Stuff like that happens down here all the time," the officer behind the counter said. "People don't realize how easy it is to flip over when you hit one of them ditches."

"I wonder what he was doing out there?" Ben asked.

"Nothing much for a visitor to see . . . ." the officer offered. "Just some remote cattle ranches. Must have gotten lost, or mixed up. It can happen." Ben nodded his agreement.

"Let's go talk to the insurance company that had the claim," Nick said to Ben, not quite satisfied.

"What do you suppose that will prove?"

"Don't know until I see their report, which should have a photo of the damaged car."

They ate a quick lunch and arrived at the local insurance agent's office shortly after 1:00. The agent on duty called their regional office to have the report faxed to him. It was a typical claims form with some of the information missing and probably not necessary. The amount of the damage was $ 7,811. The car was a small Plymouth Breeze 4-door. Damage was reported to be extensive to the right side and front of the car. Also damage on the left side. A complete itemized list of all the damage was attached. It took a while for the faxed photos to come through. The car was shown sitting upright on its wheels inside a parking lot. File numbers appeared on the lower right hand corner of all the photos.

Nick examined the photos carefully and pointed to the driver's side of the car.

"Notice the left side of the car. Those marks look like creases on the left rear fender and both doors."

"Okay, so what? These are pretty poor copies."

"Well, if the car went off the road on the right side, and rolled over in the ditch, the right side would have all the damage, not the driver's side."

"Nick, the right side does have considerable damage...."

"I know, but these marks don't appear to be related to the car rolling over. It looks as if another vehicle hit the car on the driver's side, and maybe forced it off the road."

"Yeah, I can see that now. You might be right, Pardner. That could mean that someone was following that car... or maybe, chasin' it."

Nick asked to have copies of the actual photos sent to Ben's office the next day so they could examine the details carefully.

"You'd think someone at the scene would have noticed that and put it in the report." Ben was annoyed at the oversight. He also knew the officer who did the report and planned to have a chat with him later. "You think there could be a connection with this accident and the one you're working on?"

"Maybe. If it wasn't an accident, then we're dealing with some bad people who like to make things look like accidents. That's a pretty scary thought."

"Okay, let's go on the assumption that we're onto somethin' fishy here. And someone now knows that you're here snooping around. I think you better reconsider letting me loan you a piece. I'll get you a statement that says you're officially on-duty, assigned to our department for purposes of this investigation. Nobody will question it, even if it is bending the rules a little bit. You'll need to keep that with you while you're here, just in case you should get stopped."

Ten minutes later, Ben came back with the official looking statement and handed Nick a 9 mm Berretta automatic with a full clip of ammunition. "Here, wear it in good health."

"I'll try not to lose it. And hope I don't have to use it."
He was thinking of the photos and his notes being taken from
his room. Had he had this gun then, it wouldn't have helped.
They waited until he was gone to enter his room. So someone
was monitoring his movement. The air conditioner was turned
off so they could hear anyone approaching, while they were
in his room. That meant someone was definitely worried.

Nick knew Ben had some work to catch up on. They
agreed to have dinner at Ben's house around 6:00. Meanwhile, armed with a good county road map, he decided to
drive out to the accident site and see what that ditch looked
like in daylight. And see if it was sufficient to have caused
Sal Del Vecchio's death.

State Route 21 headed west into what appeared to be
nothing but swamp land and a few farms. He saw some low
scrub bushes and some cattle grazing, nothing else. The accident report indicated the scene was between mile markers
15 & 16, at a rise in the road. The black top was badly cracked,
and the centerline was faded so much he could hardly see it.
He had driven for ten minutes and had not seen another vehicle. At the 14-mile marker, the road curved to the left and
as he negotiated the turn, he could see a rise ahead. A culvert passed under the road at that point, causing the road to
rise about 4 feet. There was a slight grade on either side.
Just beyond the rise, Nick pulled over. He could see the ditch
about 6 feet from the side of the road. The ditch itself was
dry with some wild grass growing in it. Beyond the ditch was
a bank about 4 feet high with some brush and weeds growing
on it. Beyond that, there was a trace of a barbed wire fence
long forgotten. It was hard to imagine this was Florida. It
could have been anywhere in the Midwest.

Nick stood by the ditch trying to imagine how the accident might have happened. There was a slight breeze and
with it he heard a car or truck in the distance. It sounded like
it was racing at high rpm. The curve of the road, and the rise

by the culvert blocked his view. He could hear a vehicle approaching, and it slowed down slightly as it must have been nearing the curve, then accelerated again. Closer now, it sounded more like a truck than a car, the engine had a deeper sound.

He had a sudden impulse to take a leak, and didn't want to be seen standing there in the ditch. Whoever was speeding down that road at 75 mph probably wouldn't notice him standing there, but instinct directed him to climb the mound to the other side, where he'd be hidden from the road. As he was unzipping, he heard the screech of tires and gears being downshifted, then the brakes. It was an older, blue Chevy pick-up truck, and it was stopped just behind Nick's rented Thunderbird. Curious, Nick bent down to remain out of sight. The driver and his passenger both wore straw cowboy hats. And both were carrying rifles!

"Where d'ya think he got to?" One of them said.

"He ain't far, keys are in the car."

It had been a long time since Nick had felt any fear. He felt it now. For some reason, he was prey to those two with rifles. He was no match, even with the automatic in his waist. He knew he had no real advantage, so he crawled along the other side of the embankment hoping to remain hidden. He knew they would start searching for him and running was not an option. Maybe he could make it to the culvert and hide there. It was his only chance. It seemed like 5 miles away crawling on hands and knees and trying to be as quiet as possible. The tall grass helped to hide him.

"See anything?" One of them yelled.

"Nah, but we'll find him. City guy like that can't hide out here."

Nick crawled on his stomach, trying to hold his breath. The grass seemed sharp as he clawed the dry clumps, pulling himself along. He came to the low point where the mound flattened out to the level of the ditch. To get to the culvert, he had to risk being seen crossing the ditch. He waited, and heard another sound. It was a vehicle approaching from the other direction. It served as just enough distraction to the two men, so that he was able to crawl quickly across the open ditch and entered the culvert on his hands and knees. His fear hit a new high. There was some water in the culvert, and a snake enjoying the cool spot. At the same time, an old, beat up, school bus passed by. Nick crawled backwards carefully. Which is worse he thought, being shot in the ass by some Florida redneck, or being bitten by a snake?

Just outside the culvert he found a broken branch about 3 feet long. He held the branch in front of him and crawled forward toward the snake, waving the branch. He poked the snake with the tip, hoping it would slither away. With some additional prodding, it reluctantly left the culvert in the same direction Nick was headed. Perspiration soaked through his tee shirt. Still clenching the branch in front of him, he exited the culvert on the other side. He had to assume the snake was poisonous. Shooting it would have given away his position.

Each side of the road was the same with another ditch and another mound. On this side of the road, the mound wasn't as high. Concealment would be difficult unless he remained on his stomach. Knowing there was a snake in the vicinity meant there could be others as well. That made his crawling more cautious than before. He chanced a quick peek over the edge of the mound and saw the two men walking slowly through the brush on the opposite side of the road. They walked about 20 feet apart so that they could cover a wider search area. When they didn't find him over on that side, they would no doubt turn their attention in his direction. He didn't have much time. Crawling on his hands and knees hoping he wouldn't be discovered, Nick crawled in the direction of the Thunderbird. He could just see their straw hats moving above the brush from his vantage point. He ducked his head and continued to crawl even faster. For the first time in his life he actually tasted the metallic, bitter tang of fear.

"Ya think he saw us comin'?" The voice was moving away from his position. They were going further into the high brush area, and not along the mound where he had crawled. Had they walked closer to the mound, they would surely see the path of bent grass he'd left. For the moment, he was safe, but he had to make a quick dash back across the road and remain hidden behind the truck.

His survival instinct told him to act fast and not delay. Hunched over, he ran across the road without being seen. For once, he was glad he remembered to carry his pocketknife. He opened the small blade and began cutting the valve stem until he heard a slow hiss of air escaping. He took another peek over the rear of the truck. The two straw hats were at least 200 feet into the field. With any luck they might encounter a rattlesnake, Nick hoped. He hated snakes. The two men carried their rifles high. They looked like bird hunters moving through the field of high grass.

The Chevy pick-up had been pulled off the road at an angle to the Thunderbird. Because it was parked on a slight rise, the soon to be rear flat tire wouldn't be noticeable from a distance. Nick worked his way to the rear of the truck. The license plate was missing. For the moment, that wasn't a high priority. Escaping was. He had to open the door of the Thunderbird, start the engine and speed away without getting hit. And he had to do it quickly. Time was running out. The men were walking back toward the road now. In another minute they would see him crouched beside the door. Nick reached up and opened the door slowly, remaining out of view. Then, he jumped inside and was relieved to see the keys still in the ignition. The Thunderbird sounded exceptionally loud as he started it, put it in drive and got back onto the road, hoping there wouldn't be a vehicle approaching the curve, coming at him. The Thunderbird responded to his

185

flooring the accelerator. He heard the tires squeel. He had to stay out of shooting range.

The two men heard the engine start, and they saw him. They aimed and fired hitting the side view mirror on the passenger side. Another round cracked the windshield as it hit the molding. Nick could see the flash from the barrels as they continued to fire. With the distance rapidly increasing, his chances of being hit again were improving. He found a side road and did a fast spinning turn, hoping it wasn't a dead end. Then he floored it, just as the rear window shattered. His pulse was racing almost as fast as the tachometer on the dash. If the men had been carrying shotguns, they wouldn't have been able to reach him at all. Perspiration was stinging his eyes, he wiped his face with a muddy hand and gripped the wheel. Nick knew he had just had a close encounter with death and the realization was causing his knee to jerk uncontrollably. He dropped down from 85 to 70 so he could think, while he headed back to Ben's office to report the incident.

By the time Nick re-entered civilization and normal traffic, his regular pulse had returned. He turned the air conditioner to high hoping it would help dry his shirt and face. Somehow, someone was able to keep tabs on his whereabouts without being noticed. That bothered him. The fact that he'd been followed out to that remote accident site pretty much confirmed that Sal's accident had been engineered. Probably by the same pair stalking him now, Nick surmised. They knew where he was staying. And they already knew that he'd been to Orlando, so that put Phil Freeman and Nelson in the spotlight. No one else would care that he'd been to Orlando and was now in West Palm Beach, the place he always considered to be Paradise... until today.

CHAPTER 17

Nick spotted a gas station with a pay phone and pulled in. He called Ben's office and learned that Ben had left for the day. Nick asked the officer on the phone to call Ben's house and have him meet Nick at his office as soon as possible. Nick gave the officer a quick summary of what happened, and a brief description of the men and their truck. A fast APB might pick them up, and a patrol car was dispatched to the area Nick had just departed. With any luck they may still be there, changing a tire. Nick didn't recall seeing a spare tire, but he hadn't bothered to look. He was just trying to prevent a possible chase. He should have brought his cell phone along his own gun, but he hadn't anticipated needing either one. It was another serious mistake.

Ben arrived just as Nick was pulling into the Sheriff's Dept. parking lot. Ben had a digital camera and started taking pictures of Nick's Thunderbird.

"Pardner, you look like something I'd throw away. What the hell happened out there?"

Nick walked inside with Ben, giving him a full, detailed report. He even mentioned the snake. As he walked toward the men's room, he realized his fly was still unzipped. It had all happened so fast. Nick's sneakers were still caked with mud. He looked like a vagrant. Ben brought him some aspirin and asked him how soon he wanted to move out of the motel.

They left the Thunderbird in the Sheriff's parking lot. Ben drove Nick back to his motel so that he could clean up and change clothes. Nick knew it was time to start thinking ahead. Since they knew where he was staying, he was an easy target. Taking another room across the parking lot from his current room would provide a good vantage point for watching anyone approaching this room. And, he had to think of a new plan for staying alive. Whoever was after him, wanted him stopped. They had his notes, the photos, and copies of the fueling slips in Orlando, so they had a good idea of how much he knew, and what he was after. Nick tried to remember all that he had written down in those notes. Maybe his questions about Sal Del Vecchio's accident triggered the two yokels to follow him out there. Maybe they were responsible for Sal's untimely accident back in '96. And, who had tipped them to Nick's interest, and where he was today . . . and last night? Those guys weren't following him, they were anticipating his every move! It was like a deadly game of chess. So far, he hadn't made any good moves.

Fear and anger mixed together were a bad combination. It made for irrational thinking. Right now, Nick had to start thinking clearly and fast. Time wasn't on his side. Being stalked was an entirely new experience for Nick. For once he knew how some women must feel when their ex-boy friends pursued them.

The only other time Nick could recall feeling so scared, was when he was a rookie cop responding to a robbery in progress call. He and his older partner arrived at a gas station, where two suspects were just leaving. When they saw the police cruiser, they fired at it, shattering the windshield. Nick had instinctively ducked below the dash, while his partner jumped out of the car, returning fire. The robbers went several blocks before another police car cornered them. Nick remembered how close he had come to being killed. The difference had been a fraction of a second. His reflexes had saved him that day, and it was the first time he had truly experienced raw fear. Today, was the second time. He hated the feeling. He hated not being in complete control at all times. And, he hated not having answers to some nagging questions. Questions somebody didn't want answered.

Ben was driving his wife's Jeep since he wasn't working. He parked across the road from the motel where he could see Nick's room. He and Nick checked the three parked cars. All had out of state license plates. Two were from Georgia, one from Illinois. No one was outside to notice as Nick quietly tried his door. It was locked, as it should have been. He unlocked it with his left hand, keeping the automatic ready in his right hand. He pushed the door open slowly with his left foot maintaining a balanced stance, ready for anything that came at him, or moved. Nick wouldn't get caught by surprise again. Once inside, and finding nothing out of place, he began to feel a little foolish. He washed, changed into some clean clothes, packed his suitcase, and walked back to Ben's waiting Jeep.

The motel clerk on duty looked bored as he watched a small TV behind the counter. Ben wasn't in uniform, but he still made his presence known when he walked into a room.

"You have any messages for Alexander?"

"No sir, no messages." He was an older man, probably retired and working here part-time.

"Anyone inquiring about which room I'm staying in?"

"Not while I've been on duty." The man nodded at Ben to acknowledge him. Ben smiled, but didn't bother to explain anything, he let Nick handle the situation.

"When do you usually start work?"

"Well, It depends. Sometimes I come on at three and work 'till eight. Sometimes Frank is late coming in, so it just depends. Frank is usually here until two. We don't stay open all night. Late night trade isn't that much this time of the year."

"Who's on before you?"

"The owner, Mr. Harris. He's here earlier in the day and stays until I show up. You want to talk to him?"

"Yeah, maybe later. Listen I want you to do me a favor. What's your name?"

"Ed. Ed Harris. My nephew's the owner." He smiled knowing that came as a surprise.

"Well Ed, I'd like to change my room."

"Is there a problem? Of course, we'll be happy to put you in another room, we're not all that busy right now."

"Can I get something on the other side of the pool? My real reason for wanting a different room, Ed, is the air conditioner in my room is really noisy." The motel had a U-shape layout with a small swimming pool in the middle. Cars could park in front of each room. Nick's room had been half way down on the opposite side of the office.

"It's no problem to switch you to another room."

Ed gave Nick another key and asked him to check the room before deciding if he wanted it. It was directly across from the room he had been occupying, and gave him a good view of anyone coming or going on that side of the motel. Nick put ten dollars on the counter as a thank you tip. Ed pushed his money back across the counter to him not accepting it. This older gentleman wouldn't be easily bribed by anyone. That meant the desk clerk who came on later might be the one who tipped off his visitors about which room Nick was using.

"One more thing. If anyone should ask for me, I'd appreciate it if you'd just mention that I've checked out."

"But what if they're trying to get in touch with you?"

"I'm down here on vacation, trying to get away from my ex-wife who's a pain. She may have someone else try to get in touch with me while I'm here, and I just don't want to be bothered. I want some peace and quiet . . . and an air conditioner that isn't noisy." Nick winked at the man who smiled back at him knowingly. Nick had just fabricated this story and was surprised at how logical it sounded.

"How long you plan on stayin' with us then?" Ed asked.

"I'm not sure. Couple more days at least." Nick took the new key to room 33. Ben hadn't said a word. He turned and followed Nick out.

The room was identical to the one he'd just left. Now he had to get another car and return the damaged rental unit. Nick was glad he'd taken the extra insurance, and hoped that would cover the damage. Back at Ben's office, Nick waited while Ben reviewed the details of Nick's encounter with his Captain. So far, the old blue pick-up truck hadn't been found. When Ben came out of the Captain's office, he looked like he'd just been chewed out.

"Hey, Pardner, the Captain seems to think you brought all this here trouble with you from Detroit. He wasn't too happy about me lettin' you go pokin' around out there by your lonesome, either. He says the Del Vecchio file stays as an accident, unless we get some hard proof that says otherwise. That comes direct from the top office. I guess they don't like you Yankees comin' down here and messin' around in our procedures." Ben was trying to make a joke of it and doing a poor job. "I should have gone out there with you, Nick. I'm sorry now that I didn't go along. It won't happen again, Pardner. I promise."

"Not your fault, Ben. Neither of us knew how serious these people were until now. Those two knew exactly who they were looking for, and why I was out there. It's no coincidence."

"Well, whoever it was, driving that old blue Chevy pickup, you can bet they'll ditch it now. If they come after you again, they'll be driving something else. We'll have a city patrol car cruise the area around the motel while you're staying there, just in case they spot something suspicious." Ben and Nick both knew that wouldn't be a real deterrent.

The worse part of the experience was, that Nick was just far enough away that he wasn't able to get a good look at them. Therefore, his description was very generic. Take off the straw cowboy hats, and they could be anyone. Nick felt sure they'd try again. This time, he had the advantage of knowing someone was after him. And, he had Ben for backup.

STAN

He hated to get Ben involved, but this was his turf. Nick was just a visitor without any legal jurisdiction whatsoever. Ben's Captain probably made that point to Ben as well. Ben was just kind enough not to say anything more about it to Nick.

"So far, luck has been on your side, Nick. Let's hope it stays that way." Ben suggested they drive out to the airport, turn in the Thunderbird and get a replacement rental. This time, it would be under Ben's name, just in case someone cared to check.

Nick explained to the woman at the rental counter that the car had been hit by a stray bullet and gave her a copy of the police report, along with the name of his insurance agent in case there were any additional charges for the damage. His new car turned out to be a smaller Ford Contour. It was all that was available. Nick and Ben stopped at a restaurant to get something to eat. Dinner plans at Ben's place had been understandably delayed for another time.

"I didn't tell Becky too much. I just explained that you had to meet someone and wanted me along," Ben said as they finished their first round of beers. "She understands, and doesn't complain much."

"That was my rule, too. The less they know, the better. You don't want them worrying, and you don't want them talking to their girlfriends, or their hair dresser, either."

"Life down here is pretty routine, Nick. We don't get all the killings and muggings you guys get up in Detroit. Most of our crime here is break-ins, and stolen cars of course. The drug scene isn't any worse than any place else. I think most of the drugs go North."

"You might be right about that. I keep thinking that drugs may be part of what we're confronted with here, and we just can't see it yet. This charter outfit could be a front of some sort for transporting drugs."

"If it's drugs, then we're talking mob, and they'd use heavy muscle, not a couple of yokels to go after you." That made sense to Nick.

"Yeah, my Chief said the same thing. What if they're free-lancing, and the mob isn't aware of what they're doing either? Suppose it's a small operation just starting to get bigger. And suppose this guy Vince somehow learned about it. That would be a strong motive to knock him off." Nick had almost forgotten about the original accident that had set all this recent activity in motion. It was like a series of closed doors.

"Well, if I was them, I wouldn't hit him on the boat while it was in the marina. I'd take him out into some deep water and feed him to the fish, or make an anchor out of him". Ben was caught up in Nick's speculation. "And why didn't they just wait and whack you last night when you got back to your room?"

"You're right. Killing the guy at the marina just doesn't make any sense. Maybe it really was an accident after all, and the rest is just an attempt to cover up something else far more important." And it has allowed me to stumble onto it, Nick thought to himself.

"Ya know Pardner, that's beginnin' to sound more like it. And maybe this Sal Del Vecchio stumbled onto somethin' while he was down here and got scared. Maybe he was trying to make tracks outta here, when they caught up with him. No logical reason for him to be out there."

"Whatever it is, they seem to know who I am. It's funny how they knew just where to find me. Anyone could have traced me as far as Orlando. I flew there on a commercial flight, then, rented a car. Ah, but I also told the rental car people that I would be dropping it off at their West Palm Beach office, so that established my destination. They would have to check all the local motels here, to see if I was registered. That's how I'd do it. Then tip the motel clerk for the actual room number and give him a story. From then on, all they had to do is watch for me.

"Maybe they been waiting for you to arrive and knew you were coming all along. If so, they been following you from a distance and keepin' outa sight. They gotta be local boys to do that and not draw any attention," Ben said between bites.

Nick thought about how tired he was last night after returning to his room. Had it been a little sooner, he may have caught whoever was in his room. Then again, that's why the air conditioner had been turned off, so they could hear anyone coming. They forgot to turn it back on when they left. Nick was beginning to put the little pieces together now. It was beginning to make some sense. Nelson was from this area, so he probably knew a lot of the locals, and it would be easy for him to hire someone to keep tabs on Nick.

"Just so you don't think I'm sleeping at the switch here, I have someone lookin' for that old school bus that passed by while you were out there. Maybe they can help identify the pick-up. Or maybe they saw where it went. "You think this Calvin Justine character you've been lookin' for might be involved in all this?"

"He might be. He's elusive enough. And, he's connected to Freeman. Once we get him spotted, we'll follow him and see where that takes us."

"Nick, I gotta tell ya, Pardner, I'm not sure staying at the same motel is a smart move."

"Gotta stay somewhere. And this way, I can keep an eye on the other room, in case they come back. I called my office, and they're sending duplicate photos directly to you. You should have them tomorrow. Also, they contacted Executive Aviation in Orlando for new copies of the fuel bills. It may not be all that important, I just want to collect as much evidence as possible." Nick knew that it was the small items that could make a difference in a case.

"Boy, you show up, and strange things start to happen. Is it always like this with you Nick?"

―――

194

"Nope. This is more excitement than I've seen in quite a while. Right now, I'd settle for a little boredom." Nick went on to tell Ben about the impromptu bout with Neil at Chez Lou's.

"Well now, that could explain everything. You pissed him off, Nick and he's getting back at you. I've had a few of those moments myself." They talked for another hour about their work and some of the funny things that happened along the way. Nick even mentioned his missed opportunity to get laid by a cute waitress named Mavis. He had to break their date, and it was doubtful he'd ever take her out now, with Ruth in the picture.

"I don't know what it is about waitresses, Nick. They really go for cops. I know several that would be willing to go out, if I said the word. If I was single like you, I'd have a date every night probably."

"Oh no you wouldn't. You need to keep one night free just to catch up on the laundry. And another night, to get some sleep. I hate sleeping in strange beds." Nick went on to mention that in addition to waitresses, he'd met a fair number of single and divorced women at the Laundromat he used. "You get a chance to check out their underwear before you ask them out."

"Now there's an original piece of police work. You pick out the one's with sexy panties?"

"Yep. And you make sure there's no kiddy clothes in their basket." That's how he'd met Gloria, he recalled. "It sure beats picking up women in bars". It was also one of the reasons why Nick never owned a washer and dryer, and rarely used the units in his apartment complex.

They agreed that Ben would stake out the Post Office and keep an eye out for Calvin Justine. Ben was taking the day as vacation time. Nick planned on driving down to Miami to talk with the DEA people there hoping to learn a little more about Freeman Enterprises and their Florida operation.

He also planned to stop by Freeman's West Palm Beach office and check it out.

"I guess we'll have to take a rain check on the fishin' for a few days, huh Pardner?"

"I feel like that's what we've been doing, only I'm the bait."

"Well, I guarandamntee ya, sooner or later, we'll get those dudes who shot at you if they're a couple of locals."

"Yeah, that would make me sleep a whole lot better." Nick declined a third beer. He wanted to be totally sober for anything else that might happen. Last night, he had been tired, hadn't eaten much and the drinks hit him. That wasn't going to happen again. He hated learning lessons the hard way.

Ben drove Nick back to the motel, watched him check his rental car parked across the street, in the mall parking lot. Then he watched as Nick crossed the street, and walked into the motel office. He was still worried for Nick's safety. The faded blue Chevy truck hadn't been found out on old Rt. 21, nor had it been spotted anywhere else yet. Ben had asked that a cruiser check the motel area frequently during the night. He doubted they'd see that old Chevy pickup again, yet he wanted to take every precaution. Nick's business down here was unofficial. That meant that any help Ben would give him would be on his own time. To keep his wife, Becky from worrying, he planned to tell her that he and Nick were going fishing tomorrow. That would explain his old clothes, rather than a uniform.

Inside the motel office, Nick waited until the night clerk finished a phone reservation. It was the same young man who had registered him the night before. Now he had a name, Frank.

"You must be Frank," Nick asked.

"Yes sir, what can I do for you Mr. Alexander?"

"I was staying in room nine last night, and I wondered if anyone had been asking about me?"

———

"From Detroit, right? Noooo, I don't remember anyone calling and asking for you." Frank had a slight nervous twitch that he couldn't hide. He was in his late 20s, needed a haircut. He also looked a little pale, considering the time of year. No suntan meant this fellow spent a lot of his time indoors. He had a bad acne problem. Probably could use some sun and fresh air, Nick thought.

"Think real hard, Frank. Maybe somebody dropped by and asked you which room I had? Maybe even gave you a twenty, so they could take a look at my room while I was out . . . ."

"Honest, I don't know what you're talkin' about. Wasn't anything missing was there?" It was enough of a slip to convince Nick he was right. They'd gotten to this guy.

"Yeah, they took some things, and I think you helped 'em, by giving them a key, or did you open it for them?"

"Mister, I don't know anything. This is a quiet motel, and we never have any trouble here. You got a complaint, I suggest you speak with the owner in the morning. Besides, I see where your room was switched to number thirty-three today."

"So you know about my switching rooms, do you?" That didn't surprise Nick. He'd have to know which rooms were vacant, and which were occupied.

"Yeah, Ed told me. Said you wanted to be left alone, and not to put any calls through to you. Tell anyone who asked, that you checked out." Frank was beginning to act a little jumpy. He didn't look directly at Nick, another sure sign he was nervous and lying.

"You do drugs, Frank?"

"No! Who said I did?" The man almost snapped at Nick.

"No one, just asking. Bet you know where I could get something though." Nick put a twenty on the counter and watched Frank's eyes drop to it.

"I guess it would depend on what you're lookin' for. It ain't all that hard to find down here."

———

Nick started to pick up the twenty. "I might know somebody," the night clerk said still watching the twenty, still not looking at Nick.

"Uh huh. And where could I find this candyman?"

"Well, uh, I don't see him very often. He hangs out at one of the local bars I go to. Anyone who goes there, knows he deals, so maybe you could find him there."

"So where is this place?" Nick was beginning to get impatient with this weird kid.

"I tell you, I get the twenty, right?"

"The name of the guy first." Nick's hand still covered part of the bill on the counter.

"They call him Bingo. I don't know his real name. He hangs out at a place called The Blue Pelican. He won't sell to a stranger, he has to know you. Want me to call over there?"

"Maybe tomorrow. Meanwhile Frank, if any more of your friends ask about me, you can tell them to be very careful, because I'm waiting for them. I don't want any maid service, understand? Nobody goes into my room." Nick pushed the twenty toward Frank, giving him a hard stare.

"I'll leave a note for the morning shift. You want a wake up call?"

"I've already had my wake up call. I don't plan on sleeping. In case your friends come back, I want to be sure to be awake to greet them with a nice surprise."

Nick walked out, turned right and put three quarters in the soft drink machine. He waited a few minutes, before walking back to his car. He'd spend a few hours watching from the car before he tried to sleep. He reclined the bucket seat so he could just see through the steering wheel.

He woke hearing a car start. It was 1:30. Nick saw the night clerk pulling out from the motel. Nick was surprised that he'd been able to doze that long. There wasn't any traffic, so Nick had to be careful trying to follow the kid, which turned out to be easy. The car he was following pulled into

The Blue Pelican parking lot. Nick drove past it, then turned around and came back slowly taking in the cars and pickup trucks in the parking lot. No faded blue Chevy. At least he had a spot to mention to Ben, along with a name. He drove back to the shopping mall, parked and pushed the seat back for another try at some sleep. Nick didn't recall seeing any patrol cars cruising the area. And, he'd forgotten to call Ruth.

CHAPTER 18

Nick woke early, stiff and cold. Every muscle ached, and every joint seemed to protest any movement. It had rained sometime during the night, there were water drops on the windshield and hood of the car. Nick needed some coffee badly, yet he hesitated driving anywhere to look for an open restaurant knowing he had to look as bad as he felt.

He walked over to his room and checked the door carefully. Everything appeared to be okay. He shaved, took a long hot shower and changed. Stopping by the motel office, he helped himself to the free coffee on the side table. He passed on what looked like day-old doughnuts. Carrying the coffee and sipping it slowly, he walked across the street, past his parked car to a small restaurant where he was meeting Ben for breakfast. The smell of bacon frying hit him as he entered. That smell always made him instantly hungry.

"You sure do look tired, Pardner." Ben was in a booth.

"I am. Didn't sleep very well." Nick yawned.

"Yeah, I know. My night man said he saw you sleeping in your car when he passed by."

"Nice of him to take notice."

"Seems a shame to spend all that money for a room, then sleep in the car. Don't make a whole lot of sense."

Nick told Ben about the night clerk and what he had learned about a fellow called Bingo, who might be dealing drugs. It was a pretty good bet the night clerk was one of his customers.

"The Blue Pelican is a fag joint, Nick. Good thing you didn't go in. We know about Bingo, too. He used to run with a motorcycle gang a few years ago. Works on one of the charter boats now. He's been busted a few times. Bad dude."

When they got to Ben's office, the photos had arrived. Nick pointed out Calvin Justine. Ben had a friend at the phone company who promised to give him an address for the Freeman Enterprise phone. It turned out to be in an older residential section of Lantana, a community just south of Palm Beach, with the same exchange as Palm Beach

Nick took one set of photos with him to Miami. He had an appointment to meet with the DEA people down there. Ben would keep an eye on the Post Office. Later, over drinks, they would get together and compare notes.

———   ———   ———

The DEA people were helpful. One of the agents was at the auction and able to identify Calvin Justine and Nelson as being there, and buying the Bertram, which was nearly new. He also remembered the Beechcraft King Air, twin-engine executive class plane they had confiscated and used for a while. There was nothing unusual about the transaction. Address given at the time of the auction was an apartment in Fort Lauderdale near Pier 66 marina. New owner was listed as Calvin Justine.

"Did you check this guy out?" Nick asked.

"Sure, he wasn't on our list of known drug dealers."

"I mean did you check out his actual address?"

"You gotta be kidding me. We don't have time for that sort of stuff, unless he was a suspect, and he wasn't."

"So he gives you guys a half million and change and a local address, then disappears with stuff worth twice that. And if his name doesn't appear on your list, you assume he's clean."

"Happens all the time. Sometimes the drug dealers even get their own toys back, using someone else to front for them. Guy didn't have a sheet, we checked that, too."

"I'll tell you a really funny one," another agent interjected. "Some lawyer who's obviously fronting for some drug dealers bids on this cigarette boat we confiscated. It was worth maybe four hundred thousand. The guy bids two hundred and twenty and gets it. Pays with a certified check, right? An hour later, he has a crew there taking the boat out to another marina where he has a slip. Then the crew starts going over the boat carefully and finds a secret compartment with a half million dollars hidden away."

"How would you know it was a half million, and that they found it? You put it there?"

"Yeah, you got it. It was all marked money so we could keep an eye on this guy. Actually, some of it was bogus. That way, when he spent any of it, we could take him in, which is what we did." The agent laughed at his own story.

"How did you manage to make that stick?"

"It's all about who you know. They watch us, and we watch them. Sometimes we have to lay a little trap to get close to the big boys." All this story telling was for Nick's benefit. He'd asked a simple question that suggested they weren't staying close to possible suspects. The agent wanted to prove to Nick they were busy catching bigger fish.

Nick felt he wasn't getting anywhere. He had to find Calvin Justine, and he needed some solid evidence. So far, he had hunches, and he knew he must be getting close to something because someone was worried enough about him to make an attempt on his life. He didn't want to get that close again. He decided to swing by the Pier 66 marina on the way back up to Palm Beach.

Crossing the Inter-coastal to the marina, Nick was taken with the number of large yachts. Not dozens, but hundreds the size of Freeman's. He decided that boat financing, and insurance must be a lucrative industry down here. And, where did all that money come from? He thought most of the people in Florida were retired.

The marina Manager recognized Nelson's picture. "He

used to run a small charter boat out of here a few years ago. I seem to recall he was quite popular."

"Any idea what happened to him?"

"Not really. I think he went to work for one of his clients as a boat Captain. Sold his rig to one of the other charter outfits, and split. Kinda sudden."

"He have any friends around here?"

"Oh sure. Lots of lady friends. Being a young, good-looking guy, and single, he never had any trouble finding company. Most of them had bucks, too. You know, fancy cars and furs. I doubt he had to spend much money entertaining. They entertained him."

"So he was working the carriage trade."

"Yep, that's what he was working all right. Him, and his brother. The women were crazy about those two."

"His brother, what does he do?"

"Well, far as I know, Eric still does the same thing as Nelson. They both have licenses to skipper charters down here. I don't know if Eric went with Nelson, or not. Haven't seen either of them in quite a while."

"What about the other charter boats, he hang with any of those guys?"

"Not that I recall. He was a bit of a mystery around here. Didn't seem to hang around with the other charter boat captains. He and Eric were very selective about their charters. Turned down a few, which around here isn't too smart. Business isn't always that great, know what I mean? "

"You ever see this other guy with him?" Nick pointed out Calvin in the photo.

"Maybe. Looks familiar. What did you say his name was?"

"Justine. Calvin Justine. He may have chartered one of the boats down here."

"No sir, that name just doesn't ring a bell. I can go through my records if you want, and see if he ever booked any space here. It'll take some time, if you want to check back with me later."

"I'd appreciate it. I'll give you a call tomorrow." Leaving the marina, Nick could envision himself as a fishing boat Captain after he retired. Only problem was the money. He'd never have enough to buy the kind of equipment he'd need to compete down here. Never-the-less, it was a nice thought to contemplate as he drove back to West Palm Beach to meet Ben. He checked his mirrors regularly.

"Well, how'd it go, Pardner?"

"Didn't learn very much today. Nelson used to work out of Fort Lauderdale doing charters . . . and had some wealthy lady clients. Somewhere along the line he must have met Calvin Justine and decided to quit the fishing business for bigger stuff."

"You ain't gonna believe what I turned up."

"Uh huh. You spot Calvin, or learn where he's living?"

"Both. But something is strange about all this, Nick."

"You're telling me. So, what happened?"

"Well, I hung around the Post Office trying to blend in with the decor. You'd be surprised how busy that place is. Must have been a couple hundred people in just an hour."

"Does this have a happy ending?" It was Nick's favorite expression, when he wanted someone to cut to the good part.

"Sorry. It's just that I don't usually spend any time at the Post Office. About ten-thirty your man shows up. At least he fits the picture you gave me. And he goes to the box I'm watchin'. He takes out the mail, looks through it quickly, throws out some junk stuff and leaves. I follow him out to the parking lot where I see him get into this old Mercedes. Must be ten years old, maybe older, but in decent enough shape. No rust anyway."

"Uh huh. Go on."

"Guy didn't look like money, Nick. He was wearing jeans and boat shoes, and a sport shirt. Real ordinary, nothing fancy. And his car wasn't what I expected either. Driving an old Mercedes. Not driving anything new. So I follow him. He stops for a hair cut at a small barbershop in this older neighborhood. Mostly retired people. Strictly middle class area, not uptown like you'd expect . . . if this is the guy you've been talking about. So I wait awhile. He's chewing the fat with all these old timers in there. They seem friendly. Then he leaves and I follow him to this older residential area in Lantana. Smaller homes. Nice and neat, but not luxury. Not even expensive. Shit, Nick I live in a place nicer than that. So I note the address and park up the street. Next thing I see him washing the windows outside, so he obviously lives there. Does his own chores, no hired help."

"Something's wrong here," Nick said.

"That's what I'm trying to tell you. If this guy's so rich, what's he doin' livin' there? I figured him for one of those fancy high rise jobs along the coast."

"Maybe it's not him."

"Well, here's the rest of it. My friend at the phone company comes through for me. Took her a while. Anyway, Freeman Enterprises has an unlisted phone number, and guess where that number is?"

"In Lantana?"

"Yep. Same address as the guy I followed. So, he must be working for them, but he's as ordinary as anyone else living in that area. So I figured there was still something screwy, and checked at the county court house to see who was listed as the owner of that property. Name on file is Earl Henry Thomas. He's listed as the owner since 1954, so he's been livin' there a long time. How do you figure it?"

"Like I said before, it's a real puzzler. Let's go out there and talk with this guy. Maybe he can give us the answer."

"Okay. Can we eat first? I haven't had anything since breakfast."

"Sure. Before I forget, thanks for all the help. Maybe we'll learn what it is Freeman Enterprises is really up to."

"Nick, for what it's worth, this guy doesn't look like a

205

shady character. I doubt that he's dealing drugs, unless he's using all this as a front of some kind. And, it's been my experience that anyone living at the same address for over twenty-five years, is a fairly decent citizen. I checked, and there isn't anything outstanding, or any priors on this Earl Henry Thomas."

"I wonder if he had any contact with he late Sal Del Vecchio." Nick didn't have much of an appetite. He pushed his food around, waiting for Ben to finish. All their meetings seemed to be over drinks, or food.

It was obvious that Ben enjoyed eating. He ate three slices of bread, making sure the butter was spread evenly on each piece. When he was almost finished, he took the remaining half slice of bread and sopped up the gravy on his plate. Finally done, it was difficult for Nick to see any evidence that the plate had been used, it was that clean. Nick waited patiently for Ben to finish his eating ritual. Then, as Nick was about to get up, Ben said, "Okay, I guess I'm ready for some pie. You havin' any, Pardner?"

"I don't think so. Could we go?"

"Hey, Nick, that old geezer will keep. He'll be there. No need to go runnin' all the way out there on a half empty tank now is there?"

"Your tank is looking pretty full." Nick took the check and stood up, hoping that Ben would take the hint. He did. Between Ben and Gary Mitchell, it was a wonder Nick didn't add some weight, just watching them eat.

"Eatin' and eatin' right is important, Nick. In this business, it's easy to get an ulcer. I know a lot of guys that eat chili for lunch, tacos and burgers at fast food joints for dinner, and never eat a decent meal during the week. Then, on weekends, they go out for pizza and wonder why their gut is always actin' up. Me, I like to enjoy my meal . . . ."

"I can see that," Nick said. They hadn't spent much time together, and Nick knew that some indulgence was required.

Food was apparently a very important subject to Ben, and it showed. Ben was at least 250 lbs and maybe, closer to 275. Because he was big, and tall, he didn't look fat. And he moved fast. Not the kind of guy you'd want to go up against.

"Ever play any football in school?" Nick wanted to put food behind them, and changed the subject. Ben was doing the driving in case they were being followed.

"Yeah, I played guard in high school for three years. I thought it was the easiest position on the team. All you had to do was block anybody coming at you. And the secret was to be the last one still standin' up. When the ball snapped, I stayed in position and never tried to stand up, just kept my head and shoulders down, so I could stay under the other guy. It was the easiest way to knock 'em on their ass . . . just move forward slowly, and don't get off balance. Piece of cake."

"Ever get hurt?"

"Nothin' that ever kept me outa the game. Best thing about playin' ball was the girls. They sure did flock around the team. I never had a problem gettin' a date."

They passed through a commercial district. Now the houses were close together, mostly small bungalows and ranches. Some had a one-car carport and a small front yard. It was a blue-collar neighborhood like thousands of others, all over the country. Nothing was particularly significant, just ordinary, and neat. There were many neighborhoods in Detroit like this.

An old faded tan, 4-door Mercedes was parked in the driveway of the house Ben pointed to. With the car there, he was no doubt home. It would be getting dark soon and Ben had removed his sunglasses as they approached the front door. A tall stately gentleman opened the door dressed as Ben had described him earlier. He was at least 6 ft. tall, and on the lean side. Full head of white hair, kept a little on the long side, combed back like artists used to do.

"Yes? What is it you want?" He looked more annoyed than surprised.

207

"Mr. Justine?" Nick asked to get a reaction. He got it, the man's eyes opened slightly larger in surprise.

"Sorry, you must have the wrong place," the man started to close the door.

"Just a minute. Are you Earl Henry Thomas?" This time it was Ben who asked.

"What if I am. Who are you?"

"Police, Mr. Thomas. May we come in?" Ben flashed his badge, Nick didn't bother.

"What's this about? I haven't done anything wrong."

Ben opened the door without waiting to be invited in. Nick followed. "Guess there's no need to tell the whole world your business now is there, Mr. Thomas?" Ben said.

Nick took in the living room. It was small, yet nicely furnished. One inside wall was paneled and held dozens of framed photos. Nick moved closer and saw that Mr. Thomas was in most of the pictures, in a variety of costumes. He was on stage kneeling in front of a distraught woman. It was a promotional photo for a stage play of some sort. There were several theatre posters also framed.

"Okay, what's this all about?" The three of them were standing, and Mr. Thomas had made no offer for anyone to sit and be comfortable.

"Mind if we sit down, Mr. Thomas?" Ben asked, moving back toward the sofa.

"Yes, I mind. What is it exactly that you want? And who sent you here?"

"Well sir, there's a phone number registered here for a company known as Freeman Enterprises . . . ."

"So what!"

"And, there's a Mr. Calvin Justine who is supposed to be an officer with that company. His description fits you to a tee, sir. Are you also known as Calvin Justine by any chance?"

"I don't know what you're talking about. I'll have to ask you both to leave."

Nick turned from the wall and looked directly at the man. "Are you still doing any acting?"

"No, I'm retired from the theatre. Those are just some old memories up there."

"I see you played a variety of roles. Even did some Shakespeare I see." Nick had a hunch he'd found part of the answer. "Did you happen to know, or meet a Mr. Sal Del Vecchio?"

"Sorry, don't know the man."

"He was supposed to be down here visiting with some of the people from Freeman Enterprises a few years ago. You and Nelson take him fishing maybe?" Nick watched the man's face closely. No reaction. The man was now in his acting mode.

"Like I said, I don't know the man. Never even heard the name before."

"Nelson never mentioned it?" Nick watched the man's eyes shift slightly when he mentioned Nelson's name. He had to know him. Acting, or not the eyes said a lot.

"No. I think you gentlemen are wasting your time here."

"On the contrary. It's been most enlightening, Calvin, or is that just a stage name you use once in a while?" Nick asked.

"I don't know what you mean. I told you I'm retired."

"Sure you are. Quit stalling. You're a good actor. You could play the part of a wealthy businessman quite easily, and no one would even think of questioning it. Why don't you tell us about it," Nick moved to a chair and sat down. The man remained standing and looked deep in thought for a minute. "What's the matter, lose your lines?" Nick asked.

"My only association with Freeman Enterprises is a part-time job taking messages, and picking up their mail and forwarding it to their offices in Detroit. The address here is nothing more than a mail drop. I can't tell you anything more than that. And, since I've done nothing wrong, or illegal, I'll ask you both to leave. I have nothing further to say. I've been retired for seven years and I live alone."

"Ah, but you bought a yacht and a plane from the federal government awhile back using the name of Calvin Justine. Also some limos. Everything was registered in your name, that is, the false name you gave, Mr. Thomas. And that's a Federal offense."

"I don't own a boat, or a plane. That should be very obvious to you. I live a simple, uncomplicated life . . . ."

"All the world's a stage, Mr. Thomas. I think you've been keeping your acting career alive, playing the role of a simple, retired gentleman And when needed, the role of a very flamboyant businessman, who dabbles in many enterprises. Who thought it up, you or Nelson?" Nick was smiling now. His good old hunch mechanism was working again.

"Is he in some sort of trouble?"

"He could be. There's the question of where you got all the money to pay for those expensive toys. Fishing charters don't bring in that kind of a catch, unless it's drug related, which is a natural guess down here. Just what is your relationship to Nelson and his brother, Eric?"

"You know about Eric?" The man seemed surprised and looked at the wall behind him where a framed photo rested on the bookshelf. It was a furtive glance, but enough for Nick to catch since he was watching Calvin closely.

"Why don't you assume that we know everything," Nick said walking over to the framed photo. It was an enlarged color shot of three people standing at the railing of what looked to be **'The Other Woman'**. An attractive Blond wearing sunglasses stood between Nelson and . . . . all of a sudden, it hit Nick, Eric and Nelson were twins! Both men looked exactly alike. All three were smiling. It was as if they'd just witnessed his surprised expression.

"This taken around the time you bought the yacht at the DEA auction?" Nick was still examining the photograph.

"I suppose it might have been, I don't recall the exact

moment." Calvin took the photo from Nick and put it back on the shelf. He handled it like it was an antique vase. "Who is the woman?" She was quite attractive. "I believe she was one of Nelson's friends. She used to charter his boat when she was here." "So where did all the money come from, to buy the yacht and the plane? Were you all fronting for someone else?" Nick was thinking of Phil Freeman. Maybe he put up the money and used Nelson & Calvin as his pawns. He wasn't sure where Eric fit into the puzzle. "You'll have to ask Nelson that question. I don't poke my nose into his affairs. You'll have to leave now." Calvin was moving toward the door. "Having a half million bucks to spend, didn't that make you just a little curious? His charter business wasn't that good, unless he was into the drug trade. And, he wasn't established with Phil Freeman at the time you two attended the DEA auction. That came later." Nick was just guessing on that point, trying for another reaction. "I think this is where I refuse to answer any more of your questions and seek counsel from my attorney. I'm going to ask you to leave one last time." "Fine. Be sure and give Nelson my regards when you talk to him. And tell him that I'll be in touch with him again, real soon. By-the-way, where can we find Eric?" "I thought you had all the answers. I have no idea." He closed the door behind them. As they drove away, Ben gave Nick a big smile. "Well Pardner, part of the puzzle is taking shape. You sure did nail him fast enough." "Trouble is, we still don't have a case. He's right, there's nothing illegal about the phone, or having a post office box as a drop point down here. They're using it to make a big impression on potential clients and investors. It tells me they're phony. We now know that Nelson has been using this old actor as a front man, using a fictitious name. And that makes

Phil Freeman a liar, suggesting Calvin is a partner." No wonder Phil didn't want Nick to have any contact with Calvin. His whole phony scheme would become obvious. Maybe that's what Vincent Blessing discovered. If so, it may have been the reason he took such a big drink of Lake St. Clair.

"Guess you still got more questions than answers."

"That's the way it's been from the beginning."

"Don't forget, someone also wants you out of the way."

"Yes. I wonder how much Calvin, or Earl Henry had to do with those two hayseeds out there yesterday? If I was getting close to something yesterday, I'm a lot closer now, and someone must be getting very nervous."

"Which means, Nick, you better check out of that motel, and let me put you up someplace safe." Ben felt responsible for Nick's safety while he was here.

"Why? At least they know where to find me. That night clerk will tell them anything they want to know for a price, which is just the way I want it to happen. Not too easy, so they won't become suspicious."

"You think they'll buy that trap?"

"Hey, Ben, you gotta play the cards you're dealt."

"These are some pretty high stakes we're talkin' 'bout, and right now, Pardner, I'm not sure you're playin' with a straight deck. No kiddin', this could turn into something bigger than we might imagine. Let's go talk to the Captain. He needs to know what's goin' on."

"Let's wait one more day before we do that. I wish now I had brought my car along so I could have stayed back there and kept an eye on old Calvin."

"Shit, he ain't goin' no where. At least we know where we can find him if we want him. You got a plan?"

"I think the DEA boys need to know they've been duped. Tomorrow, I'll call them and tell them about Calvin. Maybe a little pressure on him will refresh his memory on some of the details. They'll want to know where the money came from.

I'm a little surprised they didn't check him out better." Nick wondered why Nelson just didn't buy the items in his name, unless... he couldn't. That just might mean he had a record. If so, why hadn't Wizard picked up on it? Probably for the same reason old Calvin used a different name. Nelson might have done the same thing.

"If the guy's an actor, he probably stayed at some expensive address for a little while and gave the impression he was legit."

"Uh huh. I could see that as a possibility. But Nelson was using him as a front." A front for what? A high class loan sharking operation, or was it an investment firm that was selling franchises and leasing equipment? On the surface, all those activities appeared to be legitimate. And all those activities had a high cash flow, so maybe they were laundering drug money. Now there was Eric to consider. He was a new wrinkle that Nick wasn't sure about. Maybe he was part of the charter operation. If so, he could here in the West Palm Beach. He could be the one behind Nick's recent sleeping difficulties.

Nick was quiet for a long period. He just sat and stared out the windshield as Ben drove. He had seen something back at that house, and he was trying to recall all the small details. It was the framed picture on the shelf, with Nelson and Eric. And the attractive woman who Calvin said was one of his clients. She looked familiar. Nick was trying to see that blond with red hair. The sunglasses were the same pair she'd worn to Vince's funeral. Yes, it was Ruth Lambert in that picture. No wonder Nelson knew how to find him! A hard lead ball formed in Nick's stomach and he felt suddenly sick.

"Pull over!" Nick shouted at Ben, who turned and looked surprised.

Ben stopped the Jeep. Nick opened his door, leaned out and vomited beside the road. He'd been played with, lied to, teased and probably laughed at. And it hurt. It hurt like hell.

Ruth's mysterious boyfriend, the one she never mentioned, was probably Nelson. Nick wondered if Paul Deckel knew that, and had forgotten to mention such an insignificant detail.

CHAPTER 19

Ben and Nick debated on whether or not to stop at The Blue Pelican. Ben finally agreed that someone did need to check the place out, in case there were any violations. Neither he, nor Nick had any official capacity here. It would be just another sniffing mission, similar to their visit with Mr. Earl Henry Thomas a.k.a. Calvin Justine.

"You feeling any better, Pardner? You look a little peaked around the gills."

"I'm fine. Must have been something that didn't agree with me." Nick wasn't about to tell Ben how he'd been sucker punched by a beautiful woman, who had pretended to be helpful when all she had been doing was checking on his progress. He'd been a fool. He'd broken his cardinal rule about not discussing case information. And, it had almost cost him his life. Now, he had to think of some way to turn this to an advantage, however slight that might be.

"You think we can pass for a couple of queers?" Ben was trying to improve Nick's sullen mood. He sensed something was going on with Nick. He'd just wait until he was ready to talk about it. It was something about that picture the old man put back on the shelf. Nick recognized something, he was pretty sure.

"No, I think we'll pass for a couple of cops. I'd just as soon have it that way. Maybe we'll get lucky, and I'll spot those two hayseeds that used me for target practice."

"Nick, I know I don't have to remind you that everything we've done so far is unofficial. I'm not even on duty, and you have no jurisdiction down here. So let's be careful, okay?"

Nick nodded agreement. He knew what Ben meant. As for careful, so far, Nick hadn't done a very good job. From here on, he planned to be one step ahead of anyone who wanted a piece of him.

The Blue Pelican might have been a nice place at one time. The parking lot needed attention. The blacktop was in bad shape, with big cracks where a few weeds had managed to grow. More nondescript brush grew from cracks next to the cinderblock building, which had been painted a light shade of blue, a long time ago. The neon sign featured a pelican roosting on a post. This hung above the entrance flickering in a sporadic manner. A possible wiring problem. A few motorcycles and several pickup trucks indicated the type clientele he and Ben could expect to encounter.

Inside was in keeping with the outside, blue walls. A U-shaped bar was against the back wall. A dance floor in front, near the entrance, and a few booths along each side. A few tables were in the middle. The juke box in the corner was playing something Nick had never heard. Smoke hung heavy everywhere. The place needed a good airing out. The smell of stale beer hit them at once.

The Pelican wasn't very busy. The bartender looked like a skin head with his sides shaved. He wore an earring and had a mustache. He wore a T-shirt that said, *Booze is the Answer, I Forget the Question.* Nick and Ben slipped into an empty booth near the entrance. Two guys were dancing together. Nick had a hard time not staring at them. Their gyrations reminded him of two drunks trying to dance together without any music, totally without rhythm. The taller one had his arms locked around the shorter guy's neck while the short guy was holding his partner by both buns. It was the most disgusting thing Nick had ever witnessed. He was sorry now that he'd agreed to come in here. Had it been a man and a woman together, it would still be a sad scene.

"Hey, Sheila, you got a couple customers up front," the

bartender called. With that, a girl sitting at the bar with one of the customers' ambled over to their booth.

It turned out she was a he. Bobbed hairstyle made Sheila look like a younger schoolgirl. Nick had to look close to actually determine that it was a guy. Sheila was wearing lipstick, eye make-up and a big grin, displaying some bad teeth that were working on a piece of gum.

"What'll you two dudes have?"

They both ordered beer looking at Sheila, trying to decide how someone could do that for a living. Nick thought about Nick Jr. If his son ever considered doing anything so foolish, he'd . . . he'd be tempted to never acknowledge him as his son. No, he'd kill him!

"You want glasses, or you want to suck on long necks?"

"Glasses," they both said in unison.

The two dancers were still gyrating against each other, even though the music had stopped. There was a hand-lettered sign on the wall.

WE DON'T SERVE WOMEN HERE, YOU GOTTA BRING YER OWN!

"Some place, huh Nick?" Ben looked uncomfortable.

"Just when you think you've seen it all, you discover a pit like this. You think Sheila is old enough to serve us?"

"Maybe we should ask her, I mean him." They both laughed and looked around to examine the place more closely. It had to be a haven for lost soles, and those who didn't care anymore. It was probably the perfect spot to deal drugs. The desk clerk, Frank wasn't there.

"That'll be four dollars." Sheila gave Ben a wink and held out her/his hand. Rings on every finger, and dirty fingernails, some were broken.

"Here, I'll get it," Nick said, giving Sheila a $ 5 bill. "Keep the change, Hon."

"Hey, that's real sweet, guy. Just raise your hand when you're ready for another round."

217

"Is Bingo around?" Ben asked

"Oh oh, you're Narcs, right? I knew it. He ain't been in for a week, honest."

"Listen up you fake pussy, I just want to talk to him, and I mean right away. Get a message to him, understand?" Ben had grabbed Sheila's arm and pulled him closer so he could spit the words out. He was more disgusted than angry

"Whatever you want, big guy, you got it. I'll ask around, okay?" Sheila pulled away and walked back to the bar, wiggling his behind in tight faded jeans.

Nick had to keep his head down so his grin didn't show. He felt silly being here. At least he had Ben along for company, otherwise he would be totally uncomfortable. Hell, he wouldn't be caught dead in here alone. That quick thought triggered his brain enough to remind him that someone out there was willing to put his lights out, and he shouldn't forget it, for even a minute. Even in this fag joint with Ben. Staying one step ahead, he said to himself. It would be his new mantra. Coming to the Pelican was purely a fishing expedition, hoping to get a line on Frank, the motel night clerk and anybody he might be associating with, that would have an interest in Nick. In a way, Nick was the bait in their attempt to catch some interest. It was a strange way to go fishing with Ben. They had a second round and tried to talk about fishing. They were interrupted by a big bald guy, wearing a dirty tank top, dirty jeans and biker boots. He had tattoos on both arms and shoulders.

"What do you want with Bingo?" he growled.

"I guess we'll tell him that when we see him," Ben answered. This guy fit his description and looked familiar.

"You lookin' for trouble, you got it." The guy looked like he meant it. He had cold eyes and bad breath. Nick looked across at Ben, wondering how he wanted to play this.

"Pardner, you put that ugly face of yours any closer, and I'm gonna shoot you in the nuts and then raffle you off to the rest of the fags in this joint." Ben had a small 25 mm automatic in his left hand below the table pointed at the biker's groin.

"You the heat?" The Biker didn't seem too concerned, but backed away a little.

"Sure I am. Don't all cops hang out in fag joints while they're on duty? Listen asshole, tell Bingo I want to talk to him, and not to send any more cute messengers."

"Maybe you need something?"

"Maybe, we'll discuss that with Bingo," Ben said. The guy looked familiar, he was trying to place him. This could be Bingo playing a game with them.

"Well then, maybe I'm Bingo." The description the night clerk had given Nick fit this guy. He pulled up a chair and sat at the outside edge of the booth leaning both bare arms on the table. "And it don't make no difference if you are the heat in here. You try anything, you won't leave except in pieces, which we'll feed to the fish." The man smelled of fish, sweat and gasoline. Nick moved away slightly. Bingo proceeded to light a joint. It was his way of showing he wasn't very concerned about the current situation. He wasn't easily intimidated, that was obvious.

"What do you think, Nick should we try actin' scared?"

"Nah, just buy him a beer and keep that piece leveled at his equipment. Between us we ought to be able to tear up this place pretty good." Nick was trying to sound tough.

"Okay, so you don't scare easy, so what is it you want? You lookin' for scag, maybe I know where you can get some. You want pussy, the real stuff . . . you're in the wrong place. But I guess you know that by now. If you're lookin' for information, you got the wrong guy."

"Yeah, we already knew that. We're lookin' for Eric. You work the boat scene, know where we can find him?" Nick was fishing with some new tackle.

"Never heard of him. What's he to you?"

STAN

"Better you don't know. We hear he's the man to see to score some good stuff though." Ben was really winging it.

"Well since I don't know the man, I guess I can't help you, not that I would, you understand, you being cops and all...."

"Bingo, word is out that you're one bad dude to deal with. Now I realize you got a reputation to protect. But, I suggest you don't try blowing smoke in my face, or I'll lay a hurt on you, you won't soon forget. And your reputation will be ruined around here. Remember my face . . . and stay out of it, hear?" Ben was giving him his best mean look. Bingo was also putting on an ugly look with a little more success. He had the smell going for him and knew it, so he smiled at them. It reminded Nick of 2 wrestlers on TV doing a promotional thing between events, growling and flexing their muscles.

"Yeah, yeah, man, liked I'm scared. Nice to see the heat out sniffin' around and comin' up empty... as usual." He walked to the bar, whispered something to the bartender and went into the back room. It could have been the toilet, or the office.

"Time to leave, Pardner," Ben almost whispered it. They got up and left quickly. Nick was on his wavelength.

Ben pulled out of the parking lot fast, drove down the road and turned around and came back slowly looking for a spot to park. An insurance agency parking lot provided a convenient view. They could see the front door of the lounge and part of the parking lot. It was the same maneuver Nick would have done, and nodded his approval. He and Ben did think a lot alike. In the bar, each seemed to pick up where the other left off. It was a knack partners developed over time working together. Ben and Nick had gotten there quickly.

"What are you thinking?" Nick asked.

"I don't know. Somethin' about that guy worries me. He's big trouble, Nick. He knows all the action around here. And now he knows we're sniffin' around for something. He'll make a move, you can bet on it. Let's just see how long it takes. You threw him a real curve ball when you mentioned Eric. You think maybe he's hanging around here?"

"It was just a hunch. Eric was working charter boats down here with his twin brother. Since Freeman Enterprises doesn't have an actual office here, I figure Nelson flew over to see either his brother, or Calvin. My guess is it was Eric. So if he's around here, he's probably still messing around with boats and fishing. Which means Bingo just might know him, particularly if drugs are involved. We don't have any real evidence pointing in that direction, but I think it's the source for all the money that is funding the Freeman organization.

"You said they have two, twin-engine planes. How do we know they don't have several boats, too? You showed me that picture of the yacht up in Detroit. Could they have another one down here?"

Ben's question was timely. Nick didn't know what Freeman, or Nelson owned. Wizard hadn't found anything else, but then he was using limited information. The names of the players kept changing. Nick wondered for the first time, if Ruth's real name was Lambert. Was that her maiden name, or her married name? He'd have to check that out, along with where she was that Saturday night, when Vince drowned. Supposedly she was out of town. Where, and with whom? Nick had never considered her a suspect, and he was still reluctant to stretch that far. But she certainly knew a lot more than she had told Nick. There wouldn't be any sexy phone call tonight. Let her wonder what was going on. Maybe she already knew. Stay ahead, stay ahead, he reminded himself. It was his new mantra.

A motorcycle started, breaking the silence. Bingo appeared from the other side of the parking lot on a Harley chopper, moving out with a loud roar, and 3 quick shifts. He was doing 80 before Ben pulled out of the parking area.

"I don't think we'll catch up to him, Pardner, but at least we got him spooked."

"Good choice of words. I think he's about to spread the word about our visit."

"I think you're right. And, I think it's time we hauled your ass out of that motel. It's not safe. If they come at you again, it'll be heavy and I may not be able to cover you. Let's go get your stuff. You can spend tonight at my place. That way, I can keep an eye on you."

"And your wife will know where you are," Nick added with a smile. He agreed with Ben. He was right, and it was time to leave. The trap hadn't worked. Tomorrow, they could look around for any signs of Eric at the marinas. Then, he'd head back to Detroit. He didn't have any desire to do any real fishing now. Another time maybe, when it was cooler, and he wasn't so pre-occupied.

They headed back to Nick's motel. Ben used his cell phone to call his wife, alerting her of the change in plans. Nick suggested they pick up a couple of pizzas, so she wouldn't have to bother cooking. He wanted to keep his imposition to a minimum and said it would be his treat. Ben asked his wife to call in the order and they'd pick it up on their way to Ben's place, saving time.

"Nick, I've got a suggestion to make that you might not like."

"Fire away. I'm open to suggestions, and this is your turf. I'm just a visitor."

"Exactly. I say that we take what little we've got and turn it over to the DEA guys. Let them run with it. Tell them what we've learned about old Calvin, and your suspicions that the Freeman bunch is a phony set-up. Then put the file away for a while. If something new turns up, you can always look into it. Some cases never get solved for years, you know that."

"I hate to drop it yet, Ben. We've put some things into

222

motion. I'd like to see how they play out a while longer. If nothing happens, well... then I guess I'll put it on a back burner and try to forget about it." Nick knew this was bullshit, even as he said the words. He wasn't going to just forget Ruth. He was going to explore her background thoroughly. Tomorrow, he'd get Wizard busy checking her out. If only he had her Social Security number, he could get started while he was still here in Florida.

"You know what you haven't done for a while? You haven't mentioned your new sweetie. You should have brought her down with you. Does she like to fish?"

"She used to live down here. She knows enough not to fly down here in July. And, I suspect she knows a lot about fishing. I'm planning to ask her when I get back." Nick couldn't bring himself to tell Ben how he really felt right now. He wasn't sure he knew. Foolish was the best description, and it kept hitting him.

"Sounds like one smart lady."

"Oh yeah, she's smart alright." Smarter than I am, at the moment, Nick thought. But now it's time to stay ahead, stay ahead, he reminded himself.

STAN

CHAPTER 20

Ben pulled in behind Nick's rental car, still parked across the street from the motel in the mall parking lot. They agreed that Nick would get his clothes from his room and check out, while Ben drove over to get the pizzas. Ben would stop back so Nick could follow him home. Ben waited, while Nick made a brief inspection of his rental car, then drove off leaving Nick to negotiate crossing the street to the motel.

There were more cars now in the motel area. Nick stopped by the office and told Paul, the desk clerk that he was checking out and would be dropping off the key in a few minutes. Nick was about to unlock his door when the door next to his room opened. He could hear loud music and was happy he wouldn't have to cope with the noise later. 3 men wandered out, all holding drinks, looking like they had been partying for a while. As he turned to insert his key, Nick was aware of one man walking in his direction. Nick was on full alert. He knew how to handle drunks.

"I sure hope we don't keep you awake tonight. Care to join us for a drink?" The man leaned against the building. He seemed friendly enough. He took another drink from the beer bottle he was holding.

"No thanks, I'm just about to leave. You won't be disturbing me."

"Sure you won't have just one for the road then?"

Nick shook his head and opened his door. Before he could close it, the man had pushed in behind him with lightning speed. He pushed Nick, forcing him to lose his balance. Instinct told him to roll away before getting up. That quick move saved him a kick in the ribs. He took a glancing blow on his shoulder from the beer bottle as he tried to get into a kneeling position. The man took a second swing, Nick ducked lower then rose quickly hitting the man in this mid section. As he started to reach behind for the automatic, the other two men materialized, grabbing him from behind. A fist slammed into his stomach, then another quick blow caught him on the temple producing instant dizziness and nausea. They taped his hands behind him. His gun was taken.

Nick knew he was in trouble and hoped Ben would arrive soon. His shoulder was throbbing. His stomach and head ached.

"Shit Zeke, I thought Detroit cops were tougher than this," one of the attackers said.

"I don't know about that. Bingo says he might be gay. Maybe we'll get a chance to find out later."

Nick fell to the floor and pretended to pass out. He was trying to buy some time. These men knew who he was, and they were waiting for him to return. Paul probably alerted them that he was coming. And somehow, they had a connection with Bingo. Even though Nick didn't recognize any of the men, he felt certain that two of them were most likely out on Rt. 21 yesterday. Now they were lifting him to his feet and forcing him out the door. One of the men backed a van up to the door and had the back doors open. Nick started to yell, "I'm a police off..." when something struck him from behind. This time his lights went out. No stars, no pain, nothing.

The commotion caused a few other motel guests to peek out their doors. All they saw was a white van pulling out of the parking area, speeding down the highway. Nick's motel room door remained open. His suitcase was still on the bed. Paul saw the van pull out and quickly picked up the phone to make a confirming call that would subsequently keep him in a mellow mood for the rest of the week. Bingo always rewarded his buddies when they did him favors, like now. He

225

was still on the phone when Ben's Jeep pulled in. Ben was unaware that anything had happened.

Nick was slipping in and out of consciousness. He was lying on his stomach, his hands taped behind his back. His feet were free, but useless. Someone was kneeling beside him, reaching into his pocket, taking out his money and his wallet. Nick had lost track of time. He knew he was being driven somewhere in a truck that reeked of fish. He was beginning to hate that smell.

The truck stopped suddenly. The back doors flew open and hands were pulling on his legs, dragging him out. He saw several commercial fishing boats tied to the pier. And he heard a familiar sound. La la la loop, la la la loop. It was the sound of twin diesel engines idling, waiting for the command to increase their rpms.

"Okay, get him onboard and untie those lines. Move it!" The man at the controls of the sport fishing boat looked exactly like Nelson. So this had to be Eric.

For a brief moment, Nick caught a whiff of fresh coffee beans. Then as a breeze emerged off the water, he smelled diesel fuel and fish. They pushed and kicked him, forcing him over the side and into the well area of the boat. Nick remained on his knees with his hands still taped behind him. It was a hopeless situation to be in. His mantra, Stay ahead, stay ahead hadn't worked for him. This gruff bunch of deckhands were being directed by Eric who was obviously in charge.

"Well, well well, lookie who we got here. It's the tough cop who thought he could scare me. Ha, ha, hah, you don't look so tough now, honey. I hear tell you came all the way down from Detroit city, just to do a little fishing." Bingo was sporting a broad smile standing over Nick. "You wanted to meet Eric, right? Well, turns out he wanted to meet you, too. I don't think he wants to shake hands, however. Ha, ha, hah."

"Shut up, Bingo. Come up here and take over," Eric yelled

above the engine noise. The boat was entering open water, soon there would be more bouncing and vibration as the speed increased.

This was a working charter boat, much smaller than **The Other Woman**. Nick estimated that it was somewhere in the 37 foot category. He never saw the name, as he was half hoisted, half pushed onboard. Nick remained down, lying on his side. His back to the fighting chair, hoping to find a rough edge where he could work on the duct tape that held his wrists together. Salt water sprayed over the side as they skipped through the chop in the water. Nick could feel each jolt through the deck.

"Now you know what happens to nosey cops down here. They just disappear," this was the one they called, Zeke, who was leaning over Nick's face. He was the same man at the motel, who had offered Nick a drink.

"I think I'll take that beer you offered earlier," Nick was trying to use humor to cover up the fear he felt. This was a one-way ride that wouldn't last too long. He was out of options.

"How about some used beer? I've got a bladder full I can give you." The man was starting to unzip his fly when Eric stopped him.

"You already had your fun. Go find that extra anchor and bring it back here," Eric ordered, looking down at Nick and giving him a wicked smile. If Nick hadn't discovered that the men were twins, he would have thought this was Nelson.

"So you're Nelson's twin brother, Eric," Nick said looking up and relieved that Zeke hadn't pissed all over him. That would have been the ultimate insult to his predicament.

"Usually I say, 'at your service' whenever someone says that to me. However, since you're not a paying customer, we'll forget the formalities. Right now, you're just excess cargo that we're about to get rid of. In case you're wondering where we're going, we're headed for the Bahamas, only you won't be making the entire trip with us. Bingo, is our local shark expert. He likes to experiment with different types of bait. It's a little research project he's conducting." The smile became a sneer. And like Nelson, he had cold eyes.

"You think getting rid of me will end the investigation? You're wrong. You, your brother, Phil Freeman and old Calvin are in big trouble. What happened, Vincent find out about you and your operation?" Nick wasn't about to start crying and plead for his life. If he was about to die, he'd do it with some dignity at least. "Why didn't you dump him out in the lake?"

"You don't know as much as I thought. We didn't have anything to do with Vince's death, not that he didn't have it coming to him. The man was a fool to think he could threaten us... and play games with Ruth. That piece of shit deserved what he got, but it wasn't me or Nelson. His ticket was about to get punched, somebody beat us to it."

"Then why the hit on me, if you're so innocent?"

"Because you've been asking too many questions, digging around in things that are better left alone. Until you started poking around, nobody was aware of our operation. You got Uncle Earl very upset."

"So who put the hit on Vincent, if you didn't do it?"

"Don't know, don't care. It's Nelson's problem now, not mine. I don't get involved with Phil anymore than necessary. That's Nelson's department."

"Well Phil's just an errand boy for Nelson anyway, isn't that right?"

"Figured that out all by yourself, did you? By-the-way, before we pitch you to the sharks, I have one small chore to perform. Neil would love to be here right now, but since he isn't, he asked me to give you his regards." With that, Eric kicked Nick in the ribs, breaking at least two. "I was suppose to break your hand, but ribs are just as good. The sharks won't know the difference. I guess it's time we got you bloodied up."

———

Zeke arrived with rope and a medium-size anchor. The way he carried the anchor, it had to weigh at least 40 lbs. Zeke kneeled and started to tie a knot in the rope through the anchor. "How much line do you want to use?" he asked Eric.

"Use it all. I don't want to lose that anchor, so be careful how you tie it."

Zeke began singing the song, Mack The Knife, "When the shark bites, with his teeth, Dear...." All the while smiling at Nick, who was having a hard time taking short breaths. Every time he tried to take a deeper amount of air, the pain struck like a bolt of lightning. He was still trying to loosen the duct tape against the seat base. He'd found a rough bolt head and snagged it several times trying to pull and stretch the tape. His wrist was raw from the rubbing. So far, Zeke hadn't noticed, since he was still busy trying to tie a bowline through the anchor. The rocking motion of the boat didn't help. He seemed content taking his time, something Nick had very little left.

"...Our boy's done somethin' rash." Zeke was having rope problems.

Eric went back to the cockpit to confer with Bingo. Power was reduced and the boat slowed noticeably. The rocking motion intensified causing Zeke to lurch sideways. Nick took advantage of the opportunity to kick him in the head. It was a solid blow snapping Zeke's head back. Blood started pouring from his nose. Nick managed to roll over, then get on his knees. Before Zeke could get up, Nick gave him a head butt. It produced a loud yell, causing Bingo and Eric to turn around. Nick crawled over to Zeke's slumped body and turning, he was able to grab the fishing knife from its scabbard on Zeke's belt. He quickly cut the tape, grabbed a life ring and jumped over the side, into the saltiest water he'd ever tasted. If he was going to drown, he didn't want to do it tied to an anchor. He was gulping salt water and air and coughing. He was also aware of a new sound.

229

He heard the womp womp womp sound of chopper blades approaching. At the same time, the boat picked up speed and was turning around. Bingo stood by the rail with a giant gaff hook. Eric was in the cockpit, and another man was sitting in the bow with a rifle aimed in his direction. Nick wasn't sure if he'd fired, or not because of all the noise. He hung onto the life ring with one hand and waved at the chopper now hovering overhead.

A minute later, a Coast Guard Para-medic was in the water, fastening something around Nick. The last thing he remembered was screaming, as a strap was pulled tight around his chest, then he passed out.

CHAPTER 21

"Hey, Pardner, how come you went fishin' without me?" It was Ben leaning over Nick as he opened his eyes, realizing he was in a hospital bed, and alive.

"They were waiting for me, Ben. Did you get Bingo and the rest of them?"

"Oh yeah, we got them, and the boat, and the two guys at the pier, who were happy to give us all the details. We also got the desk clerk at the motel. Big round-up."

"What about Zeke?" It seemed so long ago to Nick. "Sorry, Pardner, I don't know about any Zeke, he the guy you were fighting with on the boat?"

"You could hardly call it fighting. He was one of the guys who followed me in the pickup." That too, seemed like a long time ago. Nick wanted to give Ben a report, but he was too tired and about to fall asleep. "How long have you been here?"

"I think Mr. Zeke may be poisoning some sharks about now. I don't know how he went over the side, pushed, or fell maybe. You've been out for about twelve hours. You want some cold pizza?" Ben was trying to think of something funny to say.

Nick tried to laugh, but it hurt. Even with all the tape on his ribs. Ben gave him a sip of water and told him to get some sleep. He'd be back that evening and give him a full run-down on all that had happened. He offered to call Ruth for him.

"Noooo, please don't do that! I don't want anyone in Detroit to know what's happened down here. Let them think I'm dead."

"But why not your sweetie? She must be worried sick,

not hearing anything from you for what is it, several days I think."

"Ben, please, I know you mean well, and I appreciate everything you've done. You saved my life, man. But don't try calling Ruth to tell her anything."

"Okay, I guess you want to tell her yourself, huh?"

"Yeah, face to face. I don't want to miss the surprise."

"Hey, you trying to tell me something? Is she part of all this?"

"Unfortunately, yes. I think she's involved. There are some things I have to check out when I get back. I'll know more then."

"That's what all the pukin' was about, wasn't it? She the gal in that picture you were studying at Calvin's place?"

Nick didn't answer, just nodded. Then he fell asleep. Ben sat there for a long while watching Nick's steady breathing. The man had gone through a hell of a lot in a short period of time, then had it capped off with betrayal. If Nick was keeping her posted on his whereabouts, no wonder it was so easy for those bozos to keep tabs on him. The punk at the motel was a minor player, but he'd still pay a stiff price for becoming involved, even if he didn't have a choice.

When Ben asked the Coast Guard to scramble a rescue chopper, his Captain was furious. Ben had never seen him so angry. He hadn't been happy with Nick's visit and his nosing around. Then, when the Coast Guard had put 3 men on the boat to bring it back, they later discovered a false bottom in both fish wells. And a lot of cocaine residue. It was enough to confiscate the boat and turn it over to the DEA task force in Fort Lauderdale. The bust made Ben's Captain very pleased. He even suggested that Nick's name be kept out of all the reports.

――― ――― ―――

―――

"Welcome back to the real world, Pardner!" Ben was sitting across from his hospital bed when he opened his eyes. Even with the blinds closed, Nick could tell it was daylight. "Hi," it was all he could manage without some water to quench the dryness in his mouth and throat.

"How you feelin'?" Ben was standing next to the bed looking down at him, holding a copy of the local newspaper. After a few gulps, he managed, "Great. My ribs ache, my knee is sore, I feel like my stomach was recently pumped, but other than that, I feel just fine. Best sleep I've had in ages." He gave Ben his best smile attempt. "What time is it?"

"What difference does it make? We ain't gonna do no fishin' today. It's too late! Maybe in a few days, when you're feelin' better."

"Ben, I gotta tell ya, the only kind of fishing I want to do for awhile is from a pier, not a boat." He heard Ben let out a long chuckle. "So what's going on? Fill me in."

"Why don't you wait until after you've had something to eat. Everything I have to tell you can wait a spell."

"Are you kidding me? I almost get killed, and now you want me to wait? Come on, I want all of it . . . now!" Nick managed to sit up and felt more comfortable.

"Well, the good news is, the doc says you're a tough old bird, and in pretty good shape . . . considerin'."

"Considering what?" Nick rubbed his cheek and knew he needed a shave badly. His mouth had a bad taste, too. And he was aware of the uncomfortable hospital gown he was wearing.

"Considerin' all you went through. He thinks you may have a mild concussion. You got a couple a cracked ribs there, and a few bruises that I can see, but no broken jawbones. If it were broken, you wouldn't be jabberin' right now." Just then a nurse came into the room and took his temperature and pulse. She left without a word. Nick watched her leave. Good

233

looking legs and rear end. He arched his eyebrows up and down like one of the Marx Brothers used to do. Once again, Ben gave a hearty laugh watching his friend. "It's a good thing they didn't cut off your pecker out there."

"Hey, Ben, old habits die hard." He knew what was coming next and waited.

"Yeah, well when I die, that's the way I want to go . . . with a hard on! Nurses around here are pretty cute. You best stay awhile, you just might get lucky."

"I'm lucky already. I owe you a big one, Ben. You saved my life, such as it is lately, thanks. How'd you know where to look?"

"One of the guests at the motel called the police about a fight in the parking lot. They saw the Fish Distributor's name on the van when it drove away. I got there soon after they left with you. Missed you by maybe two minutes. Then I headed directly for the dock area and missed you by a couple minutes. The two bozos there were persuaded to cooperate. I threatened to shoot his dick off and he told us you were going for a one-way ride, and described the boat. Then it took me a few minutes to get a chopper from the Coast Guard. And it took a few more minutes to get a track on the boat. The two we arrested at the pier, told us that Bingo was headed for the Bahamas, so we knew the general direction, but there were a lot of boats out there."

"I never expected any of this to happen. And I never expected to make it, once I was on that boat. With me out of the way, they were home free."

"Let's hope that's just what they're still thinkin'."

A food tray arrived, and Nick was surprised at how hungry he was. Between bites, he gave Ben a report of all he could remember from that night. He had overheard some bits of conversation about Eric meeting another, faster boat, presumably near the Bahamas. Bingo was to bring the fishing boat back, and have it ready for a trip the next day. Ben told

Nick that Bingo was in custody, being held at some remote facility. The boat wasn't going anywhere, since traces of cocaine had been found in two hidden compartments. The DEA folks had been watching Eric for several months. Bingo would no doubt try to make a deal and testify against Eric. They were holding him on several charges, including kidnapping and attempted murder, so it wasn't likely he'd get off.

The DEA people had Eric. Ben thought he was being held in Miami. They also had a search warrant for **The Other Woman**, back in Port Clinton. Agents up there were coordinating with the Miami office. Ben didn't know what they had uncovered, if anything. There was a technical loophole. The fishing boat Nick was on, was owned by Eric, not Freeman Enterprises. Therefore, there was a bit of a stretch, in trying to make a case against Freeman Enterprises, or any of their employees. Freeman could claim he had no awareness of Eric's drug activities. Trip logs might suggest otherwise, now that they knew about 2 different aircraft being used.

A police stenographer arrived later and took a complete statement from Nick. Ben called a newspaper friend and asked for a favor. He and Nick decided it might work to their advantage if some of the details were not disclosed. Nick's name wasn't to appear anywhere. The kidnapping and attempt on his life would not be mentioned. Only that a boat was taken into custody, suspected of making drug runs to and from the Bahamas. The crew had been arrested, and were being held for questioning. No names yet. A more detailed follow-up story would come out later.

Nick felt rested enough to check out of the hospital. Ben had his suitcase. Ben had also returned the rental car Nick was using. Ben's Captain was pleased to learn that Nick was planning to leave. And since all the publicity so far was favorable, Ben's time off, while he was with Nick, wasn't being counted as vacation time. Ben's wife was happy about that.

Nick called his office to check in. The DEA people had

already called, mentioning that Nick had been helpful. They also mentioned that Nick was in the hospital, nothing serious. Nick told Gary that he was flying back that evening, but not to mention it to anyone. Ruth had not called his office, so there were no messages for him. He surmised, that Ruth wasn't worried about him.

"Ben, I think I've done all I can do down here. It's time for me to get back to Detroit so I can finish all this from my end, and leave you free to do your thing here."

"Yeah, well, my Chief won't be upset about your leavin'. Since you arrived, there's been more excitement here than we normally see in a year. Putting Bingo away is a major plus for us. And we earned a few attaboy points with the Feds. Never hurts to have those guys on our side. And our friend, Mr. Calvin seems to have taken an unexpected vacation. His neighbors said that he put some suitcases in his car and left. Phone has been disconnected."

"I wonder if Freeman Enterprises is still answering their phone? I think I'll drop by for a friendly visit when I get back. By-the-way, Eric called him Uncle Earl, so that was the relationship. I still have Vincent Blessing's case to close. Eric claimed they didn't have anything to do with it."

"What did you do, have a nice chat with Eric while you were takin' that short cruise?" Ben chuckled. "You're thinking that maybe this Ruth was involved?"

"Yep. I think she was there. I still don't know why, or what the motive was. I think he learned something that got him killed. Now I want to check out Ruth's background, which I should have done sooner."

"Hey Pardner, we all make mistakes now and then. You were just thinking with the wrong head. You'll get it all straightened out sooner, or later. Keep me posted, okay? And, next time you come down, leave all that investigation baggage at home, so we can just drink, fish and relax."

Ben drove Nick to the airport. Nick still had an open re-

turn ticket. He had Gary Mitchell go into his desk and retrieve all the numbers for credit cards, and his driver's license,
so that he could get replacements when he returned. When
he shook hands with Ben for a final time, Ben handed him a
small gift-wrapped package. It was a new wallet with 5 twenty
dollar bills inside along with a thank you note: *So you can get
your car out of the parking lot.*

"Thanks, Ben. I'll pay you back."

"Oh no, the money isn't from me. My Captain said to give it
to you. Consider it expense money for helping me down here.
He's not the hard ass everyone seems to think he is.

On the flight back to Detroit, Nick thought about all the
events that had taken place since the start of this seemingly
simple accident investigation. Since Ruth knew Nelson and
Eric when she lived in Ft. Lauderdale, she no doubt knew
about their drug activity. She'd been on **The Other Woman**
soon after it had been acquired. So she knew the yacht. And
she probably knew Nelson's Uncle Earl a.k.a. Calvin Justine
as well. The old man was used, to play the part of a wealthy
businessman, and to take phone messages and pick up mail.
He must have enjoyed playing the tycoon role. Nick and Ben
agreed that Calvin might not have been totally aware of his
nephews' activity. His modest life style proved that. Nick
wondered if maybe Phil Freeman was being used in a similar
fashion, as a front man. But then, he had a bodyguard, so
maybe he really was a partner in the organization. He certainly wasn't needed for the drop-off in Orlando. He just needed
an alibi. That suggested that Phil knew Vincent was to be eliminated. He might have had Mr. Muscle do the job, since he didn't
make the trip with Vince. Maybe it just got handled poorly.
Yet Eric insisted they didn't have anything to do with it.

Ruth knew Nick was flying to Orlando to check on Phil's
alibi. She also knew that he was going on to West Palm Beach,
to check out Calvin Justine. Finding Calvin would let the cat
out of the bag, about Freeman not actually having an office

237

in West Palm Beach. That wasn't anything more than a minor embarrassment, but it suggested a phony operation. Maybe that's what Vincent discovered? Ruth no doubt knew all this, and would have mentioned it to Nelson. It was still a puzzler that nagged him. Because he was deeply concentrating on the recent events, he was surprised by the flight attendant's announcement that they were preparing to land at Detroit Metro. It had seemed like a 15-minute flight.

Nick recalled Zeke, one of his abductors, singing, 'Mack the Knife' just before his panic attack. Well, he thought, old Nickie's back in town. He hummed the song, not quite remembering all the words. "Who's that peeking, 'round the corner? Could it be, our friend's back in town?" Not wasting any more time, he drove directly to Birmingham. It would take 45 minutes to get there using the freeways, if traffic wasn't too heavy. Rush hour was over. Ruth should be home by now… and very surprised to see him.

Nick thought about Sal Del Vecchio's accident on that lonely road. It would no doubt remain an accident in the file, unless one of the bozos they captured owned up to killing him, which was unlikely. Vince's accident could well remain just that as well, if Nick didn't get some added proof. Not for the first time, Nick wondered how many accidents every year, were actually homicides? It depended on so many elements. Who arrived on the scene first, what was their level of experience, and how busy were they working on other assignments with a higher priority? Nick asked himself if it would have made a difference, if Vince had fallen overboard while out fishing in the lake? How many hunting accidents were murders in disguise, because someone was fooling around with his friend's wife? And how much time could anyone like Nick afford to spend looking into all those small, seemingly unrelated details? If it hadn't been for his interest in Ruth, would he have continued? He didn't have an answer, and he needed one.

He hoped the surprise element might work to his advantage. So far, Ruth probably didn't know he was still alive. He wondered how she would react to his unexpected arrival. His head ached. He knew he should have remained in the hospital a few more days, but this couldn't wait. There was a small window of opportunity that time provided. The longer he waited, the less advantage he'd have. Nelson might already know about Eric's arrest, and might guess that Nick was still alive. All this might be revealed in the next few minutes. Nick was hoping that Ruth's initial reaction might tell him what he wanted to know.

CHAPTER 22

Ruth's car wasn't there, and nobody answered the door. The blinds were closed, so he couldn't see inside. No key under the doormat, or over the door molding. Nick decided to wait until tomorrow to see her, maybe he'd catch her at work. He drove to his apartment, looking forward to familiar surroundings, and sleeping in his own bed.

A full night's sleep, worked wonders for Nick. He reverted back to his old routine, slipped into his sweats and ran his just a short distance, because his ribs started to hurt. Nothing appeared out of place in the neighborhood. There were cases in the office that he needed to review and perhaps reassign to someone else. He owed the Chief an update. And then there were the hundreds of miniscule details that still needed to be sorted out. Each was significant if viewed in the proper sequence.

When Nick returned to his apartment, Sergeant Mitchell was waiting, sitting in a patrol car.

"Welcome back, Nick. I hear you had quite an ordeal on your fishing trip, but you and your buddy did catch a big one."

"Glad to be back, Gary. Glad to be alive." Nick gave him a short version of what happened, and what he'd learned in Orlando and West Palm Beach. "Freeman Enterprises isn't as big an organization as they'd like everyone to believe. It's drug money. The DEA is working on it from that angle now."

"Here's what I got from my trip over to Port Clinton." Mitchell handed him a copy of the motel registration card indicating 2 people had stayed 2 nights. "The woman had red hair and 'very attractive' according to the motel manager. The other person remained outside in the car, so he couldn't give me any description. They didn't actually arrive until Sunday morning, even though they had reservations for Saturday night, and paid for both nights. So they checked in and paid the bill on Sunday morning. And here's a list of phone calls that were made."

Nick spotted the call to Vincent Blessing's office. It had been made at 9:30 AM on Sunday. There was a call to West Palm Beach also. This didn't come as any surprise now. Had Nick checked Ruth's alibi earlier, he might have uncovered all this prior to leaving for Florida. He vowed never again to stray from routine procedure. He invited Gary into his apartment. It was only the second time Gary had been inside. He detected a slight change in Nick. He seemed friendlier and hadn't called him 'Mitchell' once. Nick made coffee for both of them.

"I ran a check on Susan Deckel's driver's license. Remember, her husband mentioned that she'd had a few tickets in the past? Well, it appears one of those tickets involved running a red light. She caused a pretty bad accident and suffered a broken hip. I remember her husband mentioned that she has bad migraine headaches. That could be the result of the accident."

"I've really eliminated anyone in the family from being involved in the boat accident." It was an unintentional slip.

"So now you're thinking it was an accident after all?" Gary was surprised.

"No, just used the wrong reference that's all. I've been thinking about accidents a lot lately. You find out anything else?"

"Yeah, your buddy, Wizard called. He dug up some interesting stuff. Ruth Lambert was married to a doctor...."

"I knew that. What did he find out?" Nick wasn't' sure he wanted to know. He still had mixed feelings, and wished there was a better explanation than what he was going on.

"Well, it seems Doctor Lambert liked to treat only rich

patients. He was supplying them with party dust. Got busted on charges of possession and distributing. He's still behind bars doing time. Ruth Lambert divorced him five years ago."

"Did she divorce him before, or after he was caught?"

"After he went to jail." Gary smiled, knowing he had anticipated Nick's question.

It wasn't the same story Ruth had told him about the reason they divorced, but it no longer mattered. She had lied to him about several things. Now everything she had told him was suspect. If Doctor Lambert was a conduit in the drug trade, then he needed a source of supply, like Nelson and Eric. Maybe Ruth was the contact between them. Was she responsible for her ex-husband being behind bars? Nick wondered if Vincent Blessing knew of Ruth's earlier past, before working for Jeremy Keller. And did Keller know? Ruth had pointed him in the direction of Keller and that had taken any focus off her as a suspect. Nick had focused on her, for all her charm and sensuality. She caught him at a vulnerable time. He didn't feel vulnerable any more, just sore and angry.

"You read the paper this morning?" Gary asked savoring the coffee, and this rare moment of confidence sharing. He liked the new Nick a lot better than the old one.

"No, anything interesting?" Nick wondered about the story Ben had given his friend. The wire services might pick it up.

"Yeah, it seems someone fell overboard off a boat while fishing down in Palm Beach. The newspaper says there were two guys missing, one was from the Detroit area. No names. Somehow the Feds became involved after the Coast Guard reported suspicious activity. The boat was confiscated and several arrests were made. Drug activity is suspected. I guess you're one of the suspects who fell overboard." Gary was back to his old joke routine. This time, Nick didn't mind. "Sounds a little like the case we're investigating up here."

Over their second cup of coffee, Nick gave Gary a few

more details of this fishing trip with his hands taped behind him, laying on the deck and hoping for an opportunity to get free. He admitted that he really didn't expect to make it through the ordeal alive. He knew Gary would take great pleasure in retelling Nick's story to the guys at the station later. Nick figured that was the best way for everyone, except the Chief, to learn the details of his trip.

Gary sat there taking it all in, shaking his head in wonder. "Holy Shit! Sort of gives new meaning to the phrase, fish, or be bait." Gary couldn't resist a touch of corn and was surprised when Nick laughed, then winced. His ribs would be sore for several weeks.

"So now you know why I didn't want anyone to know that I'm back. I'm hoping that by showing up unexpected, I just might surprise a few people. We asked the reporter who did that story not to mention my name. Someone here might assume I'm one of those who fed the sharks." Nick went on to tell Gary about Zeke sitting in the boat half singing, half humming 'Mack The Knife'. Only someone like Gary could truly appreciate that segment of the story. For once, Gary didn't laugh as expected.

"So what's the plan now? And is there anything I can do to help?"

"First order of business is to stop by and visit Ruth. I'd also like to talk to Paul Deckel one more time. He just might know something about Vince's attempt to blackmail Freeman, if that's what he was trying to do. And Eric mentioned he'd cheated Ruth somehow. Paul might know something about that." If Vince had cheated Ruth out of something, he'd made a very big mistake. The lady was every bit as dangerous as Phil Freeman, or Nelson.

"What about Freeman? You planning on seeing him again?"

"It's doubtful. The DEA boys seem to have a line on him now. If they confiscate his boat, and start checking on all the trips made, they may be able to make a good case against him and Nelson. We don't need to get involved." Nick appreciated Gary's new attitude and willingness to help. Maybe their relationship would improve. So far, it was going in the right direction. As they were leaving Nick's apartment he had an afterthought to share with Gary.

"You know, Gary, if Vincent Blessing really did accidentally fall overboard, he sure caused a lot of trouble afterward."

"Yeah, he sure did. And you got to take a few days off, to go fishing. See any good-looking women while you were down there?

"I never had time to really notice."

"See Nick, that's your problem...."

"Don't start Gary. You're pushing your luck here," Nick laughed. Things were getting back to normal fairly fast. Another week and it would be same old, same old. Maybe he'd swear off beautiful women for a while and just settle for attractive waitresses... and no hassles. He owed Mavis a call. Maybe he'd just stop by later and say "Hello" and take it from there.

"The Chief is gonna win a bundle on this one," Gary snickered.

"What are you talking about?"

"Well . . . we had this little bet going in the office, on how long this one would last. The Chief says you always have trouble keeping a girlfriend for more than a month. I was on your side. I bet five bucks it would last longer than a month. I think some of the other guys thought so, too."

"Thanks for the vote of confidence. I think I'd better ask the Chief who he feels the prime suspect is on this case, and see if he's willing to put up some money."

"I still think it's Freeman. Guy's been lying from the start. And when it looked like you were getting too close to him and his operation, he tried to have you taken out. Probably used his bodyguard to do the job."

"Maybe. Freeman isn't the only one who's been lying to us." In the past week, he had experienced fear, anger, pain, anguish, sorrow, lust, love, rejection and foolishness. That was too many emotions at one time to cope with. He was lucky to be alive and that counted for a lot. Now, he had to count on someone not expecting him to show up. He would start with Ruth first.

Nick arrived at Ruth's townhouse and found she wasn't home. There was a FOR RENT sign in front. The front door was ajar. He entered and startled a cleaning lady who was vacuuming. She didn't know where Ruth was, nor had she seen her. Ruth had left her a note on the kitchen counter saying that she would be gone for a few days and to empty the refrigerator.

Nick asked to use the phone, to call his office. He explained that he was a friend of Ruth's and had been trying to reach her, which wasn't entirely true, but it gave him a reason to look around. The cleaning lady continued to work in the hallway. There was a clear plastic bag with trash sitting in the kitchen. Nick checked his answering machine for messages and hung up. For the second time it hit him that nothing in this place had a personal touch. No photos, just prints. Ruth could rent it furnished and leave everything except her clothes. Nick wanted to check the closets, so he said he was going to use the toilet, and walked down the hall in that direction. He sidestepped into the bedroom. The bed was made and everything looked clean and neat. When he opened the closet, it was empty! No clothes, no shoes, nothing. That was a surprise. He wondered if the cleaning lady had also noticed the clothes gone. Opening a dresser drawer, he found that empty, too. When he crossed the hall and went into the bathroom, the towels were in place, but the cabinet was empty.

Ruth would be gone for more than a few days, she had moved out. Nick walked back to the bedroom and looked for the answering machine, it was gone. If she moved, it wouldn't be too difficult to find her, as long as she stayed in the Detroit area. If she took off, it would be more difficult. And, it also made her the prime suspect in Vince's death. Nick could hardly wait to see her again, and hear her new excuses for moving so quickly. It would no doubt be a very logical reason, like everything else. She'd no doubt try to use all those feminine tricks on him again, hoping he'd be too horny to think straight. This time anger would prevail over lust.

As he left, Nick jotted down the phone number on the FOR RENT sign. It might help him track Ruth. On an impulse, Nick walked back into the townhouse, giving the cleaning lady a scare, for which he apologized. He wanted to look through the trash bag in the kitchen. Something had caught his eye while using the kitchen phone. There it was, an empty cassette case with singer Patsy Cline featured. It was the missing case for the tape he'd found on the yacht. The cleaning lady watched him remove the case carefully. He told her he'd left it there earlier.

Next stop was the Blessing residence. Ruth's red Mustang wasn't there, either. Emily greeted him at the door. She didn't seem particularly surprised to see him. Probably hadn't read the paper yet.

"I'm sorry, Lieutenant, I haven't seen Ruthie in several days. She said she was looking for a new office."

"May I come in for a minute and look at Vince's office again?" Stepping inside, Nick could see boxes and papers in disarray. It was quite unlike the way he'd seen it the last time he was here.

"I must say, she's left things in quite a mess. I do hope she plans to straighten up the office." Emily seemed a little embarrassed about the condition of the office.

"Did Ruth take anything with her from the office?"

"I suppose she did. I didn't actually see her take anything, but it certainly looks like she might have, doesn't it? Heavens, I've never seen this room look so messy!"

It appeared to Nick that Ruth must have been looking through files, then discarding them in the process. Perhaps there was something important in Vince's files that had been overlooked. If so, only Ruth would know where to look, and it wouldn't require making such a mess.

Nick left his card. "If you hear from Ruth, please have her get in touch with Sergeant Gary Mitchell at once. It's very important."

"Does any of this have something to do with the way Vince died?" It was the first concern he'd heard from her.

"Yes, I think it does, Mrs. Blessing. Nick decided to spare her any details. No sense worrying her, she wasn't in any danger. "Is your daughter still staying with you?"

"Well, she's just visiting for a few more days. Right now, she's at the clinic. She has a therapy session. Her hip still gives her a lot of pain, poor dear. This past year has been difficult for Susan. Now with Vince gone, she's having a terrible time coping, I'm afraid."

"How long ago was it, that she was in that car accident?"

"It was just about a year ago. The car was badly damaged. It's a wonder both of them weren't killed. Paul was very fortunate to only get a few cuts and bruises."

"Was Paul driving, or was it Susan?" Nick made a mental note to have Gary get a copy of the accident report, so he could review the details. There was a small discrepancy here.

"Yes . . . ." She seemed to reluctant to go on. "Paul was driving. He felt so bad about it."

"And did your husband blame him for the accident?"

Emily just nodded, clenching her hands tightly. She looked pained and Nick was sorry he had brought it up. He thanked her, patted her hand and left her standing in the hallway.

Nick cruised around Birmingham's shopping area, hoping he might spot Ruth's red Mustang convertible. He didn't know the license number. He made another mental note to get it, along with the Paul's accident report. He'd have Gary meet

him at his new favorite restaurant. Maybe catch Mavis work-
ing. He'd treat Gary to lunch. That would surprise him. When
Nick arrived, he learned that Mavis had taken the day off.
Her kid was sick. So far, his day was off to a bad start.

Gary arrived with a few surprises also. First, the mustang
convertible Nick was looking for was a leased car. Gary found
the license number on the motel registration card. Car was
leased to Nelson Klept, not Ruth Lambert. Ruth Lambert
did own an older model Honda Prelude. Second surprise was
the accident report involving Paul Deckel. He was charged
with reckless driving. There was a note that the drunken driving charges had been dropped. Apparently good old Vince
had used one of his club buddies to help out on that one.
Susan had indicated he could 'just pick up the phone and call
one of his friends'. Nick could picture the fury that must have
caused Paul later.

"The case just gets more complicated at every turn, huh
Nick?" Gary was enjoying the sandwich and salad. Nick said
he was treating, that was a first. He knew Nick had a thing
for the red head. And he knew it was still a sensitive subject
he'd have to skirt... for a while. What a pun opportunity. He'd
save it for another time, when Nick was in a better mood.

"Yes, it's been a real can of worms. Know what I think?
Vince just fell overboard and messed up their plans. The guy
didn't even know about the drugs. He was just trying to get
Freeman to invest in his franchise idea, for starting a new
magazine. Probably didn't even know that Freeman and Keller
knew each other. Freeman probably stole Sal Del Vecchio's
pizza franchise idea and made some money with it. So, he
saw another similar opportunity, and may have discussed it
with Keller somewhere along the line. Either that, or Ruth
knew about it and mentioned it to Nelson . . . ."

"You think Vince knew about this Lambert broad and
Nelson being close friends?" Gary asked, wiping his mouth
on a napkin. First good lunch he'd ever had with Nick.

"My guess is, he didn't know. I think Nelson and Ruth go way back. She was probably married to the doctor when she met Nelson, in Ft. Lauderdale." The pieces were starting to fall into place for Nick, now that he could think objectively. Most of this he wouldn't have known if he hadn't actually made the trip to Florida. He wouldn't have learned about Nelson's twin brother, Eric. He wouldn't have discovered the use of a second plane. He wouldn't have seen the photo of Ruth with Eric and Nelson. And, he wouldn't have guessed that Calvin Justine was a retired actor . . . and Nelson's Uncle. The question of who orchestrated the entire scheme still loomed in Nick's mind. Phil Freeman probably didn't enter the picture until later, so it had to be Nelson. And now he'd just learned that Nelson also used another name occasionally. Instead of Hoffman, he also used Klept. Eric handled the drug running while Nelson ran the business end, laundering the money. And, there had to be something in the past, that caused him to use a different last name and to use his Uncle, to bid on and buy all that equipment.

"You think she's involved in the drugs, too?" After asking the question, Gary decided that the answer was obvious. Of course she was, her ex-husband was doing time for passing out illegal substances to his friends and clients. She was in it, up to her big tits. "By-the-way, the real estate office has Vince's phone number listed, as the place to contact for rental information. You think she might stop back?"

"Who knows? I think she's skipped. If Eric was able to tell them, I'm still alive, and they know both boats are in custody, and they know the Feds have Bingo, then they're worried. She and Nelson had to pull out fast. She'll turn up somewhere. I was hoping she would be surprised to see me still alive." Nick had thought about that moment and just what he'd say to her. Maybe, 'Here's the tape I found on Freeman's yacht. And here's the case for it. You forgot both... along with a few other details.' The tape proved she'd been on the yacht. It didn't prove that she was there, when Vince went over the side. Nick wondered if Ruth had an arrest record? Nobody had bothered to check. There hadn't been any reason, until now. He asked Gary to get on it.

CHAPTER 23

Nick's next stop was to Keller, Katz & King Ad agency. He knew Jeremy wasn't there, but he did find Cassandra Keller in. She walked out to the waiting room to greet him.

"I seem to recall we met once before," she said coyly.

"Actually we met twice. The first time was here in your husband's office as I was leaving."

"Well, what brings you here this time? Shall I call you Detective, Lieutenant, Officer or Old Saint Nick?" She laughed, and being sober, she seemed reasonably pleasant, and certainly glad to see Nick again. She appeared to be more attractive than the last time he had seen her. The make up wasn't as heavy. "You here to see me, or Jerry?"

"I'm looking for Jeremy. I understand he took a rather unexpected vacation without clearing it with us. Did Phil send him off somewhere by any chance?"

"He's on a photographic shoot in the Bahamas for one of our clients. He'll be back in a few days. Is there anything I can do for you... while he's gone?" She winked at him. Drunk or sober, the woman was aggressive and flirty.

"You have a number where he can be reached?"

"I should say he can't be reached. And that might be the truth if you try, but I'll give you the number we have here."

"Thanks. Who's your client in the Bahamas?"

"Actually, it's for a travel agency here."

"Uh huh. And does Phil Freeman own a piece of that travel agency?"

"I never asked, but I wouldn't be surprised. It's Horizon Travel in the same building that Phil is in. He's into a lot of different things, you know?"

STAN

"I'm finding that out. Did your agency ever do any design work for him, for a Pizza franchise a couple of years back?"

"Yeah, we did. How did you know that? Phil sold that whole thing to some company down south I believe. We did all the early promotion stuff for him."

"Jeremy told me a little about it," Nick lied. "Do you have any samples of what you did on file? I'd like to have some copies, and the dates when you did all that stuff."

"Something wrong with what we did?"

"Oh no, nothing like that. It will help substantiate some facts for an investigation down in Florida for a friend of mine. This is strictly a favor, that's all. You won't be involved."

"I seem to recall you were going to give me a lift home, because you were concerned about me driving. Then you walked out on me. Just when I thought we might have a little fun. What happened there? I had a sexy dream that night about you. Do you always tease that way, then leave the lady wondering?"

"No, it's usually the other way around, Cassandra. I run up against an attractive, intelligent woman like you, and it scares the hell out of me." He leaned over and kissed her on the cheek.

"Yeah, I'll bet you say that all the time. You need to get some new material, Nick. I've got a girlfriend I'll bet you'd love to meet. She's a bit of an airhead, know what I mean? But she's got hot panties. Likes to party. Get her a little high and she'll take you for the wildest ride you've ever had. Think you might be interested?"

"I'll keep it in mind." Nick wondered how Cassandra would know so much about her friend's abilities. Then he quickly shifted back to the present. "If you should happen to talk to Jeremy, tell him I'm looking for him."

"I don't plan to tell him shit. You want to know something? This place runs a lot smoother when he's not here

---

252

barking at everybody. As far as I'm concerned, he can stay down there for as long as his Visa card will allow it." She patted his butt as he walked out.

The dates for all the projects Keller worked on were shortly after Sal Del Vecchio's death. Nick would try to use that coincidence to advantage with Freeman. That was his next stop.

Phil Freeman's car wasn't parked in his normal spot, and his secretary confirmed that he wasn't expected in for the rest of the week. Nelson was out of town on a charter. She wasn't allowed to give out any information on where to, or who with. She was the only woman that hadn't smiled at Nick lately and that bothered him. Must be the age difference, he thought. Or, maybe it was all the good looking guys that worked for Phil. Nick just wasn't in that league.

"Leave them a message that I was here, and that I did finally meet Calvin Justine. They no doubt already know that, but tell them anyway, okay?" Nick gave her his card and a wink. Her face turned a little pink. "Oh, and tell them they're paying too much for those engines on the King Air". He wondered how long it would take the DEA people to grab the plane again. Nick had already told them where it was.

—— —— ——

"Hello, Paul." Nick walked into Paul's office at his small print shop unannounced. No one was out front when he walked in. Paul looked surprised to see him.

"Lieutenant! I didn't see you come in. Is anything wrong?" Paul was nervous.

"Apparently Emily didn't tell you that I was at the house earlier today."

"No, I haven't spoken with her today. Susan is over there, staying with her."

"Yes, but Susan was at the clinic when I was there. It's

——

funny you never mentioned the car accident to me earlier, when we were talking about Susan's migraine headaches."

"I didn't think that had anything to do with Vince's accident. It happened a year ago."

"Uh huh, and you were driving, and a little drunk. Old Vince had to get you out of that scrape, didn't he? And he was no doubt pissed about his daughter getting hurt. Blamed you for everything, didn't he?"

"So what's this all about? Sure he was pissed. I heard plenty about it, too. And I wasn't drunk!"

"That's right, you weren't. I read the report. I think you were high on something. You still do drugs, Paul?"

"Don't be ridiculous, I don't do drugs." His red face said otherwise.

"Tell me something, Paul. You really hated Vince, didn't you? He was a continual pain in the ass to you. He competed with you for his daughter's affection, and she took his side in all the family arguments, didn't she?"

"Emily tell you that? I'm surprised."

"No, I put it together. Emily didn't take sides did she? She probably just accepted things as they were. I think she's fond of you."

"You're right, she is. So what do you want? The car accident is history. And I don't touch the stuff anymore. Vince said he'd kill me if I ever touched the stuff again. I'm clean, honest!" Paul was almost crying.

Nick moved around to Paul's side of the desk and moved some papers to sit, exposing the desk calendar. It was the exact same type Vince had in his office. Nick saw a note written across the page. It was the same way the note was written on Vince's calendar. Nick flipped back to July 15th, and discovered the page missing. Another piece of puzzle had just fallen into place.

"You substituted the pages on Vince's appointment calendar." Paul just nodded. He was scared.

"So, you knew he was meeting someone on that boat, didn't you?" Another nod.

"What difference did it make to you?" Nick wasn't sure where this was leading.

"Vince stole Ruth's magazine idea, and was trying to use it as his. Ruth told me all about it. She knew how I felt about Vince. She wanted my help."

"Hmmm. So you two were friends and co-conspirers then. Did Vince know any of this?" Paul shook his head, no.

"Were you more than just friends? Maybe lovers?" Nick could see Paul's face turn red. Nick had the answer, even though Paul hadn't moved his drooping head.

"So you fell in love with Ruth. It's easy to do with a beautiful woman like her. Even though, she's older than you. Did you know that Nelson was her boyfriend? He has been for many years." Now that he had Paul talking, he had to go easy. It was sensitive stuff they were discussing. Nick had to know, even though he'd prefer not to hear it.

"Not until that night . . . ." Paul tried to catch himself.

"Tell me about that night, Paul. The night Vince went over the side. Were you there?" Another nod.

"So what really happened?" Nick could almost put it together by now.

"I guess it doesn't matter now. You already know most of it. You saw how beautiful she is, and how she can drive you crazy. She liked to tease me, when I would visit her office. She'd bend over so I could see down the front of her dress, stuff like that. She knew I was looking and didn't seem to care. Sometimes she'd just brush up against me, like it was an accident, only it wasn't. And I'd smell her perfume. Man, it could intoxicate you. It drove me nuts sometimes." Nick also knew the intoxicating effect and nodded agreement.

"Did Susan ever suspect you had a crush on Ruth?"

"Maybe. She'd always ask me a lot of questions about her. Susan doesn't like her."

"So what happened?" Nick didn't want Paul to get sidetracked.

"One day, when she was upstairs with Emily. I opened her purse and found some coke. She came in and caught me looking at it. That's when she asked me if I had ever done any of the good stuff. I said I had in school, but not lately. She had plenty of the stuff, and shared hers with me. We got a little high together. God, she's fantastic when she gets high." Nick was feeling jealous just listening to this.

"One time I screwed her on Vince's couch, right there in the office with the phone ringing. She even answered it, while we were doing it. She was the craziest woman I ever knew. She can put moves on you like you wouldn't believe. Then, when she told me about Vince, and what he was trying to do, well, I said I would help her any way I could. I told her about seeing the note on Vince's calendar. She hadn't seen it."

"Go on, what happened?"

"Susan and I ate with her folks, that Saturday, then we left. Susan was having another migraine and was in a real bitchy mood. She took a pill and went to bed. I waited until Susan was asleep, then I went over to Ruth's place. I knew where she lived. I followed her a few times. I got there just as she was leaving. She was driving a different car. So I followed her. I knew she had a boyfriend, but I didn't know his name, and she never showed me any pictures of him. She didn't talk about him. And the way she was with me, I figured she must not be seeing him too often. Otherwise, why was she so hot whenever I was around? Thinking about her being with someone else sure made me feel jealous, even though I'm married. Probably sounds stupid. I remember I asked her one time, if she had ever done it with Vince."

"What did she say?" Nick held his breath.

"She said she only liked to do it with younger men. Vince was way too old for her."

"So you followed her." Nick wanted to keep him focused,

not let him ramble too much.

"I wanted to see where she was going, and who she was meeting. It turned out to be some big blond-headed guy, looked like a body builder. Maybe a little older than me, and a lot bigger. She met him in some parking lot. They talked for a few minutes, then he followed her, and I followed them. They drove to this marina. Vince's car was already there. The guy stayed in his car and parked by the entrance. Vince got out of his car when she drove up and parked next to him. I parked out next to the street, so they wouldn't see me." It occurred to Nick that Paul thought the guy Ruth met was Nelson, when it was probably Neil.

"So she was meeting Vince. Did she take him to the Yacht?"

"Yeah, she opened the gate, left it open and went inside that big boat I'd been on before."

"What about the other guy still in the parking lot?"

"I don't know. He drove off, I never saw him, or his car again. He just like left I guess. So I sat and watched the boat for maybe an hour. They were sitting inside drinking and talking. At one point I thought they might be arguing, the way he was throwing his arms around. They didn't go down to the staterooms, which I half expected to see them do. Finally, I was getting a little tired just sitting there in the car, so I got out and went for a walk. The gate was open, so I went up to the boat to see how close I could get. I could hear them talking, but I couldn't make out what they were saying. I took off my shoes and crept onto the boat, being careful not to make any noise. I kept low and it was dark, so nobody saw me. I stayed there for maybe another half hour, when suddenly Vince came stumbling out. He almost bumped into me. Scared the shit out of me. If he had turned around, he would have seen me. So there he was, pitching his guts out over the side. He was leaning way over. That's when I did it. I pushed him real hard, and he went over the side. I don't know why I did it, I just did."

"Then what did you do?"

"Man, I didn't know what to do, but I knew I had to get the hell out of there fast before Ruth came out and saw me. She'd really be pissed if she knew I was there. That would be the end of it. So I ran. I remembered to take my shoes, but I didn't even put them on. I ran across that gravel parking lot in my socks! Then, when I got to the car I got in and just sat there. I was having trouble trying to breath. I was shaking so bad I couldn't even drive. Pretty soon Ruth comes out. She turns off the lights and leaves. I saw her throw something in a can by the gate, then she goes over to Vince's car and unlocks it and starts looking around. Then the guy in the car shows up again, and he helps her look in the trunk. A couple of other cars came in and they quit looking. She got in her car and followed the guy out. They didn't see me or my car. It was totally black out there that night. I figured Vince was dead, 'cause he never appeared. Then I went home. Susan was still sleeping soundly from the pill she'd taken."

"That it? You never told Ruth you pushed him over the side?"

"No. I decided to let her think her boyfriend did it." Maybe that would piss her off and she'd dump him."

And she tried to get me to think maybe Jeremy Keller had done it, Nick thought as he reached for the appointment calendar on Paul's desk. He couldn't help but feel a little sorry for the kid. He understood the spell women like Ruth could weave. Nick knew full well what that woven spell was like. He'd been there a few times.

Nick drove Paul to the Birmingham Police Station where he could be processed. They would take his statement and hold him. Emily would no doubt post bail for him. Then all hell would no doubt fall upon him from his wife, Susan. Birmingham could have another homicide on their hands as a result. Poor Paul. The kid didn't stand a chance, no matter which way he turned.

——— ——— ———

Nick returned to his office and received a big welcome from everyone. The Chief was glad to see him, and motioned for him to come into his office as soon as the welcoming group was finished. Nick sat down in the Chief's office and started to bring him current on all the events when Gary barged in. He was holding a plaque with a set of shark's teeth in an open oval.

THE CRAZIEST FISHERMAN IS ONE WHO USES HIMSELF AS BAIT!

It was the first time that Nick, the Chief and Gary had a big laugh together. Outside the door, there was more of the same. Gary pulled up a chair and joined Nick and the Chief like he'd been invited. He wanted to hear all the details, even though he already knew most of the story. He wanted to hear it one more time.

"So Nelson was the one behind the entire operation?" The Chief asked.

"Looks that way. He and Ruth had a little deal cooked up years ago where she'd introduce some of her society friends to Nelson and Eric. I think it was more of a party boat than fishing when the ladies went out. Somewhere along the way, Nelson came into some big money. Probably running drugs. He'll never admit to any of it. And Ruth has disappeared. I doubt we'll ever see her again."

"There's an APB out for her, Nelson and Freeman. They'll turn up somewhere." Gary added.

"My guess is they're in the Bahamas. That's where their contacts are, and that's where Eric was headed."

"What was the motive behind all this? Gary asked. He was getting better, Nick noticed.

"According to Paul, the idea for **DETROIT VISITOR**

magazine was Ruth's idea from the beginning. She got the idea while working at the Keller agency. She told Vince about it later, hoping he'd help get it started. Instead, he tried to take credit for the idea. She didn't learn about that until Vince talked to Phil Freeman about franchise ideas. It got back to her through Nelson. Vince never knew that she and Nelson were bed buddies. When Freeman didn't show any real interest, Vince started talking to some of his friends at his club. One of them remembered another franchise idea, one of the members had for a pizza chain. He warned Vince to be careful, because Sal Del Vecchio died, soon after a meeting with a prospective buyer in Florida. Later, his franchise idea materialized, causing friends to suspect Sal may have been murdered. My pal, Ben Wheeler is working on that down in Florida. It's still filed as an accident. I sent him some artwork from Keller's agency to help substantiate the evidence and establish probable cause.

"Was Freeman behind any of this?" The Chief asked.

"He was no doubt involved. But I suspect Nelson allowed him to act as the front man in the operation. Nelson likes to be behind the scenes. He let his Uncle Earl, a.k.a. Calvin Justine play a small part, when they needed someone to help them pitch one of their schemes."

"Why bother with the schemes, if they were making money hauling drugs?" Gary asked.

"It's all related. Nelson needed legitimate business ties to launder the money. He didn't want to draw any attention to what he was doing, so he spread it over several different businesses. And, they probably did fairly well. Maybe that kept the mob boys from suspecting anything unusual. They may have been aware of his trips, and he may have paid them off, or done them a few favors, who knows? Anyway, he doesn't appear to be connected, just an independent operator, right under their nose. That's my guess."

"So the kid did it. Because he was crazy over this sexy,

older woman, who worked for the victim. She beguiled him so bad he couldn't think straight, is that it? An impulsive, foolish act, and he almost got away with it. Didn't realize the consequences of it all. Is there a lesson to be learned here?" The Chief asked with a smile, looking directly at Nick.

"Probably, but spare me for a few more days, okay?" Nick had a report to finish and some calls to make. The first one would be to Ben, thanking him again for all his help, and giving him the final details. Next would be Wizard. He needed to know that he was a big help. Keeping him informed directly paid big dividends later, when Nick would need him again. And then there was the call to Mavis. She really did have a cute ass. And as for his old habits, they sure did die hard.

# # #

Printed in the United States
3177

9 780738 859750